FORBIDDEN INK

LIZA MALLOY

$\mathcal{A}$dam Bricker climbed out of his cement gray Toyota Tacoma and stretched his neck before sauntering up to the counter. Although the drive hadn't been too long, the night sure was. Adam couldn't sleep on that island. The condo was comfortable and maintained alright, but it was also haunted.

Growing up, Adam had spent a few weeks each year in the island property, but when his mom had gotten sick, they'd started renting it out year-round to pay for her treatments. And then when she died, well, neither Adam nor his father felt like returning. But now, Adam couldn't put it off any longer. His mom had made her wishes clear—Adam was to spend at least one full summer on the island before settling into a career.

It wasn't just the memories of his mother that haunted Adam when he was here on the island, but the fact that he had literally brought his mother with him. She'd wanted her ashes scattered off the southernmost tip of Hilton Head Island, and while Adam wasn't about to undertake that task before his father joined him on the island in the fall, the men had agreed that her ashes shouldn't remain unattended in the house back in Nantucket.

Adam and his father had been living with the ashes in a

surprisingly small, yet gorgeous, hand-painted urn for nearly five years now. During that entire time, Adam had never once freaked out that his mother's remains were right outside his bedroom. But now that he was alone with the urn, constant thoughts about it plagued him.

During the drive down the coast from Massachusetts to South Carolina, he'd actually caught himself talking to his mother's ashes. And last night, when he couldn't fall asleep even after opening the window to welcome the distant sound of the whooshing waves, he kept singing that stupid children's song in his head: "ring around the rosie, pocket full of posies, ashes, ashes, we all fall down."

It occurred to Adam that he might be losing his mind.

"Ash! Ash!" a shrill voice called out, snapping Adam out of his thoughts.

He spun around, confused that someone had said aloud the very thing he was fixated on. He spotted the speaker, a lanky brunette probably a couple years younger than him. She was running towards another girl, her body blocking Adam's view of the second girl.

Adam started to turn back to the counter, ready to dismiss the incident as an odd coincidence, when the brunette stepped to the side, offering him a glimpse of her friend. Adam's breath hitched. She was hot, with long golden hair, bronzed skin and a body he knew he'd be dreaming about. But there was something else about her, too. Maybe it was the way the sun bounced off the wall of the marina nearby, casting a glittering haze over her, or maybe he was just sleep deprived, but she reminded Adam of what an angel would look like.

"Who's that?" he asked, turning back to Clay, the guy working the counter at the marina shop.

Clay glanced over to the girls. "The blonde is Ashlynne Marie Kensington," he replied quickly, correctly guessing which lady had caught Adam's eye.

Adam craned his neck to watch Ashlynne with her friend. They were talking about something, and they'd both just used the same chapstick. Gross. But now Adam couldn't stop looking at Ashlynne's lips, which even from here he could tell were full and probably soft as a ripe raspberry. Her smile glowed, flashing bright white teeth.

Clay laughed. "Don't even think about it, man. That girl is better guarded than the White House."

Adam furrowed his brow. "How so?"

Clay shrugged. "Overprotective father combined with not one, not two, but three older brothers who don't mind senseless fights and treat her like some blind puppy they have to save." He wiped his hands on the rag beside the surfboard he'd just waxed. "Plus she has a boyfriend. And she's underage."

Adam glanced back at the girl, still mesmerized. She certainly didn't look underage. "How old is she?"

"I don't know. She'll be a senior at the prep school here this year, so my guess is seventeen."

"I'm only nineteen," Adam informed his new friend.

Clay gave him a quick once over. "Really? I would've guessed twenty-one at least. You got all that ink in one year?"

"Nah. I may have started early." Adam knew he looked older and, for now, he was enjoying the perks. He suspected once he hit thirty he might wish for more boyish looks, but currently he was milking his mature appearance for all it was worth.

He gazed back at the girls. Ashlynne and her friend were now bouncing excitedly about something. The movement drew his eyes directly to her breasts, causing Adam's stomach muscles to clench. She was dressed in a loose white tank top almost as long as her cut-off jean shorts that showed off tanned legs that went on for miles. She wore strappy gold sandals that reflected the sunlight in a near-blinding way, but Adam could still tell she had bright pink polish on her toenails.

His best friend back home, Nate, had always said you could

tell a lot about a girl by her nail polish colors. Adam recalled hot pink being a good sign.

Clay chuckled again, interrupting Adam's ogling. "Did you not hear anything else I said?"

"Yeah. So how did the boyfriend get past the three psycho brothers and the old-fashioned dad?"

Clay shook his head dismissively. "He's working for them, not her. They're all loaded, and their families are tight. It's basically some arranged marriage type of shit. My guess is if the boyfriend had to pick her brothers or her, he'd pick them."

"So you don't think she really likes her boyfriend?" Adam interpreted, already feeling better about his summer home.

"Look, I don't know. I was a couple years ahead in school and they weren't even dating when I graduated. I'm just guessing based on what I pick up on here all summer," Clay finally said. "But I guarantee you that her family and entourage aren't going to take kindly to the likes of you." He gave Adam a once over, as if Adam didn't already know that his tattooed, muscular physique didn't exactly fit in at a polo match or yacht club or whatever shit rich people were into around here.

Adam couldn't help grinning. He didn't mind a challenge, especially one that kept his mind off the real reason for his visit to the island. "What time should I report for duty tomorrow, Boss?" he asked.

"I didn't offer you the job," Clay replied.

Adam crossed his arms and smirked.

"Jesus Christ, fine. You're hired. You better know your way around a fucking boat like you say you do, though, and you'll still have to convince my dad."

"You won't be disappointed," Adam promised. "Nine a.m.?"

Clay glanced down at his notepad then nodded.

Adam started back towards his truck, nearly slamming into a wakeboard display as he continued checking out Ashlynne's butt.

* * *

THE FIRST TIME Ashley saw the new guy, she was with Brent. They had just finished lunch at Plantation Pines, the country club where they both worked part time—Brent as a golf caddy and Ashley as a tennis instructor. Neither of them needed to work, but the jobs looked good on college applications and since their families were already members of Plantation Pines, they weren't held to the same high work ethic as those who got the jobs based on merit.

Ashley was done with her two tennis clinics for the day, but Brent was sticking around to caddy the back nine for some tourists. Brent walked Ashley to her Lexus, and as he pressed her against the sleek side door for the requisite make-out session, she noticed a guy watching them from a few spots over.

He wore khaki cargo shorts, a black tank, and a dark blue baseball cap turned backwards. He had a square jaw, striking blue eyes, and multiple tattoos dusting the muscles along his shoulders and bicep. He was, without question, hot.

Ashley felt her cheeks flush and quickly glanced away just as Brent pulled back. "See you tonight," he said, cupping her butt cheek through the ridiculously short tennis skirt.

She glanced over to see if the guy was still looking and winced when she confirmed that he was. PDA never really bothered Ashley, except when there was a crazed stalker gawking. Who was this guy anyway?

She walked around to the rear of the car and opened the trunk, swinging her racket and duffel bag inside before pressing the button to close the trunk. She made her way back to the driver's side before realizing the guy was still watching her. As soon as their eyes met, he grinned.

Flustered, she tried to determine what was going on with this guy. Based on the tattoos and cargo shorts, Ashley eliminated the possibility of him actually belonging to the country club, which meant the only place she could have possibly seen him was the marina. After a moment, she gave up guessing and asked.

"I'm sorry, but do we know each other?" she shouted, feeling silly as soon as she heard her small voice travel across the parking lot.

He smiled wider, winked, and said "not yet" before hopping into his truck and driving off.

Ashley couldn't stop her lips from curling upwards at his coy reply. And she hoped she did see him again.

She drove home, already annoyed by the summer tourist traffic even though it had just begun to pick up over the past week and was bound to get worse. There was a jeep and a truck already parked in the driveway, but she wasn't too surprised to find the house empty. Her brothers tended to travel in packs, either with each other or their friends, so the presence of their vehicles was never a good indication of their whereabouts.

Ashley dashed upstairs and changed into her black and white polka dot bikini, then stepped onto the second floor balcony to spray sunscreen everywhere she could reach. Satisfied she'd gotten enough coverage, she headed to the kitchen. She filled her thermos with iced sweet tea, made fresh each morning by the housekeeper. Her final stop was the mud room, where Ashley grabbed her beach bag, confirming it still held her sunglasses, book, and towel.

Ashley started down the private beach walk, pausing only to pick up a chair. She spotted Lisa the moment her feet hit the sand. Lisa had been Ashley's best friend since birth, thanks to their mothers' friendship, and they'd stayed that way as they aged, and not just because there weren't a ton of kids at the local prep school. Lisa was the happiest—but most brutally honest—person Ashley knew, and Ashley knew how lucky she was to grow up a few doors down from her.

Lisa didn't turn as Ashley approached, which usually meant

she was blasting music. When Ashley plunked a chair in the sand, Lisa's eyes popped open and she yanked out her ear buds.

"Okay, don't be obvious," she began, leaning forward and whispering even though no one was within fifty feet of them. "But check out the guy at eleven o'clock."

Ashley turned straight ahead to the ocean. It was pretty dead. The closest swimmers were to the right, not left. "Lisa, eleven o'clock is in the water."

She frowned then wiggled around in her chair, pointing at a guy way off in the distance. "There. Him."

From this far, Ashley could tell that he had dark hair, blue swim trunks, and was probably tall. The remaining details were fuzzy. "Okay, what about him?"

"I think he's staying a few houses down, in the third row beach house, looks like his family and maybe two friends' families."

She waited for her friend to get to a point.

"He's going to be my first tourist conquest of the summer."

"Your first," Ashley repeated. "You're planning multiple conquests this summer?"

Lisa shrugged. "Maybe. I don't want to be pinned down."

Ashley sighed. She knew Lisa was frustrated that she'd never really had a boyfriend, but that was mostly because she'd had a crush on their friend Tyler for years and he was oblivious. Apparently, Lisa had decided this summer that she was just going to start hooking up with hunky tourists rather than continue waiting for a special first time. Ashley was torn between being supportive of her and trying to remind her that this didn't sound like her style at all.

"Okay, so what's your plan?"

She groaned. "Well, I could go talk to him."

"Yep, that would definitely be a good start." Ashley glanced over at her friend. "You look hot today."

"Or I could just lay here until my phone battery dies and then head back to the house to change for dinner."

Ashley laughed. "I'm sure he'll be back at the beach tomorrow."

"Good point. And this is definitely the best way to play hard to get."

Ashley smiled and settled back against her chair, closing her eyes and letting the rhythmic crashing of the waves lull her into a short catnap.

* * *

ASHLEY'S PARENTS had some work dinner in Savannah that night, so Ashley was free to meet friends by the marina. It was her normal crowd— Lisa, Brent, Katie, Tyler, and Dawson. Lisa and Ashley staked out the good table—close to the water but far enough from the live music that they could still hear each other talking—while Katie flirted with the bartender and the guys picked up the pizza from the shop around the corner.

Ashley was about to sip her lemonade when an arm reached around from behind her and snatched it away. She turned to see her oldest brother Jackson taking a swig.

He wrinkled his nose and returned the glass, wiggling his eyebrows.

"Can't afford drinks on your waiter salary?" she teased him.

"I was just checking that there's no alcohol in this. Someone has to keep tabs on your virtue," he said.

"That ship sailed," Austin muttered, coming up behind Jackson but eying Brent.

"Do y'all need something, or are you just now realizing you don't have your own friends?" Ashley asked. She actually didn't mind if they stuck around. It was one of the things she suspected she'd miss when the twins went off to college in the fall. Although they were almost two years older than Ashley, they were only one grade ahead, thanks to her mom having insisted they repeat kindergarten. Apparently she hadn't realized their immaturity was just a part of their personalities and not something that would improve with time.

Anyway, the prep school on their part of the island was small, and all of the kids tended to hang out together, regardless of grade, so Ashley was used to running in the same social crowds as her brothers. For the most part, it was fun, and Ashley considered her brothers friends, and not just family. Sometimes, though, it got annoying, especially when Ashley felt like her friends paid more attention to her brothers than to her. Katie was obsessed with Jackson, and Tyler and Dawson were both tight with the twins.

Austin chuckled. "This is gonna be a long, fun summer," he said, high- fiving Mason.

"Don't forget your curfew, sis," Jackson teased as he sauntered off, going out of his way to pass Katie.

Katie stared obviously at his butt then turned and fanned herself dramatically. Lisa giggled, prompting a glare from Ashley.

"Oh come on," she said. "You can't help that your entire family is gorgeous, and don't try to deny it either."

Thankfully, Ashley didn't have to reply, because Brent returned with a stack of pizza boxes. They dug in as though they hadn't eaten since final exams.

The summer heat hadn't hit full blast yet, and once it did, their appetites always dwindled. By the Fourth of July, their outdoor gatherings centered around cold drinks or ice cream, and usually took place at one of their pools. Living in the south, one quickly mastered the art of eating in the water. A lot of their social outings involved going out on boats, impromptu parties on sandbars, and racing wave-runners. Lisa and Ashley never grew tired of just lounging on the beach, though.

"You in?" Brent's voice interrupted her thoughts.

"In what?"

He rolled his eyes. "Going out on Dawson's boat."

Ashley considered it, but she wasn't really in the mood. She was tired, a little nauseous from the pizza, and had planned to do some shopping tonight.

"Nah, I think I'll pass. I wanted to pick up a birthday present for my mom anyway. You should go, though."

Brent stared at her for a long moment as though trying to decide if this was a test, and then he hopped out of his seat. He kissed Ashley on the head then took off after Dawson and Tyler. "Call me tomorrow!" he yelled.

Ashley realized everyone had left the table except her and Lisa.

"I want to go check if my shirt is in at the pro shop before we head out," Lisa said. "Want to meet up in a bit?"

Ashley nodded and they cleared off the table before parting ways on their respective errands.

Ashley had just rounded the corner of the bay of shops to the north when she bumped into him—literally. Her cell phone dropped to the floor on impact and they both bent for it at the same time, bumping heads.

"Ouch," they said simultaneously.

"Jinx," Ashley said without thinking. Then she glanced up and instantly felt her cheeks flush. It was the guy from the parking lot, still looking hot as ever, but now he was laughing at her.

"Are you stalking me?" she asked.

He only grinned wider.

"Well?"

"Sorry, I was unclear on the rules of this whole 'jinx' thing, seeing as how I haven't been twelve for a while," he said with a smirk. "Am I allowed to talk?"

Okay, despite the cocky look on his face, Ashley had to give him credit for that response. "Habit," she explained. "Youngest kid in a family that includes twins who say a lot of the same things, so, I can't help it."

"So those were your brothers you were with earlier?"

She sighed. "I guess that answers my question about the stalking. Who are you and why are you watching me?"

"Adam," he said, sticking out his hand.

Ashley shook it tentatively. She was getting serious mixed signals from this guy. On the one hand, he had tattoos, which definitely conveyed the bad boy persona. And the whole creepy stalker behavior didn't bode well. But on the other hand, he had the kind of smile that made her insides melt. Lisa assured Ashley that serial killers were never hot, and Lisa was rarely wrong.

"Ashlynne," she replied, deciding he was harmless enough, at least in the middle of the crowded marina. "But everyone calls me Ashley."

"I know," he said.

Now she was thoroughly perplexed. "I thought you said we didn't know each other."

"We haven't officially met, but I asked about you earlier. Turns out you're practically famous in these parts."

Ashley rolled her eyes. "Yeah, it's a relatively small island, so the twenty percent of inhabitants who actually live in this part of it year-round tend to all know each other."

"Well you don't seem to know me."

"You live here?"

He nodded.

"Since when?"

"Tuesday."

"For how long?"

"I don't know. Indefinitely."

Ashley remained skeptical. "You aren't a tourist?"

Adam leaned back against a decorative post. "I feel like we're going in circles here."

Suddenly it occurred to her that he was likely a few years older. "I can introduce you to my brothers if you want. They'd probably do a better job of getting you acclimated to everyone here."

"I'm not interested in your brothers," he said, the look in his eyes weakening her legs.

"How old are you?"

"Nineteen."

Wow. That was younger than she would've guessed. "Austin and Mason will be nineteen in August. Jackson is twenty-one. They're all probably still around here somewhere, and since you're so good at stalking, I assume you can find them on your own."

Adam continued eying her. "Are you this hostile with everyone you meet?"

"I'm not hostile! I'm…"

"Feisty?"

"I was going to say running late. I wanted to look for a birthday gift for my mom before the shops close."

"Is her birthday tomorrow?"

"Next week."

"So you have plenty of time to extend some of that southern hospitality and charm to a lonely newcomer."

Ashley sighed.

"I promise I won't bite," he said, "unless you want me to."

She bit her lip, determined not to blush again.

They were both quiet for a moment so Ashley gathered her composure.

"Did your whole family move here or just you?"

"Whole family, but that's just my dad and me."

"Where are you from?"

"New England area. Maine, Massachusetts."

"You move often?"

He nodded. "Hoping to settle down now, though."

"Here?"

"Sure. Seems like a nice place. A little humid, but I'll get used to it, right?"

Ashley shrugged. Despite having lived in South Carolina her entire life, the humidity still caught her off guard every single spring. Starting around mid-May, a thick dampness cloaked the warm air, making each breath feel heavy and oddly invaluable. The only time Ashley didn't notice the humidity was when she was right along the water, which was why she tried to spend as much time as possible on the beach.

"Where do you go to school?"

"I graduated," he said.

"I mean college. Are you a freshman? Sophomore?"

Adam shook his head. "I'm not doing the whole college thing."

Ashley blinked several times, trying to come up with a response, but all that came to mind were more questions, probably all inappropriate.

Adam laughed, revealing perfectly straight, white teeth. "You've never met anyone who didn't go to college, have you?"

"I..." she sighed, pretty sure he was somehow mocking her even though he was the uneducated one. "So what do you do?"

"My dad is a sailor on a merchant ship. I do a little fishing, a little boat maintenance, and I really like to take people out on boats."

"What kind of boat do you have?"

"A mid-size cruiser. It's here. Care to see it?"

She shook her head. "Maybe some other time. But right now I really should get back to my friend, and as harmless as you seem, I don't think I should hop on a boat with some guy I just met."

He nodded approvingly. "Wise woman."

There was an awkward silence.

"Well, I'll see you around Ms. Ashlynne."

Ashley smiled but before she could turn around, he caught her hand and raised it to his lips, kissing it delicately. Ashley's stomach muscles clenched. Adam turned quickly and walked towards the second boardwalk.

She stood there for a moment, partly because she wasn't sure if her legs still worked and partly because she wanted to see which boat was his, but Lisa popped up behind her before he reached his destination.

"Hey! Did you find anything for your mom?"

"Uh, no," she said, glancing down at her hands to confirm she hadn't bought anything. Why was her brain not working? "I got distracted."

"Yeah. Who was the hottie?"

"Just some guy who was lost," Ashley said.

They stepped into a few shops to find the perfect gift for her mom and then headed home. Ashley couldn't decide why she hadn't just told Lisa about Adam. She wouldn't judge her for checking out another guy when she was with Brent, and she certainly wouldn't tell him, so what was Ashley's problem?

Ashley couldn't help but wonder if she lied to Lisa for the same reason she kept thinking about Adam in the first place—he was just so different from everyone else she knew.

CHAPTER 2

The next day Adam nearly worked himself to death. Clay said his old man wasn't at the marina often, so Adam figured he ought to impress him the first time they met.

Adam didn't mind hard work though. Cleaning all the boats, wave-runners, and other equipment as people returned them to the marina was exhausting, physically demanding work, but it was mindless. Clay and Adam kept the music going, chatting when they felt like it. The rest of the time, Adam just shut off his brain and went through the motions. He was intrigued by the tourists who came to the marina, and started to feel more comfortable in his snap judgments about people he met.

Adam wasn't allowed to take customers out on the boats until he finished his loosely defined "trial period," but he had a hunch it wouldn't be long now. Clay's dad, Mr. Walcraft, was definitely impressed with Adam's background with boats and his tales about his dad's work.

After work, Adam was desperate to relax and unwind, but dreaded returning to that damn condo.

"I'll treat if you show me where a good bar is around here," he said.

Clay laughed. "Like where the locals go?"

"Sure."

"Alright. Go home and shower or whatever. I'll pick you up in an hour."

They went to a bar about twenty minutes away. It seemed ridiculous to drive so far for a drink, but Adam realized this was actually the place the locals went. He immediately recognized tons of faces from the marina, all the folks who owned their own boats and equipment.

They sidled up to the bar and ordered beers. The bartender seemed to know Clay and didn't even bother carding Adam. Adam slid his credit card across the counter to start a tab before turning to check out the surroundings. There were pool tables in one corner, TVs mounted on all the walls, a few dart boards, and a scattering of tables throughout the rest of the place. Aside from the hilljack music playing, it was pretty similar to a bar back home.

Clay and Adam talked until they were ready for the next round of drinks. Clay waved at the bartender right as a new guy came in the front door. The bartender immediately acknowledged his presence, and the crowd by the door seemingly parted to let him pass to a table.

"Who the fuck is that?" Adam asked, thoroughly unimpressed by the guy. He was tall with thick dark brown hair. He was cleanly shaven and dressed like he belonged in a J Crew ad. Adam supposed he was what a woman may call handsome, albeit in a predictable and boring sort of way.

Clay glanced over. "That would be Jackson Kensington."

Adam turned back to the guy with newfound interest. He'd already amassed a collection of three girls and two other guys squeezing in by his table. "Ashley's brother."

Clay shook his head and blew out a laugh. "Tell me you're not still on that track. I'm telling you man, you do not want to get involved. Jackson and I went to school together and I assure you he is not the guy you want to fuck with."

Adam raised his hands defensively. "I'm not fucking with anybody. I think he and I might just be friends."

Clay raised his beer bottle to his lips, but Adam could tell he was still laughing by the way his shoulders shook.

Adam finished his beer, but as the girls left Jackson's table, he decided it was now or never.

"I'm gonna go introduce myself," he told Clay.

"Wanna come?"

"No thanks. We've already met."

Adam sauntered over to Jackson's table.

"Hey man," Adam said casually. "I just moved to the island. I've heard you know everybody so I thought I'd say hi."

Jackson gave him a curious once-over. His expression wasn't by any means unfriendly, but he did pause on Adam's tattoos for a really long time.

"I'm Adam Bricker," Adam said, extending his hand.

"Jackson Kensington," he replied, shaking Adam's hand. His grip was firm but not too firm, just as Adam had expected. "Where'd you say you moved?"

"I didn't. My family has owned a place by the marina for years now, but I just moved in a couple weeks ago."

"You're not from around here," Jackson said, clearly trying to decipher the accent. "New York?"

"New England area, yeah," Adam said, deciding it was easier to skip the explanation. Adam sure didn't talk like the people around here, but he stuck out like a sore thumb in Massachusetts, too. "Nantucket most recently."

Jackson paused his interrogation to sip his beer, so Adam decided to press his luck.

"So, Kensington, right? I think I met your sister a few days back. Ashley?"

The table fell silent and Jackson's eyes narrowed. "You stay away from Ashlynne."

Huh. Adam hadn't seen that coming. He glanced over at Clay, now shaking his head nervously and all but shouting "I told you so."

Adam was about to say something else when Jackson stood. He was a fairly intimidating fellow up close, having a slight advantage over Adam in both height and weight. Fortunately, Jackson didn't have fighting on his mind.

Instead, he nodded politely, slapped Adam on the back like they were old friends, and said "Nice to meet you. I'll see you around."

Adam watched him wind his way through the bar towards the back where he started talking with some brunette, and then Adam returned to his stool by Clay.

"He seems nice enough," Adam said.

Clay snorted, clearly knowing exactly what Adam was thinking.

* * *

THE NEXT MORNING, Ashley hit the courts for an hour of singles with a friend before it was time to teach her clinics. After work, she showered and threw her suit on under her clothes and drove out to the marina to see if anything fun was going on. Katie had mentioned something about wave-runners that day, so she wandered over by the boats to see if she could spot her.

Ashley hadn't gotten very far when she heard someone shouting out her name. She turned to see the new guy.

"When are you going to come out on the boat with me?"

She glanced over at his boat. There was nothing Ashley wanted more than to go out on the boat with Adam. It was a gorgeous day—bright blue skies, the slightest whisper of wind, and clearer than normal seas. And while she knew she could probably get some other friends together and be on another boat within the hour, there was something intriguing about this particular boat with this particular boy.

"I can't go with you," Ashley said, her tone conveying the unspoken "duh."

"Because of Brett?"

"His name is Brent, and yes."

"It's not like you really like him anyway."

"You don't know anything about me."

He shook his head dismissively. "I know you're not that into him."

Ashley hated that he could goad her into pressing the issue, rather than just letting it drop like she should. "Okay, what makes you think that?"

"The other day outside the club, you kept your eyes open when you kissed him."

Ashley tried to recall whether his assertion was accurate, then decided it was a moot point. "How do you know I don't just like looking at him?"

Adam grinned as though he'd hoped she would ask this. "Because you weren't looking at him when you kissed. You were looking at me."

She rolled her eyes. "Ego much?"

He shrugged. "All I'm saying is when you find a guy you're actually passionate about, you won't be able to keep those pretty eyes open." He stared at her with bold blue eyes until Ashley flushed.

"Whatever," she mumbled.

He leaned back against the railing. "So this Brett guy doesn't even let you hang out with other guys?"

"Brent," she corrected, not even dignifying the rest with a response.

"Are you allowed to have friends?"

"Of course I am. He doesn't control me. I just don't think it's appropriate for me to go out on a boat with some guy I barely know."

Adam appeared to think for a minute. "Invite him along."

"What?"

"It's not like this is a date or anything. I'm new to the area and I want to make some friends. I think me and Brent," he paused to ensure Ashley appreciated his correct pronunciation, "might just become best buds."

"He's busy," she replied honestly.

Adam shrugged. "Well, too bad for him. Come on aboard if you're coming. Can't wait all day." He stepped onto the boat.

Ashley glimpsed around her, looking for any reason not to go, and found nothing. So she hopped onto the boat before she changed her mind.

Adam grinned, clearly pleased she'd fallen for his bluff. He began untying the ropes.

"Need help?" Ashley offered, stuffing her phone into her back pocket.

He turned and gave her an obvious once over. "You know boats?"

"I've lived on an island my entire life," Ashley said. "I'm not useless." She gathered the ropes onboard that he had already unfastened then sat down on the seat while he kicked the dock to inch away before turning over the motor.

"Nice boat," she said once he'd zigzagged out of the crowded marina.

"Eh. Thanks. It's alright for now."

"Looking to upgrade?"

He laughed. "Isn't everyone?"

Ashley shrugged off the comment, uncertain what he meant.

Adam grinned as though pleased that he'd stumped her. "No, I really can't complain. This baby has been good to me. I'm looking to keep her and get a cabin cruiser someday. Something a little longer that can handle a few trips up and down the eastern coast and maybe a jaunt to the Caribbean."

Ashley nodded, wondering how much a boat like that would run. She saw the yachts lining the marina, and while most were owned by tourists or part-time residents of the island, a fair number of her friends owned some, too. Well, not her friends so much as their parents. She had no clue what they cost, but figured it was astronomical.

He was quiet for a few minutes, so Ashley took in the scenery. The temperature dropped a good 5-10 degrees as soon as they were out of the marina and into the open ocean. It was quieter, too. She thought about how, if Adam were a total creep, steering her out into the middle of the ocean with no other boats around would be a really good way to take advantage of her stupidity. Still, something about him told her he was one of the good guys.

"You seem to think Brent is too possessive of me," Ashley said finally, hoping to get him talking again.

He shrugged. "Like you said, I don't know the guy."

"So you'd let your girlfriend—if you ever had one, of course—go out on a boat with some strange guy?"

"If she looked like you? Not a shot in hell," he said with a smirk.

Ashley swatted him playfully then walked towards the stern of the boat.

"Hang on," he called out. She did as he asked and he killed the motor. "Drink?"

"Whatever you're having."

He retrieved two Cokes from the built-in cooler and handed her one. They both stared out at the water for a few minutes.

"How are you liking the island so far?"

Adam sat. "Well, it's gorgeous, but in a different way from the coast up north. Much flatter, anyway. Those trees are awesome, the mossy ones? Jury is still out on this heat, but I know I'll like the winters better here."

"And the people?"

He tilted his head to the side. "I'm not finding the southern hospitality to be all it's cracked up to be. The tourists are friendly. The female tourists are maybe a little too friendly, but the locals...not so much."

Ashley laughed at this. "Have you tried getting to know any of the locals?"

"Hey, I invited Brent today."

"How about the guys your own age?"

He clasped his hand over his heart. "Ouch, you make it seem like I'm thirty. And no, not really. I thought about it, but figured it would be a waste of my time. They'll all be gone in September, won't they?"

"Good point."

"So where do you like to go out here?" He gestured around to the open sea.

Ashley smiled. "Mostly right here."

"Oh? This precise latitude and longitude?"

She giggled. "I like the serenity out here, with nothing but water in every direction."

A catamaran zipped past as she spoke and they both laughed.

"Well, almost nothing else."

Adam nodded. "Me too. That's why I'd like a larger boat. I'd like to really get out in the water and not worry about coming back to shore each night."

"You could stay overnight on this," she said.

"Yeah, but separate sleeping quarters and a bathroom with a shower would be a perk."

Ashley agreed. "There are a few offshore islands that are nice around here if you're out exploring sometime. And if we go kayaking someday during low tide I can take you to my favorite sandbar."

He cocked his head to the side.

"What?"

"I'm not sure if I'm more surprised that you kayak or that you have a favorite sandbar."

She turned to look at him again while he was gazing out to sea. She had seen a lot of shirtless guys in her day, but Adam, well, he was perfect. Observing him without his shirt felt like a present just for her, whereas she never really noticed what clothes the other guys in her life were or weren't wearing. He was definitely more muscular than her friends and brothers, and there was something about his tattoos that just caught Ashley's eye.

Ashley realized he was watching her and she turned away quickly, feeling her cheeks blush. Trying to play it off as though she hadn't just been checking him out, Ashley glanced back over at his tattoos.

"That's a lot of ink," she said.

"I've seen guys with more," he replied. "I mean, I kept it contained to the pecs and biceps rather than do the full sleeves."

That was true, although Ashley wasn't sure she'd ever seen someone with more tattoos in person. Across the left side of his chest was a flower, on his shoulder an anchor and then along his bicep an intricate pattern of swirls.

"Can I..." she reached my hand towards the designs, unsure of the etiquette about touching other people's body art.

Adam laughed. "Of course. Why does anyone get tattoos except to encourage hot chicks to touch them?"

Ashley swatted his other arm playfully then proceeded to touch him anyway. She'd never actually seen a tattoo up close, let alone felt one. Ashley was surprised at how smooth the skin was. She expected to be able to feel the designs almost like Braille but instead they were flat.

"Did they hurt?"

"Hell yes. Feels like someone is clawing through your skin and slicing you open in slow motion."

Ashley grimaced at that vivid image. "Then why get more?"

"They all have different meanings. The anchor here symbolizes strength and, well, represents my love of the ocean, obviously." He gestured along his bicep next. "This is a heritage tattoo, basically just a design that intrigued me, but I like that it's something I can add to and continue down my arm or even around to my back if I want to someday."

Ashley cringed at the thought of him covering more of his perfect flesh with the designs. The ones he had now were undeniably sexy, but it just seemed sinful to mark up even more of his skin. "What about the flower—is that a daisy?"

He nodded. "Yeah," he said softly. He paused and cleared his throat. "My mom's favorite flower was a daisy. I got it after she passed away." He smiled. "She'd made me promise not to get a red heart with the word 'mom' scrawled over it or anything dorky."

"I'm sorry about your mom," Ashley said.

"Thanks. Me too."

She hesitated, unsure of what the protocol is when a new friend tells you about a deceased parent. "Do you want to talk about it?"

Adam cleared his throat. "No."

"Okay then," she said amenably. "So your dad is on the island now, too?"

"No. He travels most of the year. He'll be gone till fall."

"Oh. Wow. So who do you live with?"

"Just me," Adam said.

Ashley frowned, then remembered he was nineteen. Although none of the other nineteen year olds she knew lived alone either, except for when they were at college, but even then most had roommates. "Don't you get lonely?"

Adam shrugged. "I would never turn down some company if you're offering."

Ashley rolled her eyes. "I'm not." She stood and turned to the water, which was unusually calm for late afternoon in the summer. She was accustomed to brief downpours a few days a week, but the last five days had been dry and relatively sunny.

"I'm staying in the condo we've had since I was a kid," Adam said, breaking the silence. "We used to visit a couple times a year and rent it out the rest of the time."

"Oh."

"It's a two-bedroom at the marina. No real view to speak of but can't beat the convenience."

"Yeah, it would be nice to walk to work."

He grinned. "And it's not too far to stumble home from the bars."

She raised an eyebrow.

"Hey, you thought I looked older, too." He paused. "Actually, I met one of your brothers last night."

"Jackson?" Ashley guessed, knowing that, even with their fake IDs, her other brothers could never get into a local bar before they turned twenty-one since all the locals knew each other.

He nodded. "Seemed nice enough."

"Who were you with?"

"Clay."

"From the marina?" Ashley paused while Adam nodded. "Isn't he your boss?"

"Technically he's my supervisor. I think he went to school with you."

"He did," Ashley said, remembering seeing him in the halls previous years but never actually talking with him much. He was in Jackson's class.

"We've hit it off pretty well."

"Ahh so you're not completely friendless," she concluded.

Adam laughed, and they talked more about her family, school, and the lack of rain that season. By the time they turned back to the marina, Ashley realized she'd lost all track of time.

She stood to disembark the moment they bumped into the

dock. She wasn't eager to leave, but she didn't want anyone to see her with Adam and get the wrong impression.

Adam took the hint and kept his distance.

"Thanks for the ride," she said, smiling sweetly.

"Anytime," he replied. He paused long enough for her to start off the boat then called to her. "Hey, I'm still trying to get the condo set up and get myself settled in here and could use some advice on where to go around here for different things. You mind if I call you for some input some night after work?"

She shrugged and reached for his phone. She entered her number into his contacts before handing it back to him. "See you around!"

* * *

ADAM WATCHED her hurry along the gravel path and smiled. She was without a doubt the hottest girl on the island. Better yet, she was also way more easygoing and fun to be around than he would've guessed by the way everyone talked about her. And, just as he'd suspected, she was totally into him. He'd seen the way her breath hitched when she touched his chest. He'd caught her checking him out earlier, too.

Now he just had to figure out how to make her admit she wanted him.

Adam played it cool and waited two days to call her. He'd actually kept really busy at work anyhow, so it wasn't hard to do. He spent longer than he'd like to admit plotting out what to say on her voicemail so he wouldn't come off as needy. So, it had really thrown him when she'd answered right away. He nearly lost his cool when he realized his canned speech wouldn't work in a live call, but quickly regained his composure when she recognized his voice right off the bat.

He got her recommendations for good pizza places, directions to the hardware store, and some surf shop locations, but then he quickly changed the subject to her and her friends. Adam wasn't normally a big talker on the phone, so he was surprised to see that over an hour had passed when he decided it was time to go in for the kill.

"I'm off work tomorrow," he said. "We could meet up at the beach to hang out."

"I…" Ashley hesitated. "I really shouldn't."

Adam smirked. She didn't say she couldn't, or that she wouldn't, but that she *shouldn't*. That definitely implied that she wanted to and just needed some persuading.

"Why? You're worried about too much Vitamin D?"

"It doesn't feel right, making plans to hang out with you."

"Because of Brent?"

"Well, yeah."

"Bring him along. Hell, bring all your friends. Just thought we could hang out. Totally platonic."

She was quiet for long enough that Adam glanced at his phone to confirm it hadn't dropped the call. "Well, I suppose it would be okay. Brent is out of town tomorrow so he won't come, though."

"Nuts," Adam replied, failing at his attempt to actually sound disappointed. "Next time maybe."

Ashley sighed. "Why don't you meet me at my house around 1?"

Adam jotted down her address then said goodbye.

* * *

ASHLEY DROPPED her phone on the pillow beside her and smiled. Adam was fun to talk to, once she got over the initial weirdness of talking to a guy on the phone. Ashley couldn't even remember the last time she and Brent had talked on the phone. Mostly they just texted.

A knock on her door made her jump, and her phone bounced

onto the floor with a thud. Austin popped his head in without waiting for an invitation.

"We're headed to Shelter Cove. Want a ride?"

Ashley glanced over at the clock, surprised it was already this late. She hadn't officially made up her mind about going out tonight and now she wasn't even ready.

"I don't know. I'd need to change," she said, still debating.

She heard footsteps approaching behind Austin and assumed it was Mason. Instead, Brent popped his head in the room.

"You look good to me," he said.

Her eyes widened with shock. "How long have you been here?"

He shrugged. "An hour maybe?"

Austin nodded. "We were playing the new Call of Duty."

Guilt washed over Ashley. Had she seriously spent the evening on the phone with another guy while her boyfriend was downstairs?

"You were on the phone," Brent explained. "Didn't want to interrupt."

"Was that Lisa?" Austin asked.

Ashley panicked and nodded, regretting her lie as soon as Austin followed up by asking if Lisa was coming tonight.

"Uhhh," Ashley stalled. "She hadn't really made up her mind either." She glanced at Brent. "Give me five minutes and I'll be ready."

Austin nodded and started out. "One more round?" he called to Brent.

"Yeah man. Be down in a minute." Brent kicked the door shut behind Austin and pulled Ashley's face to his, enveloping her mouth with an aggressive kiss.

Ashley relented to his warm, familiar lips and kissed him back for a minute before pulling away. "I have to get dressed."

Brent grinned and made his way over to her closet. He rummaged around for a minute before retrieving a skimpy denim skirt. "Wear this with no panties and I guarantee you'll have a fun night."

Ashley wrinkled her nose at the thought of mosquitoes working their way up her skirt in those conditions. Bug spray was the universal summer perfume on the island, but it wasn't foolproof. "Let's compromise," she said, snatching the skirt from him. "It's not like we'll be alone anyway."

Brent smacked her butt then headed into the hall. Ashley quickly changed into the skirt and a floral halter top and tapped out a quick text to Lisa telling her she had decided to go out tonight and please to join them. Lisa declined, so Ashley wedged into Brent's silver F-150 between him and her brother. She assumed Austin would head home with Mason later, leaving her and Brent alone, but it was always hard to predict with her brothers. They both really liked Brent, which was great, but sometimes Ashley couldn't tell who Brent enjoyed hanging out with more—her or the twins.

By the time they reached the cove, the live music had already begun and Ashley was dying to stretch her legs.

"More room in my Silverado," Austin quipped.

"Bullshit," Brent replied. "You only bought that so you wouldn't have the same damn truck as your brother."

Ashley rolled her eyes. Pickup trucks were the norm in the area, in part because they were able to haul surfboards and kayaks or trail small boats, but mostly as a status symbol. The perpetual debate was whether the Chevy Silverado or Ford F-150 was the better truck. Jackson had one and Austin had the other. Mason, for some reason, had decided to be an individual for once and went with a bright green Jeep Wrangler.

They ordered drinks and crowded around a table where some of their other friends were already seated. The area was packed tonight, with tourists and locals all crammed together. Ashley loved this time of year when the recent graduates were all home and hanging out with them, too, but she wished there were some way to make the island a little bigger for the times of the year when it felt too cramped.

Mason and Austin had both brought flasks and slipped something into their drinks once they arrived. They offered some to Brent, but of course bypassed their innocent sister. Ashley knew Brent would switch drinks with her if she wanted, but she realized she wasn't in the mood to drink anyway. They finished the first round and then Brent pulled her to stand.

"Come on girl, let's dance," he said.

She followed him over to a corner between the bar and the wooden railing above the boardwalk and leaned into his tall form. The singer—a middle-aged guy with a guitar and a decent voice who performed all over the island every summer—was crooning a Luke Bryan song Ashley knew by heart. She relaxed against Brent as they swayed back and forth, relishing in the cooler air here by the water.

"What time are you and your dad leaving tomorrow?" she asked in between songs.

Brent wrinkled his nose. "Seven."

"We can leave whenever you want so you can get sleep tonight," she offered. "Or I'm sure I can hitch a ride home with my brothers."

"Nah, I can sleep in the car tomorrow," he said, groping her butt as the next song started. "You got any plans tomorrow?"

Ashley was glad that he couldn't see her face, as she was sure she was blushing. She hated lying in general, but hated it more with Brent. She should just tell him the truth, since Adam was just a friend, but she knew that would just start a fight. Brent wasn't overly possessive, but he wouldn't want her spending her day alone with another guy either, especially one he didn't know. And pissing off Brent wouldn't be a good step for Adam making friends either.

"I've got a tennis clinic in the morning and then I'll probably head to the beach in the afternoon."

Brent didn't answer, clearly satisfied with this mostly true response.

He pulled her close again and Ashley shut her eyes, focused on the music around them. She made a mental note to cancel on Adam first thing in the morning. She had a boyfriend. A fun, cute, and sweet boyfriend. She had no business making dates with other guys, even if they weren't really dates.

Although, the more Ashley thought about it, the more she felt like the sheer fact of cancelling out of guilt would mean it was a date, whereas if she kept the plans, it was obvious that she didn't view it as anything but a platonic get-together.

They returned to the table after the next song, but there was only one chair free, so Brent sat and pulled Ashley onto his lap. Her skirt was too short for her to get too comfortable and she had no interest in straddling her boyfriend in front of her brothers, so she perched chastely near his knees.

Austin was busy flirting with a redhead that Ashley suspected was a tourist. Mason was clearly still drinking, and Ashley wondered if he was banking on Austin driving his jeep home. She dismissed the thought, aware that they were big boys and could surely handle their own transportation decisions. The speed limits were insanely slow on their part of the island anyway, so you could almost get by driving home a little tipsy, but with the winding roads and tendency of deer to jump in the path, she'd never condone it.

She stood to dance with Katie for a few minutes, but when she made her way back to the table, Ashley realized Brent was gone. It was late, but he wouldn't have left without her. She set off down the boardwalk a little to look for him, immediately refreshed by the drop in temperature as she distanced herself from the crowd.

It was pitch black near the water, but based on the slight smell of stale fish wafting in the air, Ashley knew it was low tide. There was barely a breeze, and the waves were indiscernibly quiet. She stopped by the guardrail, debating whether to head down the steps to see if Brent was off near the boats. Suddenly, Ashley realized she was all alone, on an eerily quiet and deserted stretch of the marina. She could still hear the music in the distance, but that actually made her current position even creepier since she knew no one would hear her scream.

Just then, a hand grasped her arm. Ashley shrieked loudly and immediately heard a familiar laugh.

"Jumpy, are we?" Brent teased, wrapping his arms around her waist.

Ashley forced a smile, shaking the willies off. "I didn't realize how freaking dark it was out here. Where were you?"

"By the bar, talking to Jill," he said. "You looked hot dancing with Katie."

Ashley rolled her eyes at the stereotypical guy comment. "It's late. You ready to go?"

He hesitated. "I sorta had another drink, but if we stay another half hour or so, I'll be fine."

"You could let me drive your truck and you'll be good to go by the time we get to my place."

Brent laughed as though she'd suggested they take a magic carpet home.

"Actually I have an even better idea," he said.

He led her by the hand further down the dark path then leaned in to kiss her. Ashley could taste the beer on his tongue as it pushed past her lips, brushing delicately across her own. Ashley pressed her hands into his hips, guiding him closer to her, suddenly grateful that she had a boyfriend.

Brent smiled through the kiss and reached for her hips. Her shirt was too tight and too stuck to her sweaty skin for him to easily slip his hands under the material so he shifted his hands over the material instead, groaning happily as he reached her breasts. He caressed each one for a moment while kissing her before moving his hands to her butt. He started to raise her skirt up a bit when Ashley broke off the kiss.

"Brent! We are out in the open."

"It's dark," he whispered.

"My brothers could walk by."

He groaned, this time in frustration. "Come on," he said, taking her by the hand. They walked back to his truck and Ashley thought they were headed home, but Brent quickly shifted his seat back and motioned for her to join him.

She blushed, thinking about some of the things they had done together in this truck. Of course, they'd never before been in a public place—or at least a public place with other people actually nearby—when doing those things. He did look hot tonight, though, especially when he looked at her with those pouty lips.

Ashley leaned over to kiss him, balancing herself precariously on her side, determined not to actually climb into his seat. This seemed to satisfy Brent, who quickly resumed his wandering hands. This time, when his hand slipped up her skirt, Ashley didn't flinch. He rubbed her through her panties, pausing to whisper, "bet you regret not going commando now."

She giggled and let him continue for another minute before nudging him backwards. She unzipped his pants and he settled back happily. But when she reached for him with her hand, he stopped her.

"I was actually hoping you could..." his voice trailed off and he licked his lips until Ashley took the hint.

"Brent, I am not going down on you in the parking lot!"

He sighed then smiled. "I could settle for a hand job," he said, wiggling his eyebrows. He handed her a hand towel from the side of his door then leaned in to kiss her. After a minute of kissing, Ashley followed his cues and reached her hand back down to him, stroking him gently until he moaned sharply and reached for the towel. He cleaned himself up then cracked his car door to dump the towel on the gravel outside.

"Eww," Ashley mumbled.

Brent laughed then flashed his sexy grin. "I could return the favor."

Ashley leaned forward for another kiss, then nudged him away. "Another time. You need some sleep tonight."

He groaned but started the engine and drove her home.

CHAPTER 3

The next morning, Ashley was so distracted by her guilt that she actually got hit in the head with a tennis ball. Twice.

The second her clinic ended, Ashley called Adam to cancel, but it went straight to voicemail. She debated texting, but that seemed lame, so she decided it was fate telling her she wasn't actually doing anything wrong by hanging out with a new friend.

Adam arrived at one on the dot. Having anticipated him being at least a little late, Ashley wasn't ready. She invited him in while she finished gathering her stuff.

"Holy shit. You grew up here?" Adam asked as they walked through the mudroom into the kitchen. He spun in a circle, mesmerized.

Ashley nodded. "Want a tour?"

"Jesus, you could charge for the tour, this is like a European castle."

Ashley rolled her eyes. She wasn't oblivious—she knew her family was wealthy. And yes, she knew she was spoiled. But their house wasn't much bigger or fancier than anyone else's in the area, so it never seemed like a big deal.

"You could go bowling in here!" he continued.

"I get it—the house is big. Do you want to see the rest or not?"

Adam nodded, so she slipped out of her shoes, waited for him to do the same, then continued. "That was the mudroom, obviously. There's a laundry room and powder room off to the side there, but nothing exciting."

"Powder room?" he interrupted.

"Half bath. You know, toilet and sink but no shower."

"Oh."

"This is the kitchen, clearly," she said. It was one of her favorite rooms in the house, actually. It had white cabinets, many with glass doors, and creamy white and grey countertops that reminded her of the way the sky looked from under water. There was a large island in the center and a breakfast bar off to the other side, and a dinner table they never used along the edge of the room. If they were going to eat in the kitchen, they did so at the island or the bar. When they had a family dinner, it was generally either outside or in the formal dining room.

Adam ran his fingers along the marble and Ashley smiled, sensing he appreciated it the same way she did.

"Butler's pantry," she said, gesturing to the small bar area between the kitchen and formal dining room.

"You have a butler?"

"No, that's just what the room is called."

"Rich people are weird," Adam mumbled.

"Here's the formal dining room, the main entry, the formal living room, and the study."

"Do you study in there?"

"No. It's my dad's office, I guess."

"He works from home?"

"No. He works in Savannah. He's not home often."

"Here's another bathroom, here's the main living area, and the den."

"Ooh double-sided fireplace," he said. "Fancy."

"Yeah, it's nice. We had it fitted with a gas insert so we can just turn it on and off with a switch now."

"But then you don't get the romantic woodsy smell of a real fire," Adam said.

Ashley eyed him quizzically. "I didn't peg you as big on romance."

"I have my secrets," he said with a shrug. "So what's out here?" Adam slid open the door to the deck.

"Umm, the deck," she said. There was a large table for eating, a sofa and two cushioned chairs, a coffee table, two end tables, a gas grill and a charcoal grill. A short stairway led to the ground level.

Adam walked out to the banister and looked over. "And there's the pool, hot tub, and do I spy a fire pit?"

"Yep. Very fun for winter. Go from hot tub to fire pit and back." Ashley paused and gestured across the way. "There's the private beach path. There's a little area with benches about halfway down. It's my secret homework or reading spot. You can see and hear the ocean but it's not quite as windy."

"Nice." He paused. "What's on the ground floor?"

"Nothing, really. I guess it's the basement. But it's just the entrance from the outdoor shower and a lot of storage. The only finished rooms are the exercise room, media room, and a bathroom."

"Oh, that's all," he said with a snort.

Ashley led him up the back stairway to the second floor. "Here's Jackson's room and the guest room and his bathroom. Here are the twins' rooms and a Jack and Jill bathroom."

"A what?"

Ashley led him into Mason's room and showed him the bathroom connecting the two rooms.

"Cool. I bet that was fun for hide and seek when you were kids."

Ashley nodded. "Here's the loft and then those stairs lead up to our parents' suite."

"They have their own floor," he said, in awe.

"Well, yeah. It has its own balcony and everything, with a pretty sweet view since it's higher up. Just a bedroom, massive closet, bathroom, and sitting room. And they have their own fireplace," she added.

"Of course," he said. "So where do you sleep?"

Ashley led him back to the other side of the loft. "Here's my bedroom and bathroom."

He stepped in tentatively then paused. "How many bathrooms does this house have?"

She cringed, knowing it was a little ridiculous. "Seven," she said. "Plus an outdoor shower."

"Wow," he murmured, "just wow."

She wrinkled her nose. "And now you can lecture me on how I'm some spoiled little rich girl."

He stepped closer. "Being rich doesn't make you bad. And you should be proud of your house. It's pretty fucking amazing."

He strolled around the room then and looked at the stuff on her walls.

Ashley froze, suddenly embarrassed that Adam was in her room, seeing her fluffy, pale pink bedding and gargantuan stuffed animal collection. Brent had been in her room before, but that was different. He'd grown up around her. Adam was relatively new and so much older. It felt like she was letting him in on her childhood secrets.

"This is the girliest room I've ever seen," he said, pausing to read a poetry award on the bulletin board above her desk. "I love it."

His final comment totally threw Ashley. Her face must have shown her confusion because Adam asked what was wrong as soon as he turned around.

"Nothing. It's just weird having a guy in here."

"Oh. But you live with a bunch of guys."

"Totally different," she said. "Although that is the reason my room has so much pink. My poor mom was desperate for some feminine touches after three sons."

Adam chuckled. "Does Brent come in here?"

"Sometimes." She omitted the part about how they weren't allowed to close the door whenever he came over, which had to be the dumbest rule in parenting ever. Her parents were rarely home to enforce the no-closed-door rule, and if they were, Ashley could just go to Brent's house. Or his truck. Or her car. Or the boat. Or a different room in the house. Lord knows her mom never went into the basement.

"But that's different," he guessed.

Ashley nodded.

He flashed her a wry grin.

"What are we doing here?" she asked, regretting her bluntness as soon as she heard the words aloud.

Adam sat on the end of her bed. Ashley knew instantly that was one image she was not going to be able to shake for a while.

"We're friends, right?"

Ashley nodded.

He shrugged casually. "So are we headed to the beach?"

"Sure. Just let me get changed."

He made no effort to move.

"Nice try. I'll meet you downstairs."

Ashley quickly changed into her magenta bikini with a faux tie-on front, combed her hair, and touched up her makeup. Then she dashed downstairs where Adam was waiting awkwardly in the kitchen.

"You could've sat down or something," she said apologetically. "Made yourself at home."

He laughed. "This is nothing like my home."

"Oh, I think I left my book in Lexi," she remembered.

"Where?"

"Lexi," she repeated, "my car."

Adam busted out laughing like they were at a comedy show.

"You named your car Lexi?"

Ashley nodded.

"But it's a Lexus. That's like the least original name out there, Lexi the Lexus."

She made a face at him.

"I mean that's like if I named my truck Trucky the Truck," he continued, still laughing uncontrollably.

Ashley sighed. "Are you done mocking me?"

He tried to gather his composure. "Sure. But you won't need a book."

"Where's your boyfriend today?" Adam asked as he followed her down the boardwalk, lugging along a wakeboard, a volleyball, a deflated raft, and the beach chairs she'd insisted on.

"He's in Savannah for the day with his father."

"Learning the family business?"

Ashley couldn't decipher from his tone whether he was teasing. "Something like that," she replied.

"So you have the whole afternoon free," he concluded. He walked straight up to the water and plopped the chairs in the damp sand, clearly knowing the tide was on its way out. He watched as the metal base of the chairs sunk several inches, leaving the canvas seats hovering dangerously close to the ground. Then he grabbed the volleyball and motioned for her to follow him.

"Umm, I'm more of a passive beachgoer," Ashley said, eying the ball like it might bite. She wasn't entirely unathletic, but her preferred beach activities centered on her lounging in her chair.

Adam glanced around at the near empty beach. "Come on, who else can I get to play with me?"

Ashley sighed, but when he served the ball to her, she returned it without complaint. They volleyed it back and forth several times before she missed. She picked up the ball and hit it back to him.

"Clearly you've played before," he said.

Ashley laughed. "Yeah, it's hard to avoid every beach volleyball game when you live on a beach."

"Must be rough," he joked. He spiked the ball to the side and she dove for it but missed. He came to her quickly and offered her a hand to help her up. "I need to cool off, and seeing as how you are now all sandy, you might as well join me."

Ashley rolled the ball to the chairs and took a long swig of tea from her tumbler before wading out into the water beside him.

"You guys have a shitload of jellyfish here, you know?" he said, glancing down at the water.

Ashley eyed him quizzically and then laughed. "Are you scared?"

He grinned, his adorable dimple making her heart thump in her chest. "I'm not *not* scared," he said.

Ashley let her gaze wander down to his chest, where his taut muscles were accented by the thin black lines etched across his skin. She longed to trace her fingers across his shoulders and chest, and down to the ridges of his abdomen. Quickly, she dove under water, desperate to both hide her blushing and distract herself. She stayed close to the surface but swam a good five yards further out towards the depths of the sea. When she came up, the water lapped gently at her chest and shoulders. Adam was still in the shallow end.

"You're seriously going to make me swim? What if I drown?"

Ashley giggled, loving his willingness to drop the tough guy shell. "I'll rescue you."

Adam's smiled broadened across his face. "Now that's an offer I can't resist," he said. He lunged forward and swam towards her with perfect form. He ran his fingers through his hair as he popped out of the water, reminding Ashley of a hunky cologne model.

"Do you wear contacts?" she asked suddenly.

"No. 20/20 vision here. Why?"

"Lucky. I can't open my eyes under water. Can you dive down by my foot?"

He frowned. "What am I getting?"

"You'll see."

He shrugged and dove down. She relaxed as she felt his hand by her foot a moment later, shifting her to the side slightly so he could retrieve his treasure. He emerged and held the sand dollar above his head. "Awesome!"

Ashley smiled at the look of wonder on his face. "Is that your first sand dollar?"

"I think so," he said. "Is that why you dragged me all the way out here?"

"Yes. I had to show you there's more than just jellyfish in our waters."

"Should I throw it back?"

"Throw it that way," she gestured the direction the current was headed. "Then we won't find the same one again."

He turned and tossed it. "So we're hunting for more?"

Ashley nodded and shuffled her feet around in the sand until she found another. She pointed towards her toe. Adam dove under the water, and a moment later she squealed as he grabbed her leg. It was a playful touch near her knee, but Ashley felt its impact much higher.

They took turns locating the sand dollars, with Adam doing the majority of the retrieval, until they'd found twelve total, and one lucky starfish.

"It's really unusual to find one fully intact," Ashley commented, before tossing it gently back into the water herself.

"We must be lucky," Adam said, gazing at her with a seriousness in his eyes that made her heart flutter. He grabbed her hand underwater. "Thank you for dragging me out here."

Ashley started to say something to break the awkwardness of

his tender gesture when she spotted a massive dark grey creature swimming way too close for comfort. She let out a high pitched shriek and launched herself at Adam, certain they were about to be eaten by a shark.

Adam caught her, wrapping his strong arms around her waist and instantly offering her comfort, despite the fact that they were still well within easy access of the shark. He pulled her back a few feet as though preparing to swim to shore with her, then stopped suddenly without loosening his hold on her.

"Dolphins," he whispered, his lips so close to her face that she felt his breath on her cheek.

Ashley stared at the water again, unconvinced until the animal surfaced again, this time clearly displaying its horizontal tail before emerging fully. A moment later, a second dolphin jumped out of the water. Ashley exhaled, relaxing into Adam's arms. His chest pressed firmly against her back and his strong forearms held tight against her waist. He felt really, really good.

"They're beautiful," Adam said. "I've never seen them this close from the water before. Usually I'm up in a boat looking down."

Ashley nodded in agreement. The adrenaline she'd felt when she thought they were about to become dinner was gone, although the logical part of her knew they still should swim back. Dolphins and sharks frequented the same waters, preferred the same conditions, and shared some of the same prey, so there was a chance a shark could be nearby.

Adam apparently was reaching the same conclusion. "We should swim in," he said. He loosened his grip on Ashley and waited for her to start swimming before following.

She stepped out of the water, wrung out her hair, then sank into the chair. Adam loomed over her for a moment, blocking the sun's rays, then sat beside her.

"A lady caught a six foot tiger shark on one of our fishing

excursions yesterday," he said. "We were barely out of the marina."

Ashley grimaced. She knew all the statistics about shark attacks and their likelihood—or lack thereof—but still got goosebumps whenever she thought about massive, dangerous creatures swimming alongside her without her even knowing. While the island's beaches were smooth and gorgeous, the water was rather murky, thanks to the waves constantly churning up sand and the absence of a reef or other sea creatures nearby that tended to make the water clearer.

As if he could read her mind, Adam continued. "You ever wonder how often there has been a shark within striking distance of you out there, just watching and debating?"

Ashley shivered despite the sweltering heat. "New topic!"

Adam smirked. "Alright. Let's discuss that boyfriend of yours."

"What about him?" Ashley was suspicious of where this was headed.

"When are you gonna dump him?"

She sat up in her chair to see if he actually expected a serious response. Adam was staring back at her calmly awaiting an answer.

"Excuse me?"

He shook his head. "Don't play coy with me. You heard me."

"What makes you think I'm going to break up with him?"

"You aren't the type to cheat."

"True."

"And you're interested in someone else," he said, his voice deeper now.

"Who might that be?" Ashley asked, trying to swallow the lump in her throat.

Adam flashed that ridiculously sexy grin of his and wiggled his eyebrows repeatedly.

Ashley leaned back in her chair with a groan. "You are so cocky!"

"I prefer brazen. Or direct," he said. "Look, I can't help it if I know what I want and don't want to waste time. Life is short. And you don't always know how long you have left."

He stood and walked up to the water, pausing to retrieve a shell by his feet and tossing it into the water. Ashley sighed. She knew he was talking about his mother, and now she felt bad for calling him cocky. Well, he *was* cocky, for sure, but she'd only said that because she was embarrassed for having been called out on her crush.

Ashley did like Adam and she hated that he knew it. She wasn't supposed to like him. She was with Brent. Brent was her boyfriend. She belonged with Brent.

Ashley slowly stood and joined Adam by the water. "I'm not good at being impulsive," she said. "I am having a lot of fun with you today, but…"

Boy was this awkward. How could she explain all the ways Brent was right for her and how very, very wrong Adam was without insulting him? "I have a lot of history with Brent. He's a nice guy. And we go to school together. And our families…"

"I hear you," Adam said.

Ashley glanced at him, trying to decipher how badly she'd just hurt his ego, but he looked fine. Clearly he was even more arrogant than she thought.

Suddenly, Adam turned to her and lifted up her sunglasses. She squinted from the sudden assault of light.

"What are you doing?"

He dropped the shades back into place. "I just can't be sure with you," he said.

"What?"

"I think you like me," he explained. "I think if we were in some alternate universe where your momma wouldn't have a heart attack if you brought someone like me home and you weren't terrified of breaking away from the script your parents wrote for your life, well I think you would give me a chance. And I think you'd find yourself pretty happy with me."

"I'm happy now."

He nodded. "Brent is better for you on paper, Ash. I get that. Hell, on paper, I'd pick him too." He reached over, grabbing her hand, and placed both of their hands on her chest, alarmingly close to her breast. "But he doesn't make your heart beat like that and you know it."

Ashley yanked her hand free, flustered and uncomfortable by the direction the conversation was headed. She had never before met someone so direct, so intense, or so passionate as Adam. She didn't quite know how to handle him. And his whole theory about how she didn't love Brent really caught her off guard. Everyone else was constantly telling them what a perfect couple they were. What did Adam see that everyone else didn't?

She stood there, awkwardly, until he abruptly turned and reached for the raft. He began inflating it while she watched, flabbergasted.

When it was fully inflated, he dragged their chairs back a good fifteen feet then motioned for her to follow him into the water.

* * *

ADAM KNEW what he'd said had struck a chord with Ashley. He still couldn't actually believe he'd said all that out loud. He'd never been the type to beat around the bush, but he'd also never had to beg to get a girl to go out with him. On the rare occasion in the past where a girl hadn't immediately jumped at the chance to be with him, he'd simply moved on to another. Attractive girls were never in short supply.

But he wasn't sure what to do with Ashley. He didn't think she was playing hard to get, nor did he get the impression she disagreed with any of his conclusions about her rationale for staying with her boyfriend. But she also wasn't budging. She was comfortable with Brent. He was the easy choice. What Adam had to do was make her realize he was worth the challenge.

He had hoped their conversation about Brent would have taken a different turn but was relieved at least that she hadn't left. As long as she kept coming back for more time with him, he was still in the game.

"Come on," he said, again waving for her to join him.

She reluctantly followed. "I'm not going way out there again after all your talk of sharks," she warned him.

He grinned and offered her the raft. She placed it under her arms and lay across it, kicking her feet behind her as they headed out to sea. Adam was grateful for the coverage offered by the water since he couldn't stop his body from reacting to the sight of her gorgeous bikini-clad ass up on the raft. It seemed to Adam that half the island had a crush on Ashley and, while she certainly wasn't self-conscious, traipsing around in her bikini all day, she was clearly oblivious to how smoking hot she actually was.

Once they were past the breaking point of the waves, Ashley stopped kicking and scooted over so Adam could relax beside her on the raft. Although they were only side by side on their stomachs, Adam couldn't help but wonder what Brent would think if he saw them. Thankfully, that wouldn't happen, and he sure wasn't about to bring him up again.

"What are your plans for next year?" he asked instead, certain she had made definitive arrangements already.

"I'm applying for early acceptance into Duke."

"Wow. Prestigious. What's the backup plan?"

She scowled at the question before rattling off a few more schools, none of which sounded particularly easy to get into and all of which were along the central to southern portion of the east coast.

"What do you have against Yankees? Or Westerners?" he asked.

"My parents both went to Duke," she said. "And I don't really feel like going too far from home. I like it here."

"Where do your brothers go?"

"Jackson is at University of Florida and the twins are going to UNC Chapel Hill."

"That's a lot of out-of-state tuition," Adam commented. "Did Austin and Mason even consider the possibility of attending different schools?"

Ashley splashed her hand in the water absentmindedly. "They claim to have, but no one ever seriously thought they'd separate."

Adam kicked his feet to counter the current's effect on the raft.

"What about you? Did you consider going to college?"

"Yeah. I always assumed I'd go. I got decent grades in high school—not that I had a choice. Coach would kick anyone off the team with less than a C+ average."

Ashley turned to him. "You were on a team?"

"Basketball. Why?"

She laughed. "You just seem like such a loner."

"A loner?" Adam had never really thought of himself that way.

"Okay, poor choice of words. You just don't strike me as a team player. You're more the type to do what you want regardless of what everyone else thinks or expects."

He shrugged.

"So what happened?"

"My mom."

Ashley twitched. "I'm sorry. That was stupid of me to... I didn't mean..."

"It's fine. It's not like that prevented me from going—it just made me reevaluate my priorities. I figured I'd have fun in college but didn't see the point in wasting time with classes and studying to get a degree I didn't really need for what I really wanted to do."

"And what is that?"

"This."

"This," she repeated. "You want to spend your life adrift in the sea?"

He laughed at her skepticism. "Maybe not drifting, but yeah. I want to be out on the water."

"There are a lot of careers on the ocean you can train for at college."

"None that appeal to me," he said. "And if I change my mind down the road, I can go to college then." He paused. "I actually considered the Coast Guard for a while but figured that might be too regimented for me."

Ashley smiled.

"What do you plan to study at Duke?"

"Coastal environmental management. I want a degree in environmental science with a concentration in marine sciences and conservation."

Before Adam could respond, a wave crashed into the raft. He hopped off to steady it so Ashley didn't flip. The waves were picking up as the tide turned, and they'd drifted back towards shore anyway, albeit significantly further down the beach than they'd started. He remained on his feet, pushing the raft over the waves.

Ashley giggled as the water splashed into her face and Adam's eyes were drawn to her mouth. She had smooth, full lips that seemed perpetually stained by watermelon. Actually, Adam realized she always had a distinct fruity scent about her, too, so maybe she was just constantly eating watermelon. Somehow, he doubted that, though. She licked her lips and his pulse raced in response. Then he realized she was looking at him quizzically.

"Whatcha thinking about?" she asked.

"Honestly?"

She shrugged.

"I was thinking about what it would be like to kiss you."

Her eyes widened. It was pretty cute how clearly unexpected his response had been.

"You can't kiss me."

"Why is that?"

"Brent."

"Ah, right," Adam said, leaning closer to her. "The problem is that I am positive one kiss from me is all it will take to convince you to leave Brent, to follow your heart instead of your head."

"But you can't kiss me as long as I'm with Brent," Ashley said.

"Aye, there's the rub," Adam agreed.

Ashley slid off the raft. "You know Shakespeare?"

Adam laughed. "I'm a man of many mysteries," he said, leading the way back to shore.

He drove Ashley back home shortly after and didn't mention her soon-to-be-ex-boyfriend again. He had hoped by the end of the day, Ashley would've at least agreed to go out with him, but he still felt reasonably confident she would soon enough.

CHAPTER 4

On Friday, Ashley headed over to Brent's to "hang out." After her day with Adam, Ashley was hoping for some time alone with Brent to remind herself why she was so lucky to have him.

Brent greeted her at the door and kissed her, then retreated down the hall towards the den. Ashley followed reluctantly, already losing the good mood she'd had upon arrival.

"I was just starting the next episode of *The Walking Dead*," he called back to her. "Want me to start it over?"

Ashley groaned silently. They'd already watched the entire series together and now Brent was rewatching them. She had enjoyed most of it the first time around, but really didn't get the thrill in watching a show that's supposed to be suspenseful and exciting when you already know what happens.

"Want a snack?" he offered, plopping down on the couch.

"No, thanks." Ashley was going to have to start jogging with Lisa if she planned to spend her summer lounging on the couch eating junk food and binge-watching TV. She curled beside him on the leather couch and pulled out her phone, already bored. She wanted to talk with Brent, but then she couldn't really think of anything interesting to talk about. Summer lacked the ready-serve gossip of the school year and the sports worth discussing. Ashley knew if she just said she wanted to talk, Brent would assume something was wrong.

Ashley tried to think about what she'd talked about with Adam on the beach. Or on the phone or boat, really. Come to think about it, she'd been talking with Adam a lot lately. They had swapped stories from childhood and compared their respective small beach town schools. They'd talked about their favorite foods and sports and seasons.

And it wasn't that she didn't want to talk about all that same stuff with Brent, but they'd already had all those discussions. She already knew Brent liked college football and that he hated cold weather and that he was terrified of becoming a stuffy old businessman like his father or hers. And she didn't need to ask him about his old elementary school or his first girlfriend because she knew all of that already. She had been there for it all.

Ashley wondered if this was why married people cheated after many years with their spouse. Before, such a thing never made sense to her. But now, Ashley wondered if boredom was to blame. People just let themselves get wrapped up in the excitement and novelty of an unfamiliar person and forget why they're so lucky to have their current person.

Brent's hand squeezed her thigh and jolted her from her thoughts. Ashley wrinkled her nose. What was wrong with her? Brent was a really good guy. Yeah, he could be self-absorbed and apparently liked anything pertaining to zombies more than she thought was healthy, but he was nice. He didn't cheat on Ashley or make her feel bad about herself. He wasn't controlling or manipulative. He didn't taunt the dorky kids at school just because he was popular and he always stood up for his friends.

So why did her thoughts keep drifting back to Adam?

Ashley stared closely at Brent, profiting from his distraction by the oversized television. His blond hair was cut short, and he had deep brown eyes and a slightly lopsided grin that she'd always found both reassuring and sexy. He had an athletic build, and, like everyone on the island, maintained a decent tan year round. Ashley knew countless girls would line up for a chance to date Brent. Why couldn't she just appreciate what she had?

"I thought I'd go mudding this weekend with the guys," Brent said, interrupting her thoughts.

Ashley realized he was asking her permission. Or maybe inviting her along, but probably not. "That sounds fun. I might sleep over at Lisa's one night."

Brent glanced sideways at her and grinned mischievously. "You could sleep over here one night instead."

She giggled flirtatiously, feeling like a fraud even as she did it.

"Actually," Brent began, pausing the show and leaning over her, "why wait until this weekend? We have the house to ourselves now."

He pressed his mouth to hers and nudged her backwards until she was flat against the couch. The leather was cold against her bare shoulders and stuck to her thighs. She wriggled to the side to get more comfortable and Brent took that opportunity to thrust his hand up the back of her shirt.

Ashley was determined to focus on kissing Brent. She squeezed her eyes closed, trying to simultaneously shut out Adam's voice for taunting her about leaving them open when she kissed. How was it his business anyway how she kissed?

"You taste so good," Brent mumbled between kisses.

Ashley figured that was true. Minty fresh, right? She had brushed her teeth before coming over, just like she did every other time she knew she'd see Brent. Brent, on the other hand, tasted like peanuts. It wasn't bad, just, well, peanuty.

His housekeeper Susie made a mean peanut brittle. Ashley wondered if there was any left. She was a little hungry, now that she thought about it. She wondered what time it was. Probably not quite dinner time, although she didn't have to be home at any particular time, so she'd probably end up eating with Brent anyway, which meant they could just eat whenever.

Brent nudged her to the side and slipped his shirt over his head. Ashley stared appreciatively at his chest and abs, pleased that her approval of his body didn't feel forced. His hands moved to lift up her shirt. Ashley clamped her hand over his.

"We're in your den, Brent!"

"No one is here, Ash. I promise."

"What about Susie?"

"What about her? She won't bother us."

Ashley groaned. Even though they'd both grown up with housekeepers, Brent had an entirely different attitude about them than Ashley did. To him, it was like the woman was more a fixture in the house than a person. He didn't care what she saw or thought of him. Ashley, on the other hand, was mortified by the thought of the housekeeper figuring out they had sex.

"Let's go upstairs then," he suggested, lifting her to her feet.

Ashley tried to think of an excuse but found herself being pulled by the hand towards the spiral staircase at the back of the house. Brent kicked his door shut and locked it, then quickly yanked Ashley's shirt off.

"You left your shirt downstairs," she said.

"So?" Brent kissed her collar bone and worked his way down.

"What if Susie finds it?"

"So?" he repeated, this time with obvious annoyance. He reached down and unbuttoned her shorts.

"It has been way too long since we've done this," he murmured, shifting his focus to his own shorts.

Ashley panicked. She knew exactly where this was headed, and she really wasn't in the mood. Honestly she wished she were in the mood, because if she just did it with Brent she could stop stressing about whether she was still into him. Although if she weren't stressing about that to start with, she probably wouldn't mind just doing it even without being in the mood because, well, why not? It wasn't like it was the first time. But as it was, Ashley knew she'd just overanalyze everything they were about to do and that stressed her out even more.

Suddenly, she realized Brent had stopped kissing her. She opened her eyes just as he flopped backwards onto his bed.

"Geez Ash, what's going on with you lately? It's like you're a million miles away."

She sighed and cautiously sat beside him on the bed. "I don't know. Sorry. I guess I'm not in the mood today."

"Today? More like the entire summer."

"That's not true. We…" She racked her brain to remember the last time they'd fooled around. Her breath caught in her throat as she recalled. It had been the night she'd run into Adam at the marina.

"I think I'm just flustered about senior year and college and everything."

Brent nodded.

"And I'm getting kind of hungry," she added, knowing that was sure to distract him.

Brent was quiet for a minute. "Okay, I could eat," he finally said. He reached for his phone. "The twins are going out on the boat tonight if you want to do that."

Ashley knew from his expression that he wanted to go with them, but she really didn't feel like spending the evening on a boat with her brothers. She wrinkled her nose. "Let's go pick up some food and head over to Katie's. She said everyone would be at her pool until later. If it's lame we can head out on the boat after."

Brent considered this and then nodded. He stepped into his bathroom and emerged a moment later with swim trunks and a towel. Ashley reminded him they'd need to stop at her house to pick up her suit, and they were off.

Ashley had fun at Katie's, and by the time Mason suggested they head over to the marina, Brent didn't even seem to care that

Ashley didn't join them. Ashley stayed for a while after they left, and then got out of the pool to dry off. She grabbed a drink from Katie's kitchen and then meandered back outside, scrolling through her text messages. Most of them were lame. Brent checked that she could get a ride home with Lisa (yes), her mom wanted to know if she'd be home for dinner (no), and her coach was reminding everyone about some stupid summer tennis clinic they were all supposed to attend the next week (ugh).

Ashley couldn't help but laugh when she reached the next text. It was from Adam, of course, and it was a picture of a man with starfish and sand dollars tattooed all over his torso. Adam wrote "my next tats?"

Still giggling, she replied "OMG no."

"But I'm a friend to echinoderms and my body art should reflect that" came his rapid reply.

"Echinoderms?" Ashley replied.

"Geez," he wrote back, "for a coastal environmental management major, you sure don't know much about marine life. So whatcha doing now?"

"Swimming at Katie's," she replied.

"Skinny dipping?"

Ashley giggled again, continuing the friendly banter. She lost track of time while she was texting Adam because he was constantly making her laugh. After a while, Lisa came over and perched on the end of Ashley's lounge chair.

"Geez, you might as well have just gone with Brent if you were going to sit here and sext him all night," Lisa whined.

Ashley flipped her phone facedown, feeling her cheeks flush. "I'm not sexting!"

Lisa laughed. "Sure," she said, clearly not believing Ashley. "Tell him I said hi."

As Lisa sauntered off, Ashley texted Adam that she had to go and then switched her phone to silent. She couldn't believe she spent the entire evening texting with Adam after blowing off her boyfriend, but she did know it was time to be honest with herself.

She was pretty sure she was only attracted to Adam because he was so new and different. Ashley's life was boring and void of excitement, so it was only natural she craved the mystery Adam had to offer. But if she was as happy with Brent as she should be, Ashley suspected she wouldn't be so easily distracted by Adam. And whatever the future held for her with Adam, it wasn't fair for her to drag Brent along while she figured it out.

* * *

ONCE THE GUILT SET IN, Ashley knew she had to end things with Brent quickly. Before she could wuss out, she invited him over the next afternoon. Then, she spent the next several hours going over the worst-case scenarios in her head. She mostly focused on the long-term dangers, like the high probability that she would never find love again. Or that her entire group of friends would shun her and that she'd have a horrifically lonely and awkward senior year as the entire class sided with Brent. Ashley knew her own family wouldn't be happy about the breakup either.

Ashley was also terrified of Brent's reaction because he had a temper. She didn't actually think he'd hurt her or anything like that, but she could see him getting pissed off and punching a wall or throwing something. She felt more comfortable having the talk with him at her own house, but the nagging concern of property damage led her to select the back patio for their conversation.

By four o'clock, Ashley was so nervous that she could actually feel her pulse in her feet. When the doorbell rang, a wave of nausea rushed over her and Ashley almost wished he'd stood her up. Of course, she knew that Brent would never do something like that. He was too much the gentleman. She walked to the door slowly, already hating herself for what she was about to do.

She opened it to find him standing peacefully at the doorstep, an innocent smile on his face. He looked like he was about to go golfing, in pressed khaki shorts and a crisp white polo that appeared never to have been worn. Ashley bit her lip, realizing he looked like a cute Ralph Lauren model.

She swallowed the rising doubt. It wasn't like she hadn't already known he was cute. She wasn't breaking up with him because of a lack of attraction, so it didn't matter.

"Can I come in?" he asked with a bemused smile.

"Oh, yes. Sorry!" Ashley stepped aside to let him in.

He leaned close and folded her against him for a slow, languid kiss. Ashley was prepared for this. She knew he'd kiss her on arrival and even though her instincts said it was wrong to kiss a guy after deciding to break up with him, she viewed this as the final test. If she couldn't go through with it after the kiss, well, then maybe she was actually supposed to be with him.

As it was, though, the kiss was just a kiss. It wasn't unpleasant by any means, but Ashley definitely didn't feel any overwhelming spark.

"You okay?" Brent asked, causing another pang of guilt.

How could she break up with a guy who was this perceptive and thoughtful? She pushed the feelings aside and nodded.

"Let's go out back," she said. "Want anything to drink?"

"No, I'm good," he replied, not giving a second glance to the interior of the home.

Ashley couldn't help but compare his lack of reaction to Adam's response to seeing the home for the first time. But, it wasn't just that Brent was used to being around wealthy people, it was also that he'd been inside this exact house hundreds of times. So of course he wouldn't give it a second thought.

"Are we all alone?" he asked as they got outside. He sat in a chair facing the ocean and leaned back comfortably.

"Yeah, but my mom should be home any minute," Ashley

answered, wanting to avoid getting his hopes up about any illicit activity when they had the house to themselves.

"So…" he began, clearly already bored. "What do you want to do?"

God, this was awkward. Ashley was astounded at how uncomfortable and just wrong this whole conversation felt when she'd been nothing but at ease with Brent for years. She took a deep breath and spoke.

"I actually wanted to talk."

"Uh oh," he said jokingly.

Ashley winced. Brent leaned forward, his elbows pressed into his thighs.

"I really like you," she began. "I mean, I know you know that. I actually consider you one of my best friends. And we always have fun together and, I don't know, we just seem to work really well together." She sighed, trying to remember how she planned to explain to him why they needed to break up when she couldn't even rationalize it herself.

Brent looked uncomfortable, but Ashley couldn't really tell whether he knew the direction this was headed yet or not since his dark sunglasses blocked his eyes.

"I just feel like we're growing apart this summer."

Brent was quiet for a moment before speaking. "Yeah. I noticed that, too."

Ashley exhaled with relief. "I don't really know what it is, I mean I can't really put my finger on any one thing and say this is what's wrong or what's missing, but I just don't see that spark between us anymore."

"Spark," he repeated with confusion.

Ashley knew she just needed to say it. "I think we should break up." As soon as the words left her mouth, she held her breath and waited.

Brent leaned back in his chair, took a deep breath, then

exhaled. Ashley waited for an eternity for him to answer, but he remained silent.

"I don't want to lose you," she began, then she sighed. She felt everything she was about to say was so cliché, but it was true, and it was all she had, so she went ahead with it. "I know that's completely unfair of me to say, given the circumstances, but I still consider you one of my best friends and I really want us to be okay around each other because, well, small town. And I know you are still going to be close with my brothers and we have all the same friends and…"

Ashley paused, realizing she was rambling. But Brent still didn't speak, so she continued. "You were my first true love and I have so many great memories with you and I don't regret any of it. But you've been in my life so long that I don't even know who I am outside of my role as your girlfriend. And I feel like I'm holding you back now. I see how girls at school look at you and I don't feel like it's fair to keep monopolizing your time when I don't really know where we're headed. It's like we've just settled into this comfortable pattern and I'm scared we're going to turn into our parents and hate each other and I don't want that. I'd rather end things when we can still be friends."

She exhaled as she finally finished her monologue, surprised and pleased at how smoothly it had gone. Really she couldn't have planned it any better.

"Friends," Brent repeated, clearing his throat. He ran his fingers through his hair and glanced around. "You want to be friends?"

Ashley sensed annoyance in his voice now and really wished he weren't wearing the sunglasses. "Yes," she said.

"It's our senior year, Ashley. I thought we had a plan."

Ashley wasn't sure what to say. They had planned a lot. Not exactly firm plans, but they were both applying for early admission to Duke, so they had at least considered the possibility of staying together for a while.

Brent stood abruptly. "I should go."

"I'm so sorry, Brent," Ashley said, feeling tears drip down her cheeks. She reached for his arm, needing him to believe her. In all of her visions of how this would go down, she hadn't expected no reaction whatsoever from him. She had a response prepared if he was hurt or angry or confused—but she didn't know what to do with this since she couldn't tell what he was thinking.

Brent shook her hand off of him. "Ashley, don't."

"Don't you think we should talk about this?" she sniffled, trying to control her crying.

"There's nothing to talk about, Ashley," Brent started through the patio door.

"Brent, wait!" Ashley lunged after him, now crying like a crazy woman. "I can't live with you hating me."

He took a few more steps then paused. Without turning to face her, he snapped, "I don't hate you, Ashley," in a voice that contradicted his words.

Ashley stood there, stunned, as he walked back through her house to get to his truck out front. She waited several minutes, then went upstairs to her room, locked the door, and sobbed into her pillow until her lips went numb.

Hours later, when Ashley's mom called her to dinner. Ashley shouted through the door that she wasn't hungry. She was beyond annoyed at the timing anyway. They rarely had a family dinner, so why did the night she wanted to just avoid everyone have to be that one random time together?

"Ashley, we are all home and eating as a family tonight. Please hang up the phone and come down now," her mother replied.

Ashley rolled her eyes even though no one could see her. "I'm not on the phone. I'm not hungry and I don't feel good. I'm going to take a bath." She slowly rolled off the bed to go fill her tub, assuming that was enough to appease her mother.

"Ashlynne Marie open this door right now!"

Ashley swore under her breath. She wiped her eyes on a sweatshirt from her dresser then opened the door an inch.

Her mother stared through the crack, her expression morphing from annoyed to concerned. "What's wrong?"

Ashley sighed. "I don't want to talk about it. I had a really bad afternoon and I just want to be alone. I cannot handle a family dinner right now, okay?"

Ashley could tell her mother wanted to push the issue and find out exactly what was wrong, but she prayed she'd let it drop. It was hard enough breaking Brent's heart—she couldn't handle letting down the rest of her family tonight, too.

Just then, Mason appeared behind their mother. "If she's not coming down, I don't have to either," he said, sauntering past the door. Ashley tried to turn away, but was a smidge too slow, and he saw her tear-stained face.

"Dude, what's wrong?" he asked.

"Mother!" Ashley shrieked. She turned and stormed towards her bathroom.

"Ashley doesn't want to talk about it right now, Mason. But you need to be at the table in two minutes." her mother said.

Ashley heard her bedroom door shut with a click, so she made her way to the bathroom. As she soaked in the tub, she tried to figure out why she was so devastated. She didn't feel like she had a right to be sad, since she was the one who decided to end things. But at the same time, it felt wrong not to mourn such a long relationship. She and Brent had broken up before, but it had always been an impulsive thing one of them had decided in the midst of a shouting match, and they always made up within days.

This time, Ashley suspected it was the last time, and she was pretty confident Brent thought the same thing. She almost felt it would've been easier if he'd gotten angry.

She reached for her phone and texted Lisa "broke up w B 2day." She held onto her phone, knowing the response would come quickly, and it did.

"OMG really? Why? What did u say? What did he say? How are u feeling?"

"Feel like shit," Ashley texted back.

Lisa replied with a hug emoji and offered to come over, but Ashley texted back that she wanted to be alone tonight.

For the next half hour, Ashley replayed in her mind all of the reasons she shouldn't have ended things with Brent. But by the time the water was cold, she still couldn't really bring herself to regret what she'd done.

She was definitely sad to end things with Brent—it was the end of an era for her. But she was also excited to see where things would go with Adam, too. She wasn't naïve enough to believe they'd have more than a quick summer fling or that she wouldn't be single again by the start of the school year. And while Ashley knew that would be hard, she couldn't shake the feeling that any time at all with Adam would be worth the heartache later.

CHAPTER 5

By mid-morning, Adam had just sent the second group of tourists off on their jet skis and was starting to clean up a boat being rented later that day. Adam saw the dusty sneakers before he realized anyone had approached. He tugged his earbuds out and paused his iPod while gazing up. He swallowed when he saw that it was all three of the Kensington boys. It was fairly obvious they weren't there on friendly terms.

Adam stepped off the boat, joining them on the dock. "Morning boys," he greeted. "I don't believe we have officially met," he added, offering his hand to each of the twins in turn. They didn't accept, so he dropped his hand.

Jackson frowned. "You've been spending a lot of time with our sister lately."

Adam hesitated, unsure if Jackson planned to say anything else. During the silence, he casually looked over at the booth, searching for Clay. He exhaled with relief upon confirming his friend was watching them. "Uh, yeah. I guess so," Adam finally answered.

"She has a boyfriend," the taller twin, who Adam thought was

Mason, said. "He's good people. The kind of man that deserves a girl like Ashley."

Adam nodded. "Yeah. Brent, right?"

"So why are you harassing her if you know that?" the other twin asked.

"Harassing. Now that's a harsh word. Did she say I've been harassing her? I kind of doubt that. I'd describe it more as a friendship, what Ash and I have going."

"She has enough friends," the first twin said.

Adam frowned. "I always thought you could never have too many friends."

"Stop being smart or this ain't gonna end well, you hear?" Jackson's annoyance was palpable now. Austin and Mason still seemed just to be along for the ride.

Adam suppressed an eye roll. "Look, I've got a lot to do. Some of us actually have to work for a living. So if you have a point, please get to it quickly so I can go on with my day."

"Stay away from Ashley." Austin said.

Adam was certain that the best course of action at this point would be to nod his head in agreement and walk away. But he couldn't stand the thought of letting these dicks boss him around. So instead, he was honest. "Yeah, that's not going to happen," he said.

Jackson's eye twitched. "What did you say?"

Adam sighed as though he were bored. "I said no. If your sister asks me to leave her alone, I will oblige, but you all know as well as I do that she isn't going to do that."

Jackson stepped forward, narrowing the gap between them. "I reckon you misunderstood. We weren't asking you to back off. That wasn't a friendly request. If I see you so much as looking in her direction again, let alone talking to her, then I'll…"

"You'll what?" Adam interrupted, stepping forward. "Fly back from college and kick my ass? Oh right. You aren't going to be here in another month. So I guess I can do whatever the fuck I want."

Jackson's knuckles slammed into the top of Adam's cheekbone before Adam even registered his hand moving. Damn. Adam had known this was headed in that direction, but he'd anticipated getting a few more sassy quips in before someone threw the first punch.

Adam reflexively raised his hand to block his face and toyed with hitting Jackson back, but the gleam in Jackson's eyes hinted that he was done. Besides, as confident as Adam was in his fighting skills, he didn't figure he could handle all three alone and didn't want to drag Clay into the brawl, although he had jumped the counter and was rushing over.

Adam motioned for Clay to stop. All three brothers turned at the same time, tempting Adam with the perfect opportunity to fight back, but he resisted the urge.

"It's all right, Clay," Adam said, gently wiping his face and grimacing at the traces of blood. That was going to swell like a mother. "These gentlemen just came to tell me something and now that they've made their point, they're leaving. Right?"

He turned to Jackson expectantly.

Jackson offered a cold stare in response but eventually nodded and started to turn.

"You better watch your fucking back, Bricker," he snarled.

Clay and Adam watched them leave in silence. Once they were sufficiently far away, Clay chuckled.

"Damn, dude. You have balls of steel."

Adam shrugged. "Shit. My face hurts. You got ice?"

Clay motioned for him to follow him back to the surf shop.

They sent one of the summer guys who usually manned the inside of the store outside to keep tabs on the marina booth. Clay returned from the back room with an ice pack for Adam.

"Thanks." Adam pressed it against his cheek for a moment before noticing Clay eying him warily. "What?"

"You have been spending a lot of time with her," Clay said.

Jesus, did this whole town think he was some sort of psycho predator? Adam didn't even know how to respond to Clay.

"I didn't mean it like that," Clay quickly added, apparently sensing a change in Adam's expression. "But you know Brent isn't an asshole like her brothers are. He seems like a decent guy."

Adam wiggled his jaw back and forth, confirming the damage was limited to the upper portion of his face and then shifted the ice pack up towards his eyelid. "He may be, but she doesn't love him."

"And she does love you?" Clay was skeptical.

"No, idiot. Not yet anyway."

"What's your end game here then, Bricker?"

Adam considered this question and decided to just go with the truth. "I think I can make her happy. And I really like seeing her smile." He felt a grin break out on his face just thinking about her, and then he winced from the pain the movement caused in his cheek.

Clay sighed and rolled his eyes. "Jesus, under that inked tough guy exterior, you're actually a total girl."

Adam laughed, but deep down, he hoped it was all worth it. He could act confident with her brothers, but when it came down to it, Adam was starting to doubt that he would ever get a chance to show Ashley how good he could be to her.

* * *

ASHLEY CAME up behind Adam as he was tightening the rope anchoring his boat to the dock. Had she not been so eager to talk with him, she would've watched him work a little longer. He was wearing athletic shorts, a tank top, and his usual baseball cap, but Ashley could see the muscles flexing as he moved his arms about.

"Hey," Ashley greeted him cheerfully, giddy with anticipation at his reaction to her news.

He finished the knot and let it drop, but didn't turn around immediately.

"I wanted to talk to you about something," she said.

"Oh yeah?" Adam reached forward and grabbed a rag off the bench and stepped onto the boat, furthering the distance between them.

Ashley was annoyed that he wasn't sharing in her excitement but tried not to let it show. "Is this a bad time?"

She watched his shoulders rise with what appeared to be a massive sigh. "No. It's just…" he turned slowly, his head down.

She waited to see what he was going to say, but then gasped sharply as soon as he raised his head. His right eye was swollen and red and there was a purplish hue covering his cheekbone. Ashley hopped over the rope onto the boat and raised her hand up to his cheek, freezing an inch away so as not to hurt him.

Adam placed his hand over hers but didn't pull away, so she delicately touched the bruised area.

"Does it hurt?"

He shrugged. "I mean it doesn't feel good."

"Come here." Ashley tugged his hand until he followed her to the other side of the boat, where they at least had some privacy as they sat. "What happened?"

"Does it matter?" He glanced down again. "Come on, you were in such a good mood. What did you want to talk about?"

Ashley certainly wasn't going to let him get away with not telling her about his injuries but she knew her news would cheer him up. "I was just going to tell you that I broke up with Brent."

A soft laugh escaped his lips. Not quite the enthusiastic response she'd expected.

"Did you give him a reason?"

"Not really, just that we were growing apart, we needed senior year free to explore who we are without each other, blah blah blah. I didn't tell him there was anyone else, if that's what you mean."

He was quiet for a moment, but then seemed to perk up. "So now can I kiss you?"

Ashley hesitated. She'd picked this time to talk with Adam because she knew Brent was at the country club and wouldn't see them together. Every fiber in her body was aching to feel his lips on hers, but she could only imagine how it would feel to Brent if he heard she was making out with someone else the day after they broke up.

Yet, as Adam gazed up at Ashley with those puppy dog eyes of his, she couldn't say no. She leaned in slowly, not wanting to aggravate his injury. Their lips pressed together tentatively, then he cupped her chin with his hands, deepening the kiss, and the rest of the world melted away. Her body was a wash of sensations and she was completely oblivious to their surroundings until he pulled away, leaving her aching for more.

"You closed your eyes," he said, their heads still close.

Ashley laughed. "Yeah, I guess I did."

He grinned. "Thank you for letting me do that. I plan to kiss those lips as often as you will let me. But for now you're just going to have to relive that brief one a few more times because I have to take a group out on the boat in a few minutes."

Ashley licked her lips and nodded, her heart still thumping from the exhilaration of that kiss. She turned to step off the boat when he reached for her hand.

"Hey," he said, "Maybe one more for now." Then he pulled her close again and kissed her slowly and softly, his tongue just barely grazing hers. He held onto her bottom lip for an extra moment as he pulled away. "You taste like heaven," he murmured.

Ashley felt her cheeks redden.

"I'll call you later," he promised. She nodded, then went to find Lisa before she passed out.

Lisa was waiting near the ice cream shack, chatting with one of the guys behind the counter. He was a summer resident, meaning he worked on the island the entire peak tourist season but lived somewhere else the rest of the year. As soon as Lisa spotted Ashley, she excused herself and met Ashley at a table in the shade.

"Here," she said, handing Ashley a diet coke. "It's on the house."

Ashley raised an eyebrow.

"Apparently my flirting can get two free fountain drinks. Yours can get two cute guys," Lisa said without a hint of bitterness.

Ashley blew out a breath, having been so thrown by Adam's injury and then the kiss that she forgot all about Brent. And that was why she was meeting with Lisa, so they could rehash the breakup. Ashley gave Lisa the recap of what she'd said and how Brent had responded and listened as her friend sympathized.

"I just can't stand it if he hates me," Ashley concluded. "And I don't want to make it awkward when we're all hanging out together."

"Brent could never hate you, Ashley," Lisa reassured her. "You guys have way too much history. Just be cool around him and give him some space when you can and it'll be fine by the time school starts."

Ashley sipped her drink, thinking September was a long time away.

"So are you going to ask out tattoo guy or are we still pretending you don't have the hots for him?"

Ashley shot her friend a pointed stare but then giggled after realizing no one else was around to hear the question anyway. "I don't know what it is about him," she finally said, "but I definitely like hanging out with him. He's so different and honest and yet very mysterious at the same time. And I feel safe around him, but he's definitely got a scary edge to him."

"Scary?"

"Well, wrong word, probably," Ashley said. The line for the ice cream shack had grown and there were now people standing closer to them, so she lowered her voice a bit. "Mysterious is a better description."

"How so?"

"I went to see him this afternoon, just to say hi and mention that Brent and I broke up, just so he knew."

Lisa laughed.

"And he was all banged up."

"What?"

"Yeah, he had a busted lip and his cheek was cut and his eye was all swollen. So I knew he'd been in a fight, but he didn't offer up any details."

Lisa grimaced and shook her head. "Ash, I don't know. I want you to be careful. I know you like this guy, but how much do you really know about him? He's got this tough guy persona and now you know he's getting into fights…"

Ashley shook her head. "I don't think he's some thug or hardened criminal, but don't worry. I'm not rushing into anything," she said, even more determined to keep the kiss to herself for now.

She was just about to change the subject when she realized a tall figure was looming over their table. She gazed up and recognized Clay, the guy who was always at the marina with Adam.

"Sorry to interrupt, but can I have a quick word with you?" he asked Ashley.

Ashley glanced at Lisa, uncertain as to what he could possibly want with her, but then followed him off to the side of the snack area.

"I didn't mean to eavesdrop, but I overheard part of what you guys were saying about Adam," he began.

Ashley winced. She knew he was pretty tight with Adam and hadn't noticed him standing there when she was talking with Lisa. "I was just telling her about his face, you know the big mystery fight."

Clay was visibly annoyed now. Ashley wasn't sure what she'd done wrong.

"Not so much a mystery, actually," Clay said. "Your brothers came by to see him earlier today when he was working. I couldn't hear everything that went on but I think the gist of it was that they told him to stay away from you and he said no."

Ashley frowned, struggling to process what he was telling her. "Wait, are you saying my brothers did that to Adam?"

Clay nodded. "I don't think he was planning to tell you. It's probably none of my business but I just thought you should know. He's not just some punk running around getting into stupid fights. He didn't even try to defend himself."

Ashley realized then how her conversation with Lisa must have sounded. "Clay, I know he's not. I just..." she sighed. "It's complicated. Anyway, thanks for letting me know." She started to walk away when Clay grabbed her arm.

"Hey, don't go and confront them on your own, okay? It's not going to help anything if you end up looking like Adam."

Ashley laughed. "My brothers wouldn't hurt me in a million years. Lock me in a tower Rapunzel-style maybe, but..." she shook her head. "Thanks."

She watched him walk away then returned to the table. "I have to go," she said.

"Why? What's wrong?" Lisa stood.

"Clay overheard us talking and thought I should know that it was my asshole brothers who did that to Adam."

Lisa's face fell. "Are you kidding? What is wrong with them?"

Ashley was so angry she could punch someone. "I need to go have a little talk with them."

Lisa nodded and threw away their cups. "Yeah. Do you want me to come along?"

"No, I'm good. Thanks," she said, giving her friend a quick hug.

"Call me later."

The short drive home only gave her more opportunity to fume. Ashley would never describe her brothers as pacifists, and she knew they'd all gotten into stupid little fights before, but this was just ridiculous. She parked her car in the driveway and stormed into the house, grateful to find at least the twins were home.

"What the hell is wrong with you?" she asked as soon as she saw them seated in the kitchen.

Mason and Austin both burst into laughter. Austin pulled himself together first and spoke.

"You should be thanking us. We found out that you and Brent were taking another one of your stupid breaks and we just made sure that you weren't in a position to do anything to make him not want to take you back later when you come to your senses."

There was so much wrong with her brother's explanation that Ashley wasn't even sure where to start.

"How did you even find out that we broke up?"

Mason replied. "I texted him yesterday to ask if he knew what you were so upset about. I figured it was some fight with Lisa or stupid girl stuff like that but he said you broke up with him."

Ashley sighed, relieved at least that Brent was still texting her brothers. That had to mean something, right? She was tempted to ask if they spoke with him, and, if so, how he seemed, but she didn't think it was appropriate. Besides, she wanted to stay on track.

"Well, what the hell made you think Adam had anything to do with it?"

"Do you think we're all blind?" Mason asked, glancing over at Jackson who had just come down the stairs, apparently having heard the commotion. "Everyone has seen you hanging out with the new guy."

"Including Brent," Austin added.

"You humiliated him," Mason continued. "What did you think was going to happen?"

"What did I think?" Ashley repeated, appalled. "I certainly didn't think that my psychotic brothers would turn violent against a friend of mine when I decide to break up with my boyfriend for completely unrelated reasons!"

They all just stared at her, their expressions confirming they still felt no remorse.

"What is wrong with y'all? You can't just go around beating up people for no reason."

"*They* didn't do shit and *I* had a perfectly good reason," Jackson said, making his way into the kitchen and slumping down into a chair.

Ashley stared at her brothers, completely flabbergasted that they would even do such a thing. She looked at them each one at a time, trying to gauge whether any of them showed any signs of regret, but they all just looked so cocky that she wanted to punch them all just to prove her damn point. But then she decided that might come off a little hypocritical.

"What the hell happened, exactly? Did you guys just gang up on him and jump him?"

"No," Jackson replied indignantly. "We told him to stay away from you and he talked shit to me. So I hit him. I think he got the message now."

Ashley stood so abruptly that her chair fell backwards, hitting the floor with a loud clank. "The only message Adam seems to have gotten was that you are a bunch of assholes. I can't believe you would do this." She grabbed her keys and purse, adding "And I'm telling Dad."

"Go ahead, he'll take our side!" Mason insisted.

Ashley returned to the marina, but Adam had already gone home for the day. Luckily, Clay told her Adam's address. She left her car parked at the marina and walked the short distance to the condo. It was a simple building that she'd passed thousands of times over the years, but Ashley realized now that she'd never ventured inside. The lobby was basic, and the slow elevator deposited her just down the narrow hall from his unit on the fourth floor.

Ashley briefly considered whether she should head back outside and text first, then thought better of it. She rang the bell and knocked loudly, wanting to be heard over the music vibrating through the walls. She was about to ring again when the music quieted and she heard footsteps.

"Hey," Adam said as he opened the door, a complete look of shock on his poor bruised face.

"You didn't even look through the peephole?" Ashley chastised.

Adam brushed off her concern with a laugh. "What, in case it was a band of robbers hoping to punch my other eye?"

She felt her face flush, remembering the reason for the visit.

"Do you want to come in?"

"If I'm not interrupting," she said, suddenly feeling shy.

"You are never interrupting." He swung the door open and motioned for her to enter.

Ashley glanced around the condo. It was decorated in traditional beachy hues with bright yellow accents and crisp white finishes. There was a hallway to the right of the entry and a small galley kitchen past that. A long bar and several bar stools formed the barrier between the kitchen and the dining area, which held a glass-top six-seater table. Just beyond that was the living room, with a couch and two cushy looking chairs, a glass coffee table and end tables, and a large flat screen television. Another hallway was to the side of the living room, and a large balcony with a view of the business side of the marina was just past it.

"Would you like the grand tour?" he offered.

Ashley shrugged.

Adam motioned down the first hallway, which led to a large bedroom and bathroom. The bedroom had two queen-sized beds, which she thought was odd until she remembered that until recently, this was primarily a rental property. There was minimal décor in the room and no personal effects that she could see, save for a large urn that she was hesitant to ask about.

"This is my dad's room," Adam said. "I'm actually using the master, allegedly because I'm here more, but really it's because my dad doesn't want to stay there without my mom."

"Oh," Ashley said. That didn't feel like an adequate response, but thankfully she didn't need to say anything else because he was already leading her to his room. The master suite wasn't any larger than the first bedroom, but housed a king-size bed and a large Jacuzzi tub in the bathroom. Various articles of clothing littered the floor and a towel was draped over the chair beside the bed.

Adam cleared his throat and pulled the door shut. "Apparently, when you pull the unit off the rental market, you lose the cleaning lady," he explained with a grin. "I'll pick up the next time you're coming over."

Ashley blushed again at the thought of being in Adam's condo, alone, with him another time. She turned to face him and was immediately distracted by his swollen eye.

"I actually came to talk to you about…" she gestured at his face.

He nodded then went into the kitchen. "Want a drink?"

"No thanks," she said, following him as he retrieved a baggie of ice from the freezer.

"I'm sorry," Ashley said. "I mean, that's what I came to say."

He frowned. "Sorry for what?"

"Your face. I didn't know earlier, but…" she sighed. "Why didn't you tell me?"

"Tell you what?"

"About my brothers." I shook my head. "I'm so, so sorry. I had no idea."

"It's not your fault."

"Yes it is. If not for me, you wouldn't have gotten hurt."

"You can't take responsible for every douchebag out there," he said, adding "sorry," she supposed, to soften the blow of the nickname as applied to her brothers.

"I'm talking to my dad tonight. They won't bother you again," Ashley promised.

"I can take care of myself."

"You didn't even try to fight back."

"Would you have felt better if I'd hit your brother?"

Ashley considered that for a moment. "No."

"Me neither. And I figured it would complicate things for you, so I didn't. But just because I didn't do anything then doesn't mean I can't defend myself."

"I'm sure you can, it's just, well, there's three of them," she repeated. And apparently they'd all gone batshit crazy.

"Like I said, I can handle them. I'm not scared, so you don't need to worry about me."

She nodded reluctantly. "Still, I'm sorry."

"So you've said." He stepped closer and placed his hands on her hips, sending shivers across her back. "I know how you can make it up to me."

"I thought you said it wasn't my fault," Ashley said, barely able to focus with his lips so close to hers.

"It's not. But I want to assuage your guilt complex." He inched his lips closer.

She couldn't wait any longer. She closed the distance between them and kissed him. His hands squeezed her hips and he kissed her back hungrily. Ashley's pulse quickened and all she could focus on was the sensation of his tongue along hers, his fingers against her body, and his breath falling rapidly against her cheek.

Ashley ended the kiss before she risked doing anything stupid. "I should go. I just wanted to apologize to you in person."

Adam grinned and opened the door for her to leave.

* * *

ASHLEY'S FATHER didn't come home until after eight that night, which sucked since her nerves had been getting worse by the minute. The second they heard the garage door open, Ashley and her brothers all straightened in their seats like a bunch of dogs who'd just heard the treat jar being opened.

Ashley glanced at Mason, then shot out of her chair.

The moment their dad opened the door, she rushed forward, but he was on the phone. Ashley sighed impatiently and accepted the briefcase he thrust at her. Then he took a glass of wine from her mom in the kitchen and went upstairs and changed. When he finally came downstairs, he was off the phone.

"I need to talk to you," Ashley blurted out. "Alone," she added, glaring at Austin who was inching towards them.

He turned to their mom, eyebrow raised. She shrugged.

"Don't look at me. They've been goofy all evening and won't tell me what's going on," she said.

"Can I eat my supper first?" he asked, his expression conveying an awareness of the futility of it all.

"Your sons ganged up on a new kid in town and beat him up," Ashley blurted out.

"Ashley dumped Brent!" Mason shouted over Austin and Jackson's protests in response to her statement.

Her father walked out to the deck and stood by the railing for a moment without speaking. Ashley followed him and shut the door behind her. Finally, he turned to her.

"Is this true, you broke up with Brent?

Ashley felt her jaw drop. "Really? That's what you want to start with? Your sons are monsters. We have a band of violent thugs living in our house and you want to catch up on my love life?"

He inhaled loudly through his nose before exhaling. "Yes. That's where I choose to begin this discussion. Now, is that true?"

"Yes."

"You didn't think it made sense to discuss this with me beforehand?"

Ashley blinked a good ten or so times before replying. "No. I didn't see how it was your business."

"Interesting choice of words, Ashlynne. I do a lot of business with Brent's father. The Abbots are very influential here locally as well. It would have been respectful for you to have at least given me a heads up before doing something so drastic."

She started to speak but he raised his hand, a clear gesture from him that she was to shush.

"Is there a particular reason you came to this decision about your relationship with Brent? He seemed like a nice boy. Good parents, good upbringing, good college prospects."

"Yeah. I don't want to go out with him anymore. That's really all there is to it."

My father nodded repetitively then sipped his wine. "Then this might just be temporary."

"I don't think so."

He frowned. "I don't know what all has happened since you aren't telling me, but you should know that no one is perfect. People make mistakes and deserve second chances sometimes."

Ashley realized he probably assumed they would get back together again since they'd sort of followed that pattern before, but it was still infuriating. She glanced behind her and caught a glimpse of her brothers' smirking faces from inside the kitchen. Ashley really wanted to punch them all now.

"Now, what is this about your brothers? And why are you all tattling on each other like a bunch of kindergarteners all of a sudden?"

Ashley took a deep breath to speak more calmly. She knew her dad would tune out anything said in an emotional voice. "I learned today that Austin, Mason, and Jackson all cornered this new guy in town. Apparently they don't like him and Jackson beat him up."

"They were in a fight?"

"No, the other guy didn't touch them. Jackson punched him."

"But he's okay, this other boy?"

Ashley sighed. "Yes. I mean, he will be. He's got a black eye and bruised cheekbone."

"Well, I'll speak with your brothers about fighting later. They know we don't tolerate that behavior. What I want to know is what that all has to do with you. Who is this new kid?"

"His name is Adam. His family moved to town at the start of summer."

"What's his last name?"

"Bricker."

My father frowned. "Doesn't ring a bell. What does his father do?"

Ashley hesitated, probably a second longer than she should have to avoid raising suspicion. "I don't know them very well so it's hard to say. He travels a lot for work."

He didn't respond, but Ashley knew he was filing away every word for research later.

"Is this boy in your class at school?"

"No. He's the twins' age."

"But you're friends with him?"

"Yeah, I guess so."

"And you haven't any idea why your brothers wanted to fight him?"

Ashley swallowed the lump rising in her throat. "I'm pretty sure they think he's the reason I broke up with Brent. Well, that and they just don't like him because he isn't from around here."

"Is he the reason you broke up with Brent?"

"No," Ashley lied without hesitation.

Her father drained the rest of his wine. "I'll speak with your brothers now. You should get some sleep."

Ashley raised an eyebrow. "It's not even nine o'clock yet."

"Oh. Well, fine. It feels later, doesn't it?"

Ashley shrugged and went into the house. She kicked Mason in the shin as she passed, but it really didn't make her feel any better.

Ashley blasted music for a few minutes and then gave up trying to decompress and called Lisa to whine. As Ashley recounted the details of her conversation with her dad to her best friend, Lisa responded with the appropriate level of anger. But when Ashley was done with the story, Lisa's tune changed.

"They're just looking out for you, you know," she said.

"Who? My insane brothers?" Ashley snorted at the notion that their intentions could be anything but selfish. "No, they just like picking fights and asserting their dominance. They're like dogs. Next they'll probably start peeing on select portions of the beach to mark their territory."

"They probably already did that." Lisa giggled. "But seriously, I'm not saying they weren't totally out of line today, but you have to at least see where they're coming from. You don't know anything about this guy. He's new to town and he's obviously been through some shit."

"So?"

"He's way older, too."

"He's only nineteen," Ashley said, although she had to admit he seemed older than that. She figured his maturity stemmed from losing his mom, or maybe it had to do with the fact that he lived alone much of the time because of his father traveling. Whatever it was, Adam acted more like the seasoned college guys she knew than a teenager.

Lisa paused. "Well, he looks even older. But anyway, I'm your best friend. And you never even told me you and Brent were having problems. So it just seems weird that this new tattooed guy comes into town and the next thing you know, you're dumping your boyfriend of two and a half years."

"We weren't together that long."

Lisa sighed. "I'm just saying that I see why your brothers

assume your breakup with Brent had something to do with this new guy."

Ashley gritted her teeth together. Aside from the too-brief kisses, her day had sucked enough already, and she wasn't in the mood to argue with her best friend on top of it all. "It really doesn't matter anyway," she finally said, "and I can't believe you're taking their side."

"I'm not taking their side. They acted like total douchebags. But Brent was a really good catch—and he was yours. I totally see the appeal of this new guy, but is some exciting summer fling really worth giving up on a good guy like Brent? We are all just worried you're going to get hurt."

Ashley started to reply, but there was a knock at her door. Her mother called for her through the door.

"Shit. I've got to go," she said, ending the call.

She climbed off her bed and went to the door. Her mother smiled cautiously, as though Ashley were some rabid dog she wanted to appease. Then she gazed slowly around the room as if searching for something mysterious.

"Why didn't you tell me what happened with your brothers?" her mom asked, moving the pile of folded laundry from the desk chair to the desk before sitting.

"Because you wouldn't have punished them without talking to Dad anyway." Ashley was too antsy to sit still, so she grabbed the laundry and started putting it away. "I thought Dad would at least ground them for randomly attacking a guy they don't even know."

"Honey, Jackson is an adult. Your father can hardly ground him. And the twins didn't really do anything. Sure, they're guilty by association but they just want to impress Jackson." She cringed as Ashley wedged a stack of tee shirts into a drawer, undoing all the crisp folds the housekeeper had made when sorting the laundry.

"He could've taken away his car."

"What would that have done? Anyone in town would give him a ride."

"It would send a message at least that he doesn't condone senseless violence," Ashley replied, impressed with the maturity of her response.

"True. Your father and I discussed it and thought it would be appropriate if your brothers apologized in person to this…" her voice trailed off as she waited pointedly for Ashley to fill in the name.

"Adam."

"Adam," her mother repeated. "So if you have his number, could you see if he's free for dinner Thursday? That way we can all get to know him better and your brothers can apologize and hopefully he'll see that they aren't bad guys."

Ashley snorted.

"Or if you'd rather I could ask the twins to go invite him in person tomorrow."

"No. I'll text him."

Her mom nodded. Ashley had finished putting her laundry away but still didn't feel like sitting so she started reorganizing some of the knickknacks on her dresser. She felt her mom watching her and wished she'd just say what she was thinking already.

"Are you dating this Adam?" she finally asked.

Ashley turned to her mother and rolled her eyes dramatically. "Mom! No. I just met him. And Brent and I literally just broke up."

"You know, your brothers seem to think this new boy had something to do with your breakup."

"Well we've already established that they're morons, so I don't put much credit in what they think," Ashley replied. "It's not like this is the first time Brent and I broke up anyway."

Her mom nodded, and Ashley sensed she was uncomfortable, too. It was weird, really, since she had been super close to her mom until high school and then things had just gotten awkward between the two of them. Meanwhile, Austin and Mason had latched on to their mother in the past few years like she was their best friend. Ashley wasn't sure if it was just a phase or if something had happened to cause her mom to switch favorites, but it kind of sucked.

"Do you want to talk about what happened with Brent? You never really told me why you broke up."

Ashley shrugged. No, she really didn't want to discuss her love life with her mother, but she also realized her mom expected some sort of explanation. "Nothing much to say, really. Nothing *happened*. I just realized I don't think any differently about him than any of my other friends."

Her mom's expression softened. "Honey, you're young. At your age, romantic relationships aren't really different from other friendships. All that romance and passion you see on the movies comes later, much later, when you're older. And even then, friendship is still the most important element of any relationship."

Ashley wrinkled her nose. "Eww, mom. I am not discussing romance with you." She shuddered at the thought. It was a little funny, though, how her parents could raise four teenagers and be so oblivious to what dating was actually like. Ashley knew exactly when each of the twins had lost their virginity, thanks to them blabbing to Brent and him telling her, and she strongly suspected Jackson had slept with half of the females on the island.

Her mother stood. "Well, Brent is a nice boy. I hope you weren't too hard on him."

"He'll be fine," Ashley replied through gritted teeth.

"Let me know what Adam says about dinner," her mom said as she stepped into the hall, pulling the door shut behind her.

Ashley plopped onto her bed and fell backwards, the fluffy bedding nearly swallowing her. She tugged a pillow over her face and growled with frustration. She was debating whether it would be possible to just suffocate herself with the heart shaped pillow rather than ever deal with her family again, when her phone chimed with a text.

She uncovered her face enough to glance at the text, surprised to see it was from Adam and not Lisa.

"Was supposed to have modeling shoot 2morrow but cancelled since my pretty face is marred. Wanna hang?" it said.

Ashley panicked, momentarily gullible enough to think he was being serious. Not that Adam wasn't attractive enough to be a model, but she suspected he'd rather swim with sharks than pose for pictures.

"Can't," she replied. "I have tennis." As not thrilled as she was for the overnight tennis clinic in Savannah, she did appreciate the timing. Two days away from Brent and her family was exactly what she needed.

Adam replied with a frowny face.

Ashley texted him about the dinner, phrasing it so he would understand it wasn't a friendly invite from her parents so much as their attempt to pick at him in person. She fully expected him to decline, not to reply asking what time. Ashley hesitated. She wanted to see him again, but it didn't feel right to let him walk into the trap.

"My parents can be scary," she said.

"I can handle it," he replied, followed quickly by, "Mothers love me."

"Really?" Ashley typed back, shocked.

"Bahahahaha," came the quick reply. "Hell no. See u then."

Ashley stared at her phone, confused, then flipped on the TV as she packed her tennis gear.

CHAPTER 6

On Thursday evening, Adam drove around the block until precisely 6:25. Then he pulled into the circular driveway, parked on the far edge, and smoothed his hair one last time. He felt naked without his baseball cap, but figured it was not appropriate southern dinner attire. He wore his only pair of "dressy" shorts, meaning the only ones he owned without holes or cargo pockets. They were slate grey with patches of other colors. A darker grey Polo covered his torso. It was short sleeved, but Adam hoped the fact that it was collared would count for something. He had considered wearing a long sleeved shirt but worried he'd literally die in this heat if he did.

Ashley opened the door as he scaled the brick steps.

"Hey," she greeted him warmly, her smile widening as she saw him.

Adam's body relaxed considerably when he locked eyes with her. He'd never before really cared what a girl's family thought of him, but this time, he did. A lot. He sensed her family's approval would be hard to earn, but crucial if he wanted to be with her. Despite that pressure, it was hard to be stressed when staring at those bright green eyes.

"You look very nice," she told him.

"Thanks," Adam replied, resisting the urge to touch her and instead taking the opportunity to check her out. She wore white shorts and a black sleeveless top. Several thin silver necklaces hung at her neck, clinking together delicately as she reached for his hand.

"Come on in, I'll introduce you to everyone."

Adam swallowed the lump rising in his throat as they entered the large family room. Every member of her family was seated and staring at him. He smiled awkwardly and proffered a wave, dropping Ashley's hand.

"So you've met my brothers," she began, "But just as a reminder, this one is Austin, this one is Mason, and this is Jackson. And this is my mom, Darcie, and my dad, Wesley."

Glancing around the room, Adam was struck with the similarities between Ashley and her brothers. Although he'd met them all before and seen family photographs, the likeness was much easier to notice in real life. Ashley looked like a younger version of her mother, except that her dark blonde hair clearly came from her father. The twins both shared the exact same hair color and texture as Ashley, but bore their father's features, whereas Jackson had his mother's dark brown hair. All of the Kensington men were tall and more muscled than the average guy, but Ashley and her mother were both slender and several inches shorter than the men.

Adam stepped forward and offered his hand to each of her parents as they stood. "Nice to meet you Mr. Kensington, Mrs. Kensington. Your house is gorgeous."

"Thank you, Adam," Mrs. Kensington said.

Suddenly, an older woman appeared from the kitchen. Adam had been so focused on Ashley's parents that he hadn't noticed her before. "What can I get you to drink?" the woman asked him.

"Uh, I'll take a coke if you have one."

"What kind, dear?" she asked.

Adam froze, stumped.

"Adam, this is Sarah. Sarah, my friend Adam is new to the south. I think he actually means Coke when he says coke."

The woman smiled warmly as Adam mumbled a "nice to meet you."

"It's a southern thing," Ashley explained to Adam.

Adam made a mental note to Google it later.

"So Adam, Ashley tells us you're from the New England area. How are you liking our little island so far?"

"It's very nice, ma'am," Adam said, catching Ashley's appreciative smile as he remembered what she'd told him about southern manners. "A little hotter than I'm used to and a lot more humidity, but very pretty."

"Where exactly are you from, Son?" Mr. Kensington asked.

"I was born in Maine, but I grew up in Nantucket and then we moved to Cape Cod about ten years ago."

"Hmm. Why the move?" Mrs. Kensington asked.

Adam hesitated. "My mom got sick and there were more hospitals near Cape Cod. She still wanted the coastal vibe, though."

"Adam's family has owned a property over at South Beach for decades now. They used to visit on vacation," Ashley interrupted, clearly trying to change the topic. "That's where he's living now."

"And you plan to stay here on the island for a while?" her dad asked.

Adam nodded. "Yeah, I like it here. My father travels a lot but he'll be home more over the winter and there's a lot more outdoor possibility here in winter than up north."

"What line of work is your father in?"

"He's a sailor."

"In the Navy?"

Adam shook his head. "No, on a merchant vessel. He does some commercial fishing, too."

The tension in the room during the ensuing silence was palpable. Adam hadn't expected the Kensingtons to be impressed with that line of work, but Adam wasn't ashamed of his dad and didn't really care what the Kensingtons thought, except to the extent that it affected his relationship with Ashley.

"Well, we love fish," Mrs. Kensington finally said, her tone warm. "And on that note, I'll go help Sarah get the dinner on the table."

Adam watched her head towards the kitchen, but noticed her slip behind the main part into the area Ashley had described to him as the bar.

Mr. Kensington cleared his throat. "I believe my sons owe you an apology. I was disappointed to hear that they forgot their manners and I assure you they don't normally treat newcomers with such disrespect," he said.

He turned to his sons. "Boys?"

"Sorry," they all mumbled in unison, not sounding the slightest bit sincere.

Ashley hopped up before Adam had to respond. "I'm going to give Adam a quick tour of the house. Be back down before dinner, Mom," she called into the kitchen.

She motioned at Adam to follow, so he did, politely nodding at her father first. She loudly introduced him to various rooms on the first floor he'd already seen and then walked him upstairs. She grabbed his hand and dragged her into her bedroom, quietly shutting the door behind them.

"Sorry," she said. "Figured you could use a break. My dad pretty much interrogates and belittles people for a living so he can get pretty brutal."

Adam grinned and exhaled hard. He didn't want to talk about her family or even think about how much worse it was clearly about to get since they hadn't even started the meal yet. He just wanted to appreciate the brief moment alone with Ashley.

"You look beautiful," he said.

Redness flooded Ashley's cheeks and she glanced away, her thick long hair flipping in front of her face.

Adam swept the loose strands out of her face and gently pressed his lips into her forehead. He didn't know how long they'd be alone but he was certain he couldn't kiss her anywhere else without needing a few minutes to cool off before rejoining her family.

"Your brother looks just like your father," he said, sitting on the edge of her bed.

"Yeah. And I take after my mother. Well, except for the hair. My mom has pictures of me and the twins as babies and you really can't tell who was who because we all have the same hair."

Adam smiled. He was nervous about heading back downstairs. He knew they didn't like him, knew that nothing he said would make him good enough for Ashley in their eyes. So what was the point?

"Just be yourself, Adam," Ashley said, as though reading his mind. "And don't take anything they say personally. They don't know you. They just don't like that you're not from here and that you're…"

"Broke?"

Ashley smiled. "I was going to say different. But my point is, any flak they give you is about them, it's not personal."

Adam nodded just as there was a knock on the door.

"Come in," Ashley said.

Austin stumbled in, covering his eyes with his hand. "Everybody decent?" He asked.

Ashley threw a pillow at him. "You're a moron."

Austin uncovered his face and smirked. "Dinner's ready." He turned towards Adam. "Good luck."

When they reached the dining room, the table was set with what Adam hoped was their nice china, and not just the everyday stuff. It looked fancy enough to serve the Queen. There were platters of roast chicken, salad, green beans with red peppers, mashed potatoes, dinner rolls, and some reddish dish Adam guessed was beets.

Ashley motioned for Adam to sit beside her, adjacent to her mother. Her brothers all squeezed in across from them and her father sat at the far end. Adam got the feeling he was sitting in Jackson's normal seat, but the table was huge—big enough to accommodate twelve easily, so he didn't feel crammed in. They all sat and made small talk as they passed the food.

Determined to be polite, Adam spooned a tiny beet onto his plate and a single lettuce leaf as those two dishes reached him. Ashley was the only one who picked up on this, and she giggled uncontrollably. Adam inspected her plate, which was loaded primarily with salad and green beans, along with some beets and a small amount of chicken. No potatoes or bread, Adam observed.

"You eat like a girl," he whispered.

She turned to him and wrinkled her nose. He grinned. Ashley was even cute when she tried to look mean.

"Adam," Mr. Kensington's deep voice interrupted their flirting. "My sons tell me you took this last year off after graduation. What have you been up to?"

Adam slowly chewed the bite in his mouth, stalling until an answer came to him. He had taken some courses in diesel technician work, mostly inboard, so he could do boat maintenance and repair someday, but didn't figure this would count for much with the Kensingtons.

"He traveled down the coast with his father some," Ashley supplied. Her father nodded and waited for Adam to add something, but Adam just nodded instead as if to suggest that was all.

"What are your plans for the fall?"

Adam wiped his mouth on his napkin, certain he couldn't dodge this question. "I'll be staying in town. Working, mostly."

Mr. Kensington shot his wife a pointed stare. "Will you be attending college somewhere?"

"No, sir. Not in the immediate future, anyway. I guess there's always a possibility down the road…"

"Ashlynne hopes to attend Duke next fall," he interrupted.

Adam smiled. "She told me. Duke will be lucky to have her."

Mr. Kensington frowned, as though Adam's polite response pissed him off even more. "Ashlynne's mother and I value a good education. We feel that it is an important stepping stone in life."

Adam gritted his teeth together while maintaining the smile plastered to his face. "I respect that position. But it's not for me."

"It's difficult to know as a teenager what you want to do with the rest of your life. A college education can help you figure out what you're good at and teach you the skills you need to be successful."

"Right now, I'm happy spending my time outside and on the water. I figure if that ever changes, I can go to college then."

"There are a hundreds of careers involving the ocean that require a college degree. I'm sure you'd find more success in life if you aim higher than to spend your days renting jet skis to tourists."

Adam took a deep breath, eager to end this line of discussion. "I'd rather be a failure at something I love than a success at something I hate," he said, finally, adding, "George Burns said that. The, uh, comedian."

Ashley's dad frowned. "Yes, I know who he is." He sighed and turned to his food.

Adam noticed the twins eying each other with surprise and what appeared to be awe. He relaxed a little and ate a few more bites of food while awaiting the next assault. He didn't have to wait long.

"I hope you excuse my directness, but I have to wonder what your intentions are with regards to my daughter," Mr. Kensington said, looking directly at Adam. "My sons seemed to think you had something to do with Ashley and her long-time boyfriend Brent taking a break."

Ashley dropped her fork with a loud clang. "Jesus, dad, really? I broke up with Brent because I don't want to be with him anymore, not that that is your business. If you guys don't believe me, ask Brent."

Her father glanced briefly at Ashley then returned his pointed stare to Adam.

"My understanding of why your sons..." Adam paused, uncertain of the right word to use.

"Attacked you," Ashley interrupted.

Adam hesitated before continuing. "I got the impression they thought I was interested in dating Ashley."

Mr. Kensington nodded. "But they were mistaken?"

"Uh, no sir. I would like to date your daughter," he said, glancing at Ashley, who was smiling apologetically at him but whose eyes suggested she was about to commit murder. "I hadn't actually asked her out yet, though."

Mr. Kensington wiped his mouth on his napkin and shared a look with his wife. Adam couldn't quite place the expression on his face, but he knew it wasn't good.

"So, that's a lot of tattoos you've got there," Mason said, his mouth full of food.

Mrs. Kensington's eyes widened, though she tried to hide it by sipping some of her wine.

"Yeah, can you show us all of them?" Austin asked.

Adam bit his lip.

"He is not going to take off his shirt at dinner, you morons," Ashley snapped.

"When did you get them done? Was it like some drunken dare or something?" Austin asked.

Ashley slammed her foot into Austin's knee as hard as she could. His eyes widened in pain but he didn't make a sound.

Adam stifled a laugh, cutting it off altogether when Mason glared at him.

"No," Adam replied calmly. "I got the first one to remember my mom after she passed."

"I'm so sorry for your loss," Mrs. Kensington interrupted.

"Thank you," Adam mumbled. He never knew how to respond when people said things like that. He took a deep breath and shoved another forkful of chicken into his mouth. Apparently, the dead mom card earned him a few minutes of peace, though, as Mr. Kensington switched his interrogation onto the boys and their planned course load at school.

As they all finished eating, Mrs. Kensington and Ashley both stood to clear the plates. Adam grabbed his own plate and the salad bowl and started to the kitchen with them.

"You're a guest," Ashley said. "You don't have to help."

"My mom taught me always to help out."

Mrs. Kensington offered him a sympathetic smile and accepted the dishes as he handed them to her. Shortly after he and Ashley sat back down, Mrs. Kensington returned with a peach cobbler. It smelled heavenly.

"We used to tell my mom she should enter her cobbler into the State Fair since it's so yummy," Ashley told Adam, scooping a bite onto her spoon.

Adam nodded appreciatively. "I can see why. It's amazing. Best cobbler I've had for sure."

"It's all in the peaches. You just have to use the right peaches," Mrs. Kensington said.

Adam spooned bite after bite into his mouth, eager to finish the meal as quickly as possible.

* * *

ASHLEY STOOD ABRUPTLY. "Mom, if it's alright with you, I'd like to be excused."

"Where are you going?" her father asked.

"For a walk," she replied, turning to Adam.

He was on his feet quickly, wiping his mouth on a napkin. He lifted his plate awkwardly as if asking for direction. Ashley took his plate along with her own into the kitchen, rinsed them, and loaded them into the dishwasher. Adam followed carrying their glasses, so Ashley loaded those too.

"Well, thank you for dinner. It was, um, good food," he said finally.

Ashley started out the door and thankfully he followed quickly.

She walked quickly until they were all the way down the beach path. He struggled to keep up. Once they reached the edge of the boardwalk, she slipped off her sandals.

"I'm so sorry about all of that," she said. "You have excellent self-control."

"How so?"

"If I were in your shoes, I would've dumped my father's wine on his head. And thrown a plate at Austin." Ashley sighed. "I don't know why my entire family is being a jackass around you. They're not normally jerks."

"Your mom seems nice," Adam said after a lengthy silence.

"She's a total pushover. She'll never stand up to my father." Ashley picked up the pace again. She needed to get as far away from her house as possible. The last thing she wanted was any of her brothers wandering out to spy.

"You know they just want what's best for you," Adam said.

"I'm almost eighteen. I can decide what's good for me by myself."

Adam reached for her hand and pulled her back. "Would you slow down a minute? I'm getting a calf cramp here."

Ashley stopped abruptly, took a deep breath, then walked up to the shore, wading in until the water was ankle high. She closed her eyes as the tug of the tide pulled the sand back over her feet, causing her to sink slightly. The tide was coming in, so the next wave reached just below her knee before receding.

Adam waded up behind her. "Uh you do know sharks feed at night, right?"

"They're only close to shore at low tide," Ashley said. "Besides it's just sand sharks around here anyway."

He glanced from side to side.

"We've had loads of issues with alligators at night lately, though," she added.

"What? Seriously?"

"Yeah." She splashed her feet around. "Several live in the lagoons in front of my house. In the summer it's not uncommon at all for them to come swim in the ocean. It's always early morning that we notice them, but I assume they're here at night, too, and it's just too dark to see them."

"But they're freshwater animals."

"The lagoons have enough saltwater in them around here for the alligators to be acclimated to the ocean. My mom says it's global warming—that the lagoons are just too warm these days. But I think they're just curious and want to play in the waves. It's always young gators in the ocean anyway."

"What do you do if you see one?"

"Run, silly."

He laughed. "Now that is a hazard we did not have up north."

Ashley lost her balance and stumbled backwards a few feet. Adam eagerly followed her to shallower waters so just their feet were getting wet. She smiled at him and reached for his hand, starting to walk slowly further down the beach. Ashley shuffled her feet in the sand so as to splash the water more than necessary, just because she liked the way it felt on her toes.

"I read somewhere that the Jaws films were based on shark attacks that occurred in freshwater lakes in Jersey," Ashley said.

He shuddered. "Creepy."

They continued in silence until Ashley stepped on a hard shell and suddenly craved the fluffy white sand further ashore. They started up that direction. She wished they'd brought a flashlight because she couldn't see Adam's expression at all. Ashley assumed she wouldn't hear from him again after tonight. What guy would ever put himself through that kind of torture? On the other hand, she had nothing to lose by asking.

"Did you mean what you said tonight to my dad? About wanting to take me on a date?"

"Uh, yeah," he said with uncertainty.

"And how do you feel now?"

"About what?"

She sighed impatiently and turned to face him. "Do you still want to take me on a date even after meeting my whole awful family?"

Adam breathed a laugh. "Ashley, there are so many, many things I want to do with you right now, but yes, taking you on a date is one of them."

She hadn't expected that response. She was all prepared for an argument and then he went and said that. "Oh," was all Ashley could muster.

Adam reached for her hands and raised both of them upwards, almost as though they were dancing.

"So, um, what were the other things you want to do with me now?" she asked timidly.

He laughed. "Well, I'm tempted to throw you down in the sand and do some things that might get us eaten by an alligator or pinched by crabs. But I also really want to do this," he said, leaning in for a kiss. It was a quick, chaste kiss, and left her far from satiated.

"That was pathetic."

"Oh really?" he laughed.

"Really. I'm not sure I could date someone who kisses like that."

His face was close enough that Ashley could see his eyebrows raise in acceptance of the challenge. He dropped her hands and placed both of his hands on her cheeks, pulling her close for another kiss. This one started softly, giving Ashley just the slightest taste of what he had to offer. But then he quickly deepened the kiss, drawing her lip into his mouth, nipping it slightly. By the time his tongue met hers, his hands had slid down her body and pulled closely around her back.

Ashley positioned her hands tentatively on his hips, but soon realized that wasn't enough. She wanted more of him. She ran her hands up his torso, pulling him closer until she could feel his heart beating against her chest. Her entire body tingled with every sensation and all she could think about was wanting more. More of his lips, more of his scent, more of his taste. More of his touch as his hands roamed her body and more of his skin under her own hands.

Without thinking, Ashley slipped her hands under his shirt and slid them up his back. She felt his subsequent groan in the pit of her stomach, where the desire to have all of him was growing stronger.

Ashley forgot all about her parents, her brothers, and everyone else. There was only Adam and her—the world beyond their lips simply ceased to exist. She didn't want to imagine anything that didn't involve staying just like this, frozen in the most perfect kiss ever, for the rest of time.

Suddenly, the water splashed over their ankles, breaking the spell. Adam moved his hands back up to her face, cupping her chin gently as he pressed his lips against her forehead.

"Was that kiss better?" he asked, his voice gravelly.

She moaned in response and he swept her up into his arms and carried her further up the beach, kissing her again as he sat her down. She leaned in for him again but he pulled back.

"I hate to say this, but I should walk you back home. Your parents are going to wonder what we're up to out here..."

"Fuck my parents," Ashley replied.

Adam growled. "You are killing me, Ash. Killing me."

She sighed, realizing he was right. They started back up the beach, pausing for another short make-out session by their shoes. As they reached the boardwalk, Ashley slowed down.

"You know they're going to forbid me from seeing you," she said softly.

"Ouch."

"Just giving you a heads up."

"Okay. Well, thanks." He paused. "So can I call you later?"

"You better," Ashley said, rising onto her toes for one last kiss.

They held hands until they were half-way up the boardwalk and then separated. She walked him to his car, concerned her brothers might try something crazy, then went to the front porch. She stood there for a minute, replaying the kiss in her mind, determined to savor every last ounce of enjoyment from the last hour before heading inside where she knew it would all end. But, the mosquitoes were bad, and she couldn't avoid her father forever.

Taking a deep breath, Ashley stepped inside.

She immediately saw the light on in his study. She slipped out of her shoes and approached the open door tentatively.

"That was a long walk," he said without turning.

"Adam left a while ago," Ashley said. "I was out on the porch thinking."

"About?" He turned to face her.

Ashley shrugged.

"Your brothers won't bother that young man anymore," he said.

"Thank you," she said, and she meant it. "It was really embarrassing that they acted that way."

He nodded, and just as Ashley was starting to think she had been wrong about the direction this conversation would take, he said what she was waiting for.

"I don't want you dating him."

Ashley sighed, disappointed in her father, disappointed in herself for even considering he'd do anything different.

"Why not?"

"Ashley, you know why."

"Because he doesn't come from money?"

Her father groaned, not exactly disagreeing. "He's not like you."

"Because he doesn't have money."

"Sure. I reckon that is part of it," he said, his voice firmer now. "You are accustomed to a certain lifestyle and he is never going to be able to provide that for you. He is also older than you, and while two years may not seem like a significant difference in twenty years, it is right now. You are a teenager—a child still, and he is legally an adult. He is more experienced than you and he has not led the same sheltered life as you."

"Whose fault is that?" Ashley interrupted.

Her father raised his hand, indicating his refusal to even acknowledge Ashley's point. "He has no plans to attend college or better himself in any way. He has no ambition, and no awareness that he even should work towards something better for himself in life."

He paused before continuing, "I also think you understand that this is a small town and people talk. You can't expect to jump from Brent Abbott to some stranger without people gossiping and without getting a reputation. You are on the cusp of adulthood. This is a year when you need to focus on your academics and figure out your priorities for life. You do not need distractions."

"I don't see why Brent is acceptable and Adam isn't. How is Adam irresponsible because he's choosing to work for a living, but Brent is a model human in your mind because he's going to let Daddy pay for an education so he can play beer pong and sleep around for four years before doing any real work?"

He slammed his fist onto the desk. "Ashlynne, you can date

Brent or not. At the end of the day, that's your call. But you are not going to date some vagrant trolling up and down the east coast looking for attractive younger girls to defile. I won't allow it!"

He turned back to his computer before he could see her cry.

CHAPTER 7

The phone woke Adam the next morning. He hadn't slept well the night before, having spent the better part of the night replaying the time he'd spent kissing Ashley and fantasizing about doing other things with her. He was tempted to ignore the phone, but considered the possibility it would be her and rolled over to check the caller ID.

It was his dad. And according to the clock, it was after ten, so Adam figured he should probably answer.

"Hey dad." He tried to sound like he wasn't just climbing out of bed, but his gravelly voice betrayed him.

"Late night?" his dad replied with a chuckle.

"Not really."

His dad paused. Adam stumbled into the bathroom while he waited for his dad to say something.

"What did you do?"

"Went to dinner at a friend's house," Adam said, covering the phone after he spoke so he could pee.

"Oh, like a party?"

"No! Just dinner. Her parents were there." Adam winced the moment the words left his mouth. He'd been so determined to disprove his father's assumption that he'd inadvertently refer-enced Ashley. Adam had about a second to hope his dad hadn't picked up on the slip before he spoke again.

"So you were with a girl," his dad said. "And you're already meeting her parents."

Adam scratched his head, unable to think of a suitable response. He and his dad generally got along just fine. And Adam knew his dad trusted him, since he was fine with letting him live on his own. But since his mom had passed, Adam often felt like his dad was trying to fill the protector and disciplinarian roles his mom once held along with the friend role he was more accustomed to. It just came out awkward.

"Yeah, I don't know," Adam finally said. "We're not really dating or anything yet. She's just a girl I met on the island. She has brothers my age, too, so I was just kind of getting to know them better."

"Uh huh," his father said. "Is she pretty?"

Adam laughed. "Of course."

His father chuckled too, then asked him about work.

By the time they'd hung up, Adam felt relaxed. He maybe didn't have the most stereotypical relationship with his dad, but he was good with it.

* * *

ASHLEY SLEPT IN LATE, then holed up in her bedroom even after waking, determined not to see anyone. But around eleven, there was a soft knock at her door.

"I'm sleeping!"

There was a click as the door unlocked and then Austin poked his head in.

"Go away," Ashley snarled, pulling the pillow over her head and debating whether she could install a chain on her door. At present, whenever she locked it, anyone could still come in simply by shoving that little key hook thingy in the hole.

"I come bearing gifts," he said. The bed sunk a little as he sat down.

She peeked at what he had brought. "How sweet, you made me a Pop-Tart," she said sarcastically. But she was hungry, so she snatched it.

"I brought tea, too," he said.

"Did you need something?" Ashley asked, knowing something was up if Austin was trying so hard to be nice.

He frowned. "I was just feeling a little guilty."

"You should. You are an asshole."

"I heard what happened with Dad."

This wasn't surprising. The downside of the open layout of the first floor was that anyone could spy from almost anywhere.

"You and Adam were gone a long time last night. What did you guys do?"

"We were talking," Ashley said, resenting the implication.

Austin sighed. "You seem to like him."

"He's a nice guy, Austin. You would know that if you had given him a chance. I think you guys would have been friends if you weren't such a douche to him."

Austin shifted on the edge of the bed. "Look, I don't think he's some epic villain like dad does. I just didn't want him preying on my innocent little sister."

"I'm not that innocent."

Austin grimaced. "Adam is my age, a little older even. I know what guys my age think and do and I don't think you should be mixed up with that."

"Austin, you were every bit the jerk two years ago you are today and I guarantee you that Adam is no more after my virtue than Brent was, so you can calm down." Ashley finished off the pastry and dropped the plate on his lap. "But I really don't need any more lectures, so you can go now."

"Ash, I was trying to apologize, okay? I don't like seeing you mad at me."

"Then don't be a jerk."

He stood up and nodded. "I can manage that. Now get your ass out of bed. We're going to the beach."

She lounged in bed for another ten minutes before deciding she might as well join them. It was a Saturday, so Lisa and Katie were sure to already be there. The beach was theirs on Saturdays, as most tourists left in the morning and the new batch didn't arrive till late afternoon.

Ashley pulled her hair into a messy ponytail, slipped on a fuchsia bikini and brushed her teeth before wandering downstairs. Her father was home, which was surprising, but he was in the midst of some discussion with Jackson, so Ashley easily avoided them both. Mason and Austin were already in their swim trunks and shoving each other around the kitchen while their mom tried to talk to them. Ashley weaved through them all to fill her water bottle, then grabbed her beach bag and started out the door.

Mason sidled up to her before she got off the back deck. "Leaving without your favorite brothers?"

Ashley rolled her eyes. "Afraid you'll get lost?"

He made a face but walked faster to keep up with her. "So Austin says we're forgiven."

Ashley stopped abruptly. "Hardly. You never even apologized."

He raised his hands defensively. "Uh, twin thing. Apology from one counts for both. Duh."

Ashley glared.

"Fine. Sorry we were mean to the tattoo guy."

"He has a name."

"Yeah, yeah. So you don't even feel a little bit guilty about what you did to Brent?"

Ashley was starting to rethink her plan to go to the beach

today. "I didn't do anything to Brent. And what was going on with us has nothing to do with Adam."

Now Mason rolled his eyes. "Oh please. I saw the way you looked at him. And he actually told Dad he wanted to go out with you. I mean, the dude has balls for sure, I'll give him that. Clearly no brains, but…"

"I can date whoever I want."

Mason cocked his head to the side. "Does that mean I can date whoever I want?"

"I couldn't care less who you go out with," she said, stopping to slip off her sandals as they reached the end of the beach walk.

"Glad you feel that way, Sis. I thought I might ask out Lisa today," Mason said with a cocky grin.

Ashley glared at him, pretty sure he was kidding, but not positive. He laughed hysterically.

"You know what? It doesn't even matter if you're serious," Ashley said. "Lisa would never go out with you."

He couldn't reply, because they'd reached the edge of the water, where Lisa and Katie were lounging. A couple girls from the twins' class were there too, along with a few guys. Further down the beach there were a few families with younger kids, but for the most part, the entire stretch of sand was theirs. Ashley set her chair next to Katie's before plopping down on her stomach over her towel. She had no interest in conversing with anyone at this point.

She drifted off to sleep after a while, and when she woke a little bit later, the atmosphere was markedly rowdier. Music blared and a game of beach volleyball elicited random shrieks from the players. Ashley yawned and stood slowly, stretching her sore neck.

Lisa and Tyler were amongst those playing volleyball, which made her chuckle. Lisa hated playing games on the beach almost as much as Ashley did, but apparently if it got her closer to Tyler, she could handle it. Brent was nowhere to be seen, which didn't surprise her, and Katie was talking to Jackson, who'd made himself comfortable in Ashley's chair.

Ashley stepped towards them, resisting the urge to gag at Katie's flirtatious mannerisms. The entire world knew she had the hots for Ashley's brother, and while Jackson clearly loved the ego boost he got from encouraging her crush and flirting back, Ashley seriously doubted he'd ever hook up with someone so much younger.

"You're in my chair," she said to him.

Jackson turned to her and lowered his sunglasses. He was lips were curled up, but the smile didn't reach his eyes. "Good morning sleepyhead."

Ashley glared in response.

"Okay then," he said, standing and flashing Katie one last cocky grin. "I came down here to talk to you anyway but I didn't want to disturb your catnap."

"I don't feel like talking to you," Ashley replied.

"Too bad, because I have some stuff to say," he said. He gripped her elbow and gently tugged her out of earshot of her friends. "Look, I know you're pissed, but Dad is right about this new guy."

"Adam," she said. "His name is Adam. And you lost your right to have any opinion about him when you punched him."

Jackson sighed. "I didn't go there intending to hit him. Mason told me you broke up with Brent and we'd all seen you talking to this new guy, er Adam, a lot lately. We just wanted to talk to him and get to know him. Nothing would've happened if he hadn't been such a cocky bastard. You weren't there and you don't know what he said."

She jerked her arm free but didn't move.

"I'm sorry I hit the guy, okay? He just pissed me off is all. But that doesn't change the fact that he isn't good for you. Did you know I met him earlier?" Jackson paused, but not long enough for her to answer. "At a bar. Where he was drinking. Why would I want my sister hanging around some guy that has a fake ID and doesn't see anything wrong with underage drinking?"

"Oh, because you were such a saint at nineteen."

"We're not talking about me. You're not nineteen. You're seventeen, and you're a girl. I hang with the wrong crowd and maybe I end up getting in a fight. You go out with the wrong crowd? Ashley, you are so naïve. You don't even know half the shit that could happen to a girl like you getting mixed in with these older guys."

"Maybe if you gave Adam a chance you would see that he's not the devil you've made him out to be."

Jackson shook his head. "Fake ID, underage drinking, smarting off to me for no good reason, and stalking an underage girl? Yeah, I think I've got plenty of evidence. He's trouble and you hanging around him just to make some point and piss off Dad isn't going to pan out well."

"That isn't why I spend time with Adam."

"Well, it's no matter now. You ain't hanging out with him anymore or you will regret it."

"Are you threatening me?" Ashley realized her voice was getting louder, but by this point she was pissed off. Austin and Mason had come to join them, and Lisa had stepped away from her game, apparently coming to offer her moral support.

"Ashley, don't be like that. You know damn well I'm only concerned about you." Jackson shook his head, clearly displeased with how this conversation had gone.

"What exactly do you think he's going to do to me?"

"Shoot, I don't know. Get you drunk, convince you to mar your skin with a bunch of ridiculous tattoos, knock you up, get you hooked on drugs and leave you in the ghetto where a bunch of his thug friends can have their way with you."

"Do you hear how ridiculous you sound? Or how offensive this is to me? I'm not a moron. I don't need you telling me what is and isn't safe."

"Well, that's debatable," he began. "But I'll tell you one thing. If I see him hanging around you any more, there are going to be consequences for him."

"What—you'll punch him again? Because I don't think he'll just sit there and take it the next time you guys come at him."

"There's other ways to get a guy's attention," Jackson said, his expression dark. "He seemed pretty attached to that truck of his."

"You aren't that big of a dick," she said.

He laughed sardonically.

"Fine. Let me simplify things for you," Ashley said, staring him straight in the eye so close that he could probably blind her by spitting. "If you or any of your friends hassle or hurt Adam or do anything whatsoever to his truck or boat or anything else even remotely jerky, I will be on my knees for him the second I find out—just to piss you off."

Mason and Austin both started laughing, but Jackson looked appropriately appalled. Ashley started to turn when Jackson grabbed her wrist.

"I'm not going to mess with Adam because it's obvious he can't take a hint anyway, but let me tell you little sister, that if I ever catch you on your knees for any dickhead around here, there won't be anything left for you when I'm done with him."

He dropped her wrist and stormed off. Ashley exhaled nervously, taking a moment to calm down, then realized he had basically, albeit in a jerky way, agreed to leave Adam alone.

Lisa was staring slack-jawed. "Did you just threaten to give Adam a blowjob if your brothers messed up his truck?"

Ashley nodded.

"Wow. That's a new one."

They both waited a minute, then giggled.

They went back up to Lisa's house for lunch that morning and then she had a manicure scheduled later. Ashley debated going with her since Adam still hadn't called, but decided against it.

Ashley texted him as she walked back from Lisa's, asking if he was working. His response was instant, saying he had planned to but that it was dead at the marina. Ashley told him to get a swimsuit and come to her place asap.

She changed into a different bikini, did crunches until she felt like barfing, then reapplied sunscreen right as her phone beeped. It was a text from Adam.

It read, "I'm here. Is it safe to come in?"

Ashley smiled and hurried down the stairs. Adam was leaned against his truck, wearing navy blue swim trunks and his usual baseball cap, looking so hot that Ashley actually felt her body temperature rise above the sweltering temps around her.

"Hey!" she greeted him cheerfully. She tossed him two bottled waters then gestured for him to follow her to the storage room. "Kayaks," she said, pointing. "Can you attach those to your truck?"

He grinned and nodded, lugging them one at a time. While he was working on that, she went back inside and threw some snacks into a waterproof cooler bag. Low tide should hit right around five, so they would be good to have a mini picnic on the sandbar.

She climbed up into the truck beside him and fastened her belt as he took off toward the marina.

"How did it go with your dad after I left?" he asked hesitantly.

"Not good. Pretty much as I expected."

"But I don't understand. I outright told him at dinner I wanted to go out with you and he didn't seem too appalled by the idea."

"Yeah, that's my dad for you. He's got his public face and his private one."

"He literally said you can't go out with me?"

"Yes."

"But we're going kayaking today."

"Yep." Ashley glanced over at him, realizing she might need to clarify. "My dad is rarely home. I have no intention of letting him decide who I go out with."

Adam was quiet. Too quiet.

"On the bright side," she began, eager to lighten the mood, "Austin apologized for everything. I mean, really apologized. And I think Mason is feeling pretty bad, too."

"And Jackson?"

"Well, he doesn't seem remorseful, but we had a talk and I'm confident none of them will mess with you anymore."

She showed him where to park at the marina and he unloaded the kayaks. Ashley tossed a life jacket in each one, then stuck their keys and phones into a waterproof cooler underneath the towels.

"Are we planning on taking on water?"

Ashley shrugged. "I'm a stickler for the rules."

He eyed her suspiciously. "Apparently not all rules."

She stripped off her tank top and shorts and threw them in the kayak, pretending she didn't see the wide-eyed gawking Adam was doing. Grinning with pride, Ashley waded out a few inches then climbed in.

"Want a push?"

She had planned to use an oar, but saw no reason to do things the hard way. "Sure. Thanks."

He walked her kayak out a bit then shoved it until it was floating freely. Ashley waited for him to get in and off shore, then started paddling to the north.

"Are we headed to your secret island?"

"Yes, sir. Fingers crossed it's empty today."

"Why? You planned something we need privacy for?"

Ashley grinned mischievously. "No, I just didn't pack enough food for anyone else."

They paddled along for about twenty minutes, not really pushing the pace. They talked about their high schools and Adam told Ashley about all of the places he had lived. Ashley took him by the marsh to see if she could show him some rogue freshwater gators, but none made an appearance.

"Now you might actually have to paddle," Ashley said as they neared the sandbar. The current was pulling away from the tiny landmass so it took a little more effort to get over it. A few minutes later, though, they were both dragging their kayaks onto the sand.

"Well, here you have it," Ashley said, gesturing around her. The entire sandbar was about half the size of a football field and mostly flat, with a few rogue bushy trees on mounds that stood up out of the water even during high tide most days.

"This is really cool," he said, glancing around. "It's like being on a deserted island with the hottest girl I've ever seen."

Ashley bit her lip, certain she was blushing beet red at the compliment. She looked down at herself, confirming she didn't have a boob hanging out or anything. Ashley never felt model-pretty or anything, but she had no major complaints about her appearance. She had smooth, thick, dark blonde hair that faded lighter in summer. Her skin was clear and her eyes were a cool shade of green. She had dark, long eyelashes that she loved and ears that were maybe a bit small for her face. Her boobs were awesome—finally—but she seriously thought she was going to die when she was still completely flat- chested at fifteen.

Living on an island where she was in a bikini most of the summer, Ashley knew she was lucky to be naturally thin, especially since her workout regime consisted of 300 squats a day and as many crunches as she remembered to do, but no real cardio outside of tennis practice. Ashley was 5 foot 5, which wasn't terribly short, but since she was attracted to tall guys, it would've been nice to have an extra inch or two.

Adam stepped closer and flipped his baseball cap backwards. "So what's the plan now that you have me here?"

"I brought snacks," Ashley said nervously, rushing over towards the kayaks.

He caught her as she walked past, holding her still for a moment without speaking, just staring at her and smiling. And then he kissed her. There was nothing tentative about this kiss at all. It went from zero to fireworks in a nanosecond and Ashley had the fleeting realization that they were probably going to drown on this tiny island because she'd never be able to stop kissing him long enough to kayak back to shore at high tide.

His hands wrapped around her, holding her without any space between their bodies. They were both slick from the heat, but Ashley didn't mind the temperature one bit. She rested her hands on his hips, dying to slide them lower, just to see if his butt felt as amazingly firm as it looked. Instead, she raised her hands, first to his shoulder blades and then to his sides, gently tracing her fingers along the edge of his ribcage and abs. He squirmed a little, apparently ticklish.

Ashley smiled through the kiss and he responded by kissing her harder. As his tongue teased in and out of her mouth, Ashley felt breathless and tingly and wild with desire. Unable to resist any longer, she slipped her hands lower and rested them on the peak of his butt. She felt his lips curl up into a grin against her mouth as he lowered his hands to her thighs. He bent his legs a little then hoisted Ashley into the air. She squealed but quickly wrapped her legs around his waist, groaning softly as his abs pressed firmly against her aching core. She hoped the counter pressure would help soothe the burning tension that increased with each moment this kiss went on.

Adam planted his hands on her butt to support her, then gradually moved them to her thighs. After a moment, he pulled back and grinned at her. "Where have you been all my life?"

"Right here," Ashley whispered, still breathless.

He slowly lowered her to the ground and cleared his throat.

"So, um, you were saying something about a picnic," he said, making his way towards the kayak. He retrieved the towels and spread them out on the sand and then began arranging the food she'd thrown together.

Ashley watched him, mesmerized by his firm abs and chest. She had never before been tempted to squeeze a guy's chest, but with Adam, well, Ashley fantasized about doing exactly that and then running her tongue along the developed ridges of his stomach. What was wrong with her? She was a total hormonal mess. She had never been this crazy with Brent, and everyone agreed he was hot.

Ashley became aware that Adam was watching her and smirking.

"What?" she asked.

"You were totally checking me out."

"Whatever," Ashley said with a shrug, feeling her cheeks flush again.

"I love when you blush," he said. "It's sexy."

"It so is not," she replied, sitting beside him and stretching her legs out.

"What are you thinking now?" he asked.

"I was thinking that you're a really good kisser."

He grinned again. "I was thinking the same thing about you."

Before Ashley could even panic about blushing again, Adam's lips were on hers. This kiss was less frantic, more tender. He placed one hand on her cheek and the other behind her back, waited a minute, and then slowly lowered Ashley to the towel she'd placed over the firm sand. Her heartbeat felt like it tripled at the sensation of him looming above her, his perfect body so close to hers.

He pulled back slightly and Ashley opened her eyes, smiling despite the pause in the kiss, as his face was mere inches from hers. Adam had the boldest blue eyes she'd ever seen and this masculine jaw line and cheek bones that made her wonder if he'd ever modeled. And his lips—his perfect, soft lips. Ashley knew he'd shaved this morning, since last night's kisses were scratchy from stubble and now he was smooth.

"You are really beautiful, you know," he whispered.

She fought back a moan. How could one person be so sexy and so sweet all at once? Ashley roped her arms around his neck and kissed him again, first lifting her head to meet his mouth, then pulling him down to her as she settled back against the towel. He rested his hand on her stomach, and while she liked the way he was softly running it back and forth across her abs, she wished he'd climb on top of her. She yearned to feel the weight of him against her, but she knew it was a bad idea. Ashley didn't want to rush into things with Adam, well, any more than she already had, and based on how she was already feeling, Ashley was going to need a lot of self control to pull away from him.

Apparently, Adam felt the same way. He ended the kiss abruptly and rolled onto his back beside her. He tugged his cap down over his face and groaned.

"What?" Ashley asked, flipping onto her side and placing her hand casually on his tight stomach, suppressing a shriek as she discovered it felt every bit as firm as it looked.

"If we were actually stuck together on a deserted island, we would starve," he said.

"But I brought food."

He laughed. "Yeah, but we wouldn't be able to stop making out long enough to eat."

Ashley giggled. "Oh. Right. Plus the tide will start coming in after a while and our island will cease to exist."

Adam uncovered his face to check that the kayaks were still secure.

"I'm not normally like this, I swear," he said.

"Not like what? Sexy and sweet?"

"You think I'm sweet?"

She nodded. "You can't fool me with that tattooed tough guy persona you try to maintain."

"Hmm. No, I mean I don't normally start making out with girls before I even take them out on an official date."

"Oh." Ashley closed her eyes so the sun didn't blind her. "Well I'm really not either. I haven't even… I mean, Brent was my first real boyfriend anyway, so there haven't been a lot of guys to make out with in the first place. Anyway, I'm not complaining about the kissing. You can keep doing that as much as you want."

He laughed, but sat up and started rifling through the food.

"Did you go out with Brent for long?"

Ashley did the math in her head. "I guess almost two years."

"Oh. Wow."

"It was kind of an off-again, on-again sort of thing, though, you know? We'd go out a few times, then we'd have a fight about something and we'd break up, and then we'd get back together."

Adam nodded. "I see. So this is like a weird rebound thing until you get back together with him?"

Ashley frowned, feeling awful that he even thought that. "No, that's not what I'm saying at all. I just mean I don't think things were ever that serious with Brent. We were in the same friend group and everyone seemed to think we should date, so we did. Part of me thinks my father orchestrated the entire relationship."

"Your dad really liked Brent?"

"Oh yeah. I mean, if he'd ever seen us making out or something I'm sure he would've shot him. But he does a lot of business with Brent's dad and our families go to the same country club and all that crap."

Adam laughed.

"How about you?" Ashley asked. "Do you have a girlfriend or two back home?"

He cocked his head to the side. "First off, this is my home now. And second off, no. I'm not like that, Ashley."

She rubbed his forearm apologetically. She hadn't meant to offend him, but he looked like the kind of guy who'd have girls lining up left and right to be with him. "So just a string of broken hearts along the east coast then, huh?"

Adam leaned forward and kissed her, but this time, he ended it right as Ashley was starting to forget what they were discussing. "I've had my fair share of dates," he finally said. "But none as pretty as you."

The way his gorgeous blue eyes sparkled as he said that about killed her. Ashley was pretty sure that she would've done anything Adam asked her to right then and there. It took all of her self-restraint not to climb on top of him. From the way he was looking at her, she suspected he'd be pleased if she did do that, but she wanted to retain at least a little mystery.

They snacked and chatted for a few more minutes before dropping the pretense of needing food and making out until the tide started to come in.

CHAPTER 8

The next two weeks were exhilarating for Adam. He woke up thinking about Ashley. He spent his time at work trying to catch glimpses of Ashley. He arranged his entire social calendar around when he could see or even talk to Ashley. And he definitely fell asleep fantasizing about Ashley. He was whipped. The worst part was that he didn't even care.

Since breaking up with Brent and being officially forbidden to date Adam, Ashley had made it clear that she was in fact just as interested in Adam as he was her. She called and texted often, she traipsed around the marina in her sexy little shorts whenever he was working, stopping by to chat as long as she could without distracting him from his work, and she would meet up with him at random isolated locations for the best fucking make-out sessions. But she didn't go on an actual date with him.

Adam didn't want to push his luck, so he didn't really pressure her, but he didn't really get what her end game was either. She never acted all lovey with him around her friends, but she didn't exactly hide their involvement either. It was almost like she wanted her brothers to know, but didn't want to really flaunt it. Adam decided he didn't really care, in the end. Being with

Ashley was awesome, whether or not other people knew they were together. Adam felt mature for being happy about getting to have her even though he couldn't throw it back in anyone's face.

Even though pretty much everyone on the island knew Ashley, it wasn't like they had a shortage of places they could go together without being seen. They could always hang out at his condo, too, but Adam viewed it as a last resort. With zero possibility of anyone walking in on them, it was too hard for him to control himself around her. The last thing Adam wanted to do was prove everyone right and be the crazed hormonal older guy taking advantage of Ashley's sweet innocence.

Not that she acted that innocent with him. She was just as bad as he was, losing her train of thought mid-sentence as her eyes wandered down his body or kissing him a half hour after she had to leave for work. And—GOD could she kiss. Ashley kissed Adam like she was slipping through quicksand and he was her only shot at air. Even when it was just a short, chaste kiss like she was afraid someone would see them, her whole body would curve towards him.

Ashley made it obvious that she wanted to be touched every bit as much as he yearned to touch her, and that was killing him. Since Ashley bounced into his life, Adam had taken a lot of long showers. Today, he knew, would be no exception.

It was late afternoon, and they were out on his boat. Adam had worked all day and Ashley had divided her time between the beach and her friend's pool, but she'd picked up a massive collection of fried shrimp and French fries from one of the beachfront restaurants and met him by his boat just as he was saying goodbye to Clay. They'd headed out to sea for a good fifteen minutes or so before stopping to eat, then drove out a little further since there was increased boat traffic at this time of day as many returned home for the evening from whatever excursion they'd been on.

"Whatcha thinking about?" she asked playfully, running her fingers through her silky mane.

Adam felt his lips curl up as he looked at her. She had slid her sunglasses onto her head now that the sun was nearing the horizon, and her green eyes sparkled like fancy emeralds. "You are so beautiful," he mused, unable to look away.

Ashley giggled and crossed her arms over her chest. "That's what you've been thinking about this whole time?"

Adam snapped out of his trance. "Well, no. But it's true." He paused, glancing out over the water, then turned back to her. "I guess I was thinking about us, and wondering what we're doing here."

"Picnic on the water?"

"No, I mean big picture, you and I, what we're doing together."

Ashley sighed and shook her head. "I am constantly forgetting that under those abs of steel and biker boy art that you are actually a total girl."

"Did you just call me a biker boy?" Adam asked.

She giggled, tracing her hand along the aforementioned abs of steel. Adam's breath hitched as her hand reached lower. He clasped his hand in hers, stopping it in its path. Geez, maybe he was the girl in their relationship.

"Seriously, Ash. I like you. And you deserve more than making out on a boat. I think I should take you out on an actual date sometime."

Ashley was still running her eyes across his chest and biceps and didn't answer. Adam decided he should probably put a shirt on the next time he planned to have a serious discussion with her.

"We could go someplace off the island if you don't want to risk your family or anyone seeing us."

Ashley swiveled around abruptly, leaning back against him. Adam turned towards her, wrapping his arms around her.

"We could do that if you wanted," she said. "Although I think most people would consider romantic, private boat rides at sunset to be the ideal date, but if you're thinking Applebee's, I'm okay with that."

Adam laughed so hard he nearly slid off the bench. "It was slow today at the marina due to the rain earlier, so I was reading that restaurant guide. You know there's a ton of four-star restaurants around here?"

"I do know that. I've lived here my whole life, remember? When my family goes out to eat, we don't hit up some buffet or get burgers at Red Robin, we go to all those fancy places. I grew up on $40 steaks and lobster tails and restaurants where the chef knows my father by name." She absentmindedly stroked Adam's forearm as she spoke, her finger tracing the outline of his heritage tattoo. "So I don't have any overwhelming urge to go to places like that, but if you do, let's go."

Adam rest his head on top of Ashley's and considered this. "No, now that you mention it, actually, I really don't want to do that. I hate dressing up. I hate pretentious places."

Ashley snickered. "So why were you suggesting it?"

"I don't know. Because I feel like I should be taking you on dates instead of just sneaking around with you."

Ashley was quiet for a while. When she finally spoke, her voice was softer. "I'm sorry we've had to sneak around. I'm not embarrassed by you or anything, I just..."

"Ash, I know. Your parents don't want you seeing me. I get it."

"The twins already know," she said. "I mean I think they do. But Jackson... Well, he's leaving for school soon enough."

Adam wasn't sure what exactly that meant for them, but he wasn't about to press the topic more. If she didn't need more traditional dates, he sure as shit wasn't going to mess with it. He'd stumbled into the perfect combination of his two favorite things—being out on the water, and being with Ashley. He had nothing to complain about.

Adam tilted his head to the side to kiss Ashley's neck. She breathed a laugh and arched towards him, ticklish. But she took the hint and swiveled around to face him. He did a quick glance around to confirm they were still alone on the water before pulling her face to his and kissing her. He lost himself in the sensations of her. Her hair tickled his face and shoulders, her tantalizing banana sunscreen scent invaded his nostrils, and her smooth fingers caressed his arms and chest, causing his blood to pool in all the right places. He nipped her lip gently before their tongues met again and Adam growled softly, taken by her spell.

Ashley, apparently feeling the same way, swung her leg over his so she was straddling him, propelling all Adam's senses into overdrive. She leaned forward so her perky boobs pressed against him and Adam groaned, feeling her hardened nipples through her thin tank top. Against his better judgment, Adam reached under her shirt, lifting it over her head. As they broke the kiss, he pulled back to check her out briefly. She was wearing her white string bikini, one he'd seen many times before, but it was definitely his favorite because he could easily imagine he was looking at her in her bra and panties, not her swimsuit.

Ashley smiled mischievously and shifted her legs so they were wrapped around his back. Tightening his grip on her with one hand, Adam let his other hand roam up her side, stroking and massaging her through her bikini top as best as he could from this angle. A purr-like sound escaped Ashley's lips and suddenly Adam felt her hand on him. He was already hard, of course. He was so fucking hard by this point that he figured he'd probably die if she touched him anymore. She stroked him twice through his shorts before he reached her hand to stop her, moaning into her mouth.

Adam felt her smile against his lips but she obediently roped her arms back around his neck. Within a moment, though, he felt her pressing against him, grinding against his aching length. God she was hot. And she was killing him. Adam wanted nothing more than to give her that release she so clearly craved, but they were on a fucking boat where anyone could zip by and see them. And he wasn't going to be that guy. He was not going to do what everyone expected and take advantage of her perfect body, even if resisting was so painful.

He nudged her off his lap, still supporting her with his arms, and groaned. "You have no idea how much I want you, Ashley, but…"

"Oh, I have a pretty good idea," she replied with a sultry laugh.

Adam dropped his head backwards, squeezing his eyes shut, praying the thick evening air would somehow calm his raging hormones enough to let him do the right thing even when she was being so damn sexy.

Ashley pressed her lips lightly against his jaw before standing. Adam opened his eyes to look at her, relieved to see she was smiling.

"You know, if you don't want me to seduce you on our romantic sunset cruises, you should probably wear a shirt," she said.

Adam swatted her with her own top, eliciting a sharp squeal. He wasn't sure what he'd done to deserve this, but clearly he'd found the perfect girl.

* * *

ASHLEY FELT like she was living a divided life. When Adam was working, she went about her normal summer activities—playing and coaching tennis, lounging at the beach, and pool-hopping with Lisa. As soon as Adam got off work, though, she'd head over to the marina, joining him for a cruise on his boat or a walk on the beach. The summer heat had reached its peak, with the humidity competing against the mosquitoes to see which could be more annoying. Ashley really wished she could just have Adam over to her house, where they could spend their evenings in the pool together. But she knew her parents would never allow that, and even if they weren't home, Jackson would find out. If he weren't leaving for school in a couple weeks, Ashley probably would've just said screw it and let him find out about Adam.

What was the worst her parents could do—ground her? Doubtful. But the risk was enough that she figured it was worth keeping their involvement a secret a little longer. Besides, Ashley wasn't even sure what would happen with Adam once school started up again.

She suspected the twins knew she was seeing him, since she no longer spent her evenings with the rest of their mixed group of friends. Austin asked her why she didn't hang out with her normal crew as much lately, and she claimed it was just awkward being around Brent, and that she was trying to give him some space too. That seemed plausible enough. When Lisa asked her about Adam, she told the truth, if not the whole truth. She said they hung out a lot and that he kissed like a god, but that they weren't officially dating.

When Ashley wasn't with Adam, she found herself thinking about him a lot. She was obsessed, and in a way that she'd never been with Brent. Ashley wasn't sure if that was a good thing or not. She also found herself insanely jealous, which was also a new feeling for her. Before, when girls flirted with Brent and he flirted right back, it never bothered Ashley. She figured everyone knew Brent was hers, and she was pretty confident he'd never cheat anyway out of fear that her brothers would kick his ass.

Adam was a whole different story. He struck Ashley as a player, and whenever they talked about their pasts, he was vague. He claimed he'd never really had a girlfriend before, but it was obvious from the way he touched her and kissed her that he had a decent amount of experience with girls. Plus he'd already proven that he wasn't afraid of her brothers, and, since they didn't like him anyway, he certainly wouldn't be worried about losing their friendship or getting on their bad side if he treated her wrong.

Despite that, Ashley didn't think Adam would ever do her wrong. She'd never before seen a guy look at a girl the way Adam did her. It was like he was memorizing her. Plus he was just a good guy. Ashley suspected Adam always did the right thing, even when no one was watching.

But Ashley would be lying if she said it didn't bother her that people didn't know he was with her. It wasn't like she wanted him branded, but every time she watched a girl pathetically throw herself at Adam, Ashley wanted to run at them screaming, "he's mine, bitch!" And there were a lot of girls who flirted with him. The locals weren't too bad, but tourists were all obsessed with him.

Once, when Ashley and Lisa were walking around the marina eating ice cream while Adam was working, she counted eight separate women who somehow managed to touch Adam. He was popular with high school girls all the way through women who looked like they were well into their thirties. It was pathetic, really. When she was close, Ashley would watch the women flirting and gauge Adam's response. He always smiled, but he never fully reciprocated, and when he knew she was around, he was constantly winking, blowing kisses, or licking his lips in her direction.

"He's been ogling you for a half hour now," Lisa said late one afternoon as she and Ashley were having drinks at the marina. They stood at a tall table on the outside perimeter of the bar, waiting for the rest of their group. Ashley had seen Adam when they arrived, but he'd been busy, surrounded by a group of pre-teens about to head out on some tour with Clay's dad. She had intentionally stood with her back to him so she wouldn't be too distracted to talk with Lisa. If she could see Adam, Ashley knew she'd just gawk obsessively.

Ashley turned as Lisa spoke and immediately made eye

contact with Adam. He was over a hundred feet away, but the intensity of his gaze made her insides feel weak. She couldn't tear her eyes away until someone stepped in front of Adam, blocking his magnetic pull on her.

"Seriously," Lisa said. "He's hot. Maybe you should just sleep with him and get it out of your system."

"Lisa!" Ashley chided. She wouldn't mind sleeping with him, although that wouldn't do anything to get him out of her system.

"Are you at least going to go talk to him before your brothers and Brent show up?"

Ashley glanced back at him. "He's busy."

They didn't have time to continue the conversation because Austin showed up then, along with two girls and another guy from his class.

"Where's Mason?" Ashley asked.

"I'm not his keeper," Austin said with a shrug.

Ashley rolled her eyes but said nothing. They ordered some more drinks and discussed what foods they wanted from which of the many restaurants at the marina. Ashley offered to go pick up the food from the seafood place at the end of the harbor, knowing it would give her a chance to walk past Adam.

She grabbed her wallet and started off, but was disappointed when she didn't see Adam by the kiosk near the pier. Right before she reached the restaurant, though, she heard his voice.

"Hey sexy," he purred, his breath tickling her neck.

Smiling, she swiveled around to see him. "Hey yourself. Where were you hiding?"

Adam shrugged, glanced around, then pulled her off to the side of the path by her hand. He scooted her against the wall and kissed her.

Ashley knew they were only partially out of view, but as his firm body pressed against her, she decided she didn't care one bit. Adam kissed her like it was his job and when he finally broke away—too soon—Ashley felt so dizzy and breathless she nearly sank to the ground.

Adam steadied her and smiled. "I've been dying to do that all evening," he said. "Call me later?"

She nodded, and started off on her way. She stepped into the seafood restaurant, holding the door open for the patron behind her and then froze, realizing who it was.

"Mason! Geez. You shouldn't sneak up on people." Ashley turned away and tried to play it cool, uncertain of how much he had seen.

"Sneak," he repeated. "Interesting choice of words."

Shit. "What do you want?"

"Crab legs," he replied. "Extra dipping butter."

Ashley hesitated. She hadn't expected his dinner order. "Is that all?"

Mason laughed. "You mean, like, is there something you can do to get me to keep my mouth shut about you letting the tattoo guy molest you outside the tee shirt shop?"

They inched their way closer to the bar where they'd place the carry-out order. Ashley suddenly felt very warm.

"Mas, don't be a jerk," she whined.

He laughed. "Fine. We already knew anyway."

"We?"

Mason nodded. "Not sure about Jackson since he's hardly ever around, but Austin saw you making out on the beach last week."

"What was he doing on the beach then?"

"Hey, you're not the only one who can get some late night sand action."

"Eww," Ashley replied, unwilling to think about either of the twins getting any action. It was their turn to order, so Ashley went through her mental list of everyone's requests before turning back to Mason.

"Well, thanks," she mumbled.

"You owe me," he said, scampering off instead of offering to wait and help her carry the food.

Ashley blew out a sigh, but then let her mind drift back to that awesome kiss with Adam. Just thinking about it made her heart pump wildly. And she decided if the twins knew anyway, she didn't need to keep sneaking around.

* * *

THE FOLLOWING SUNDAY WAS GORGEOUS, but Ashley insisted that made it perfect weather for a movie. She only had a few days left before school started, so it surprised Adam that she wanted to spend their time inside, but she claimed that the solitary theater near the tip of the island was overcrowded with tourists any time it rained.

Adam bought the tickets while Ashley hit up the concession stand. They met back by the theater where Adam laughed seeing her weighted down with a massive popcorn, two large drinks, Twizzlers and Milk Duds.

"Are we preparing for the apocalypse?" Adam asked, taking the drinks and the candy from her.

"I like options," she replied.

She led the way into the theater, her tiny pink shorts offering Adam a fantastic view of her perky butt. Adam tried to recall if he had ever seen her wear the same outfit more than once and decided that he had not, with the exception of a couple repeats in her swimwear. Given that he'd seen her—at least from afar— almost every day for the past ten weeks, that was pretty impressive. She must have a massive wardrobe. Adam figured he was going to miss her summer clothes when the weather finally cooled off and she had to start covering up some of that perfect skin she flaunted so easily these days.

Ashley stopped by a row about halfway up in the theater. "This good?"

Adam nodded, noticing the theater was nearly empty still.

They sat in the middle of the row. Ashley immediately slipped off her sandals and curled her knees up to her chest, leaning in towards Adam.

He glanced over at her and grinned. God, she was adorable. He tossed a handful of popcorn into his mouth, then saw her open her mouth expectantly. Laughing, he fed her a few kernels.

"You ready for school next week?"

She groaned. "Ugh, why did you remind me?"

"Sorry. I thought you might be excited. Senior year and all."

Ashley tilted her head back and forth contemplatively while grabbing another handful of popcorn. "Yeah, I guess that'll be good at least. But I'm going to miss spending all day on the beach."

"With me," Adam added.

She smiled at him. "Yes. With you. It just sucks that as soon as the weather cools off and it's perfect for being outside all day, they make us start spending the day inside." She paused. "Seniors can leave for lunch, at least, so that's nice. Lisa and I are going back to school shopping tomorrow."

"Like for backpacks and stuff?"

Ashley laughed. "No. Fall clothes, jewelry, purses."

"Ah," he said, feeling silly. "Where do you go for that? The mall?"

She shook her head. "No way. There are a few cute shops on the island, but we'll probably do most of our damage in Savannah."

The theater darkened further as the previews began, blasting too loud for them to continue conversing casually. Adam was perfectly content sitting quietly next to Ashley, though. He glanced around, noticing the theater had filled considerably in the last few minutes. He reached his arm around Ashley's shoulders and she glanced up, smiled, and leaned in closer, resting her head against his chest. Adam bent down to kiss the top of her head, pausing just before to appreciate the tantalizing fruity fragrance of her hair.

He loved the way her shoulders shook when she laughed, and he even enjoyed the way she fed him Milk Duds, though it wasn't his favorite candy. She shifted a few times throughout the movie, but always stayed nestled close to him. Adam realized he had never felt this comfortable with a girl before.

Halfway through the movie, Adam whispered to Ashley that he'd be right back and ducked out of the row to head to the bathroom. As he neared the back of the theater, he recognized a few faces in the crowd. He looked away quickly, hoping they hadn't seen him, but as he crossed the lobby, he saw the theater door open again behind him and knew someone had followed him out.

He briefly considered waiting right there, certain he was much less likely to get in a fight in the crowded lobby than in the quiet men's room, but he wasn't inclined to change his plans just because of a chance of violence. He swung open the door to the bathroom, noted it was empty, and quickly made his way to the urinal. He had just flushed when the door opened again. It was Brent.

Adam's body tensed as he approached the sink. Thankfully, it appeared Brent was alone. Adam wondered why he'd left the rest of his posse in the theater. Brent came closer and leaned against the sink.

"I saw you with Ashley," he said casually, in a non-accusatory tone.

Adam nodded and shut off the faucet.

"Are you guys, like dating now?"

"Uh, yeah, I guess so," Adam answered, thankful the obnoxiously loud hand dryer offered a moment of interruption from the conversation.

Adam started towards the exit, then paused. It was obvious Brent had more to say, and since the guy wasn't actually being a dick like Adam had expected, he should probably stick around and hear him out.

Brent sighed. "Look, I assume you know the history with Ashley and me. I suppose I'm just curious on the timeline here."

It took Adam a moment to piece together what Brent was asking, but then it clicked. "You want to know if Ashley cheated on you?"

Brent winced at the word but eventually nodded.

"You could ask her."

"I'm asking you," he said, his tone slightly more aggressive now, but his voice softening some as he added, "she didn't really give me any specifics when we broke up."

Adam felt sorry for the guy. It had to suck losing a girl like Ashley, and especially if they'd been as on-again, off-again as Ashley said, it was possible Brent hadn't even realized this most recent breakup was for real until he'd seen Ashley with Adam.

"I asked Ashley out when I got into town and she said no. She told me she had a boyfriend and wanted nothing to do with me. I asked her out again after I heard you guys broke up. We've only gone out a couple times so far."

Brent seemed relieved by this, but he frowned anyway. "You guys seem awfully close."

Adam chewed the inside of his lip, trying to come up with a response to this but finding nothing. Finally, he said, "she didn't cheat on you, man."

Adam waited for Brent to respond, but all he did was nod. Adam exited back into the lobby and went directly into the theater. He paused just inside the door, letting his eyes readjust to the darkness, then looked for Ashley. He spotted the seats he thought they'd been in, but when he'd left, they'd been the only ones in the row. Now there were two other people, seated on either side of Ashley. Adam made his way down the aisle, quickly ascertaining that the unwelcome visitors were her twin brothers.

He paused by Austin. "You're in my seat," he said, noting the extreme look of annoyance on Ashley's face.

"Sorry," she mouthed to him. He shrugged. It wasn't her fault.

"I'm comfy here," Austin said.

Adam groaned then stepped around Austin. He had initially planned to just escort Ashley to a new row, but she stood partially and patted her seat. Grinning, Adam slid beneath her and pulled Ashley back onto his lap. This was clearly the ideal seating arrangement, although he could do without her brothers right beside them.

Mason laughed, while Austin squealed "gross." Then they both got up and returned to their seats.

As happy as Adam was to have Ashley curled tightly against him, he couldn't help but feel bad for Brent and he knew it wouldn't lessen the blow any for him to see his ex literally on top of another dude. So Adam chastely kissed her on the cheek and shifted her onto his old seat.

Ashley pouted at Adam and he leaned over, whispering, "Brent is here with your brothers."

She must have figured what he was hinting at because she stopped pouting and reached for his hand instead.

They went back to Adam's condo after the movie. Clearly, something was up with Ashley. She wasn't her normal chipper, flirty self, and she wasn't responding to him the way she usually did. He reached for her hand and pulled her back to him.

"Hey, what's going on? You seem…different today."

She shrugged. "School, I guess."

He stared at her as she made her way around his room, touching everything as though she were memorizing it.

"Look, I don't know what your school is like, but mine was actually pretty cool senior year. And once you're accepted to Duke, you can just coast. Are you sure that's all it is?"

Ashley didn't answer but she finally came and sat beside him on his bed. She wasn't making eye contact and she looked sad.

"Ash," he began, placing his hand on her cheek.

She squeezed her eyes shut.

"Spill it. What's wrong? Is this about your brothers seeing us today?"

Ashley opened her eyes and sighed. "No. It's stupid, I know, but I'm just going to miss this."

Adam frowned. "My bedroom? That's what you're going to miss?"

She shook her head. "No, hanging out with you. I know it's all my own fault—if I hadn't been so stubborn we could've had the whole summer to spend together instead of just these last few weeks, but…"

"You were stubborn," he agreed. "Never has anyone been so resistant to my charm."

She offered a half smile in response.

"Isn't school over at three? I have to work anyway, so it's not like we'll have that much less time together than we do now."

Ashley rolled her eyes then returned to looking sad.

"Okay. I don't get it."

She gave him a frustrated look. "Adam, this summer has been fun, but we both know it can't last. You could have any girl you want and you're not going to sit around all day pining for me all day when I'm stuck in high school classes. You're going to have tons of hot girls your own age stalking you at the marina all day who'll have more to talk about than their latest government class project or calculus test."

Adam couldn't help but laugh as soon as he realized what she was worried about. He supposed it was reassuring that even someone as perfect as Ashley was self-conscious.

"Are you laughing at me?"

He nodded, biting his lip to stop the chuckles. Then he pulled her closer, tugging on her leg until it was over his so he could lift her onto his lap, facing him. She still looked down, causing her hair to cascade over her face. Adam plucked the strands off her face and tucked them behind her shoulder so he could see her better.

"I'm laughing because you're crazy. I spent all summer chasing you down like a stalker begging you to go out with me. You are way out of my league, and yet here you are, worried that I'll suddenly fall for some moronic tramp on a jet ski just because you're gone a few hours a day. If either of us should be concerned, it's me. You are going to be spending all day every day with your hunky ex-boyfriend that everyone agrees is the perfect man."

A smile cracked on Ashley's face. "Did you just call Brent hunky?"

"Yes I did."

She giggled, then promptly looked solemn again.

"Seriously, Ashley, I really like you. I'm not interested in dating anyone else right now and I wasn't planning on breaking up just because school is starting."

He paused, realizing he might have misinterpreted it altogether. He knew she had to keep her grades up for Duke and maybe she didn't think she could handle both him and school. "Unless you're saying you just don't want the distraction..."

"Oh no," she said. "I welcome the distraction."

He raised an eyebrow. "Alright then. Want to meet me at the marina for dinner after your first day?"

She winced. "My parents will freak out if I don't eat dinner at home after the first day. How about Thursday?"

"It's a date." Adam hesitated. "And then on Friday, my dad actually gets here. He'll be here for a week or two I guess, and then he's going back to Nantucket for a couple weeks and then headed back out to sea."

"Oh," Ashley said, her face not revealing any emotion.

"I sort of told him about you, so he'd like to meet you if you're around this weekend."

She smiled. "I would love that."

Adam relaxed, glad the tension in the air was gone. Then he realized he had a beautiful girl straddling his legs and started to feel a different type of tension altogether growing. "Hmm," he said, "That actually might mean this is our last chance alone here for a while."

Ashley clearly knew what he meant as she leaned in for a kiss.

CHAPTER 9

On the first day of school, Ashley woke up feeling hung over, just like every other year. After three straight months of rolling out of bed around ten, six a.m. was brutal. She only hit the snooze button once, though, wanting to ensure she had plenty of time to look her best today.

She had set out a flirty but casual floral sundress and strappy sandals before bed, so she could omit the time usually wasted pacing around in her closet wondering why none of her clothes were cute enough. Ashley wore her tiny diamond studs, a simple silver necklace, a natural makeup palette and pale pink lip gloss. She dried her hair and clipped the front off to the side with a tiny barrette.

In honor of the first day, her mom had made her pancakes—a far cry from her normal breakfast of toast or cold cereal.

She smiled adoringly at Ashley as she slouched at the island to eat. "I love when you wear dresses."

Ashley nodded to indicate she already knew that, since her mom mentioned it every time Ashley wore a dress. It wasn't that she didn't appreciate the compliment or the yummy breakfast, but it was early and she was tired.

"What time are you picking up Lisa?"

Ashley glanced at the clock. It was already 7:03. "Shoot. Five minutes," she said, shoveling one last bite into her mouth before scooting the plate across the counter to her mom who pulled her in for an excessively tight hug and kiss on the cheek.

"You are going to have a fabulous year," she said. "You are so smart and so kind and absolutely gorgeous. Anyone would be lucky to be your friend."

The random pep talk seemed odd until Ashley realized her mom was likely thinking of Brent, and how Ashley was starting the school year single.

"Thanks," Ashley mumbled, starting to the door.

"Ooh wait!" Her mom rushed over with her phone. "I can't forget my first day of school picture. I can't believe this will be my last one. My baby is a senior!"

Ashley rolled her eyes but smiled for the photo. Twelve years of first and last day photos had taught her one thing—cooperation is the quickest way to survive the senseless torture.

Lisa, of course, wasn't quite ready when she reached her house, so it was 7:30 by the time they pulled into school. But considering first bell wasn't until 7:35, Ashley considered that a win. She parked in the special reserved Senior Lot and they both gushed about being seniors. Then Lisa turned to her, suddenly looking somber.

"Are you sure you're okay? I mean, about everything with Brent?"

Ashley shrugged. "Yes. Why wouldn't I be? It's been a month since we broke up."

Lisa eyed her sympathetically. "I know, but we weren't in school then. You can't really avoid him here."

"I'll be fine," Ashley assured her.

After stopping at their lockers, they parted to head to their respective homerooms. Ashley glanced down to double check what room her schedule listed and slammed into someone. Of course it had to be Brent.

"Hey," he said casually.

"Hi! How are you?" Ashley realized instantly her tone was way too peppy, but she couldn't stop herself.

He shrugged. "Not bad."

"How was the rest of your summer?" Ashley winced as soon as the words left her mouth. Why had she phrased it that way?

Brent gave her a curious grin. "You mean after we broke up? It was alright. We took that Alaskan cruise I'd told you about."

"Oh yeah. How was that?"

"It was cool. Really cool. And I hardly saw my parents, so it wasn't a big deal being trapped on a ship with them."

Suddenly, Mrs. Jacobs, the English composition teacher, stepped between them. "Okay, you two lovebirds, summer is over. Get to class."

Ashley cringed, but thankfully the teacher quickly moved on to the next bunch of dawdlers.

"Guess we might get that a lot," he said. "I didn't really tell many people about us."

"Yeah, me neither."

He cleared his throat awkwardly. "So, you still seeing the new guy?"

Ashley held her breath and nodded.

"Your brothers really hate him," Brent said.

"They don't know him."

"Do you?"

Ashley wasn't sure how to respond to that, so she finally said, "Adam's a good guy."

Brent appeared to consider this for a moment before speaking. "The twins told me to watch out for you."

She breathed a laugh. "That doesn't surprise me. And I think I'd prefer your methods of supervision over theirs anyway. But you really don't have to worry about me."

Brent nodded awkwardly.

Ashley took a deep breath and then said what she should've said weeks ago. "I'm really sorry for everything that happened with us, Brent. I really liked you, but we had been growing apart for a while and I started to feel like we were only together because of our parents. I should've told you sooner and ended it then instead of waiting, but I just didn't know how to..." she sighed. "I didn't mean to hurt you."

Brent gazed down at his shoes. "Yeah, I know. I sorta felt the same way."

"I know we'll still see each other anyway since we've got all the same friends and everything, but I really would like it if you and I were friends still," she said.

The second bell rang, officially declaring them late for class. Thankfully, it was the first day, and no one really cared about promptness yet.

"Yeah, me too," Brent agreed. He leaned in for a quick, awkward hug, then ducked into his classroom. Ashley heard a few guys cheering and greeting him jovially and she rolled her eyes, wondering how she'd ever worried that Mr. Popular would be lonely without her.

Adam sent Ashley a couple texts that day letting her know he was thinking about her, which she appreciated in light of her embarrassing meltdown the day before. She wasn't normally so insecure, but everything with Adam just felt too good to be true. She kept expecting something to go horribly wrong. She texted back that she'd call him that night and she did, right after dinner. Ashley dragged her backpack down to the edge of their dock under the guise of doing homework. She actually did have some homework, but since it was the first day, she had been able to finish it all right after school.

Adam answered immediately and she felt herself smiling at the comforting sound of his deep, melodic voice. She recounted every last detail of her day to him, then asked about his day. They talked about what they were wearing, what they'd eaten, and how they'd slept the night before. As the sun set and the bugs started appearing, they hung up. Ashley packed up her bag and headed inside, saying goodnight to her parents and heading upstairs.

Once she was alone in her bedroom and settled into her pajamas, Ashley called him back. They talked until after midnight, when Ashley was so tired from the unusually early wakeup in the morning that she started drifting off.

The next day, Lisa drove Ashley to school with the knowledge that Adam would pick her up. She walked with Lisa out the side entrance of the school, the closest one to the senior parking lot, and paused by the rest of their friends who were all making plans to head over to the marina. Ashley was watching for Adam's truck, so it caught her off guard when she saw him sauntering towards her.

He had on his favorite cap, athletic shorts and a grey sleeveless shirt that showed off almost all of his tattoos and plenty of muscle. He looked like he was headed to the gym, honestly, and damn was he sexy. He stuck out like a sore thumb in the sea of preppy rich kids surrounding Ashley. Their school didn't have an official dress code, but the majority of the student body dressed like they were headed to a golf tournament after school.

Ashley lost focus on Lisa's story as she locked eyes with Adam. He raised an eyebrow and grinned as he approached her, pulling her close for a hug. Ashley was initially bummed that he hadn't kissed her, but then, as she realized that nearly every member of the senior class was gawking at them, she appreciated his restraint.

"You look hot," he whispered in her ear. "Maybe there's an empty classroom we could sneak into for a few minutes."

Ashley pulled back, certain her friends could guess what he was saying by how red her cheeks were surely turning. She glanced down at her outfit- black tailored shorts and a turquoise tank top with sparkling beads arranged in a pattern around the chest. A long silver necklace with a teal charm hung around her neck, the charm having fallen down her shirt.

"I would kill to be that necklace right now," Adam whispered again, grinning proudly at having embarrassed her further.

"So, uh, Adam, you headed to the gym or something?" Tyler asked.

Adam shook his head. "Nope, just left there." He turned to Ashley. "Don't worry, I showered and changed, but apparently the only clean clothes in my gym bag were other gym clothes."

Ashley shrugged. "You look good."

Adam glanced around. "Then why is everyone staring?"

"Probably because they haven't seen a tattoo before," Ashley said.

"Or because they've never seen you with a guy who isn't Brent and they're waiting for him to come out and kick Adam's ass," Lisa blurted out, saying what they were all probably thinking.

"We should go," Ashley said to Adam, even though she knew Brent wouldn't be an issue.

"We're all headed to the marina for hot dogs and burgers if you guys want to come," Tyler said.

Ashley glanced at Adam and shrugged. "Yeah, we might see you there."

The second Adam shut his door, he was leaning in to Ashley, covering her mouth with his. His hand held her face close. Ashley inhaled sharply, enjoying the fresh scent of his shower gel and the warm tingly feeling spreading through her body as he touched her.

He pulled back and started the engine before she could fully lose herself in the kiss.

"You're too good at that," she mumbled.

Adam grinned. "Where are we headed?"

She shrugged. "Up to you."

"Don't you want to meet up with your friends?"

"We don't have to."

They reached a stop sign and Adam gazed at her, clearly trying to decipher her mood.

"I don't mind hanging out with your friends," Adam said. "They're cool. And I could eat."

Ashley did think it would be good for her friends to get to know him better, but she also figured Brent would be there and that could get awkward. So she briefly explained her indecisiveness, and Adam replied, "Let's go for a while, and then we'll head back to my place. Surely you can keep your hands off me in public if you know you'll have me all to yourself later."

When they arrived at the marina, Ashley scoped out tables while Adam bought them both sodas. He ordered a burger and fries for himself, but Ashley insisted she wasn't hungry.

By the time the rest of the gang arrived, it wasn't awkward at all. Brent did come, but he was way across the table with seven or eight of their friends in between them. And if he felt uncomfortable hanging out with Ashley and her new man, well, he was hiding it well.

Adam was telling Tyler a story about a couple of tourists who crashed their jet skis the prior week while Ashley nibbled on Adam's fries. Tyler laughed as Adam finished the story and Adam turned to Ashley.

"Thought you weren't hungry," he said.

She wrinkled her nose. "Sorry."

"I like when you eat. Here," he held up his burger for her and she reluctantly took a bite. "Not bad, right?" He scooted the plate of fries directly in front of her and kissed her quickly on the side of the head. "Take them. I'm getting more."

Ashley watched him head back to the counter to order more, noticing how good his butt looked in his shorts. As she turned back to the plate of food, she caught Brent staring at her. He offered her a friendly nod, then turned back to his own plate of food.

"So things with Tattoo Guy seem to be going well," Lisa said, watching him saunter off as she slid up next to Ashley.

"Adam," Ashley corrected, even though she knew that Lisa, unlike her brothers, didn't mean anything offensive by the nickname.

"Is it weird dating someone older?"

Ashley shook her head. "No. We'll see if he gets annoyed with me being in school all day or gets bored with my high school stories, but we're actually really in sync so far."

Lisa grinned. "And I bet he's really good in bed."

"Lisa!" Ashley blushed and glanced side to side to make sure no one else could've heard her. "You know we haven't had sex yet," she whispered.

Lisa was visibly disappointed.

"I'm not a total slut. I haven't been going out with him that long."

"I know, I just figured since he was older and more experienced things might move faster." She paused. "Wait, can you even have sex with him, or will it like count as statutory rape since he's older?"

Ashley started to answer, then realized she wasn't exactly sure. Before she could put much thought into it, though, Lisa had looked it up on her phone.

"Hmm," she said with fascination. "This says the age of consent is sixteen in South Carolina. So you are free to enjoy everything Tattoo Guy has to offer."

Ashley giggled.

"He looks like a really good kisser," Lisa said.

"He is such a good kisser," Ashley agreed.

Lisa groaned. "I really need a boyfriend."

Ashley glanced at Tyler, sitting beside Lisa but totally absorbed in something Dawson was saying. "Ask Tyler to home-coming. If he says no, play it off like it's a whole group outing you were inviting him to and not a date," she whispered.

Before Lisa could answer, Adam was back. They finished up their fries, then headed back to his place. Once they were alone, Ashley made a beeline to Adam's bedroom. Her conversation with Lisa was still fresh on her mind and she was acutely aware of the damper Adam's dad would put on their love life when he arrived the next day.

Adam followed happily, kicking the door shut behind him even though they were alone in the condo. He stepped out of his shoes and jumped onto the bed, pulling Ashley down with him. She giggled before quickly losing herself in his kisses.

Ashley never had any reliable sense of time when kissing Adam. She could be certain they'd been kissing for hours, but then whenever they stopped, if was never enough. Today was no different. Laying on her side facing Adam was fun, and Ashley eagerly stuck her free hand up the side of his shirt, relishing the feel of his smooth skin against her fingers. Adam reciprocated by slipping his hand up the hem of her top. Ashley instinctively sucked in her stomach as he brushed along her belly and then his hand rested against her ribs before inching further up her body.

When his hand reached its destination, Ashley nearly bit Adam's lip as all of her nerve endings became so acutely sensitive. She writhed against his hand, needing more but unsure how much she could even take without combusting. She pulled back from his mouth and saw that he was smiling. And then he opened his gorgeous blue eyes and Ashley felt like her heart was going to fly out of her chest. She swung her leg over him and sat upright, Adam quickly following. He raised an eyebrow and looked at her in a way that made her want to rip off his clothes, and he must have felt the same way, because he quickly leaned in and unfastened her bra. The straps still hung loosely on her shoulders, trapped by her shirt, but now when his hand worked its way up her body, he touched bare flesh.

"Oh my God," Ashley breathed into his mouth, certain she would die if Adam touched her there again. And then he did, again and again. She didn't die, or even pass out from hyperventilating, but Ashley felt an indescribable pressure building deep within her. She pulled her hands off Adam's back and reached for the bottom of her shirt, desperate to yank it off. She needed to feel his skin against hers.

"Stop," he said, grabbing her hands. He pulled his lips away but left his forehead pressed against hers as he spoke. "If your shirt comes off, I'm not going to be able to control myself."

"Good," she said, breathless.

"Ash, I'm serious. We have to take a step back here."

Humiliation washed over Ashley as the extent of the rejection hit home. She turned her head so he couldn't see her face.

"No, Ashley, I don't mean it like that," he placed a hand on her cheek. "I want you so bad."

She couldn't even look at him. Obviously he didn't mean that, or he wouldn't have stopped her. And talk about mixed signals— he was the one who unfastened her bra.

"Seriously, Ashley would you look at me?"

She shook her head, feeling tears welling in her eyes now.

He sat down on the edge of his bed and pulled her onto his lap. "You are without a doubt the sexiest and most beautiful woman I have ever seen. When I kiss you, all I want is more of you. I want you so bad I can't think straight when I'm with you." He paused. "And that's why you have got to keep your shirt on. If I see any more of you, I am positive I will not be able to stop myself from taking things further."

The sincerity in his voice pulled Ashley out of her pout. She gazed up at him. "What if I don't want you to stop?"

She watched his eyes register what she was saying and he definitely looked surprised. Ashley wondered what she'd done to make him think she was so sweet and innocent.

"I don't know, Ashley. There's your parents, and..."

"My parents? Geez, I certainly don't think they have any say in what goes on between us."

"It would only make them hate me worse if they found out."

"They wouldn't find out," Ashley insisted, omitting that they probably couldn't hate him any more than they already did anyway.

"You're not a…"

"No," she said, sparing him the trouble of saying the word. "Brent and I…" she mumbled awkwardly, not wanting to finish that sentence. "Wait, are you?"

He shook his head. They both took several deep breaths.

"So you're saying you want to have sex with me," he finally said.

Ashley giggled at his directness. "Umm, I've wanted to have sex with you since the first time I saw you."

He grinned. "Ditto." He gave her a squeeze. "Okay, but not here. Not like this. You deserve romance. I want it memorable."

She rolled her eyes. As if she'd ever be able to forget sex with him. "You are such a girl."

"And you love it," he said, wiggling his eyebrows.

Ashley concentrated on slowing her breathing, now that she knew nothing too exciting was going to happen today. To counter her disappointment, Ashley focused on the fact that she was snuggled up on his lap. And as an added consolation prize, her position gave her definite proof that she wasn't the only one in the mood for more.

They were quiet for a moment, and then Adam cleared his throat again. "So, are you on the pill?"

Since all of the blood had drained from her brain to other parts of her body, it took Ashley a minute to realize what pill he meant. "No."

"Okay. Do you want to wait until…" he paused, probably hoping she'd finish the sentence for him, but she was still clueless. "Until you can get it?"

"No. I can't…"

"It's alright," he said. "You don't have to explain. We'll use condoms."

Ashley nodded, but wanted to explain anyway. "It's a small community here. My parents know like every doctor on the island. I don't trust that whole doctor-patient confidentiality thing enough to get a prescription. I don't even know if they have to keep if confidential before I'm eighteen."

"Yeah, I don't know."

She leaned back against his chest. They were quiet for a moment. Then she shifted uncomfortably. "Can, um, you fasten my bra for me?"

He laughed but quickly agreed.

"I should go," she said. "My parents will expect me to do some homework. So, um, when does your dad get into town?"

"Tomorrow, not sure when exactly."

"You still want me to meet him?"

Adam nodded. "When are you free?"

"We're driving the twins to college Sunday, but Saturday is open."

"How about lunch Saturday? We'll get take-out."

She leaned in and kissed him again, causing the blood to rush right back to all of her sensitive parts. She ended the kiss and headed out before she tried to molest Adam again.

CHAPTER 10

*E*ven though it would seriously hamper his romantic life to have his dad back in the condo, Adam was excited. He was used to being on his own for long stretches of time while his dad was out to sea, but this had been the longest period, and it had felt even lonelier since he was in a new place.

His dad looked tired yet thrilled to see Adam when he arrived Friday just after lunch. Adam was still working, but his dad came to watch him for a while and actually hit it off with Clay's dad.

It was comforting, finally having someone in town who seemed pleased by Adam's life choices and who wasn't constantly judging him. They went out to dinner that night, with Clay and his father joining them. Adam had a really good time. He had forgotten how funny his dad could be, and he enjoyed taking turns with Clay recounting some of their funnier stories from that summer at the marina.

Right around the time the check came, Adam's father turned to Clay.

"So, do you know this girl my son's been hanging around with?"

Clay's jaw dropped and he turned to Adam, clearly surprised Adam had said anything to his father.

Adam shook his head in disbelief that his dad actually brought her up now, but then smiled so his friend knew it was okay to answer.

"Yes. She's a nice girl," Clay said, biting back a laugh.

"I didn't realize you were seeing someone," Clay's dad said. "Someone I know?"

Clay and Adam both replied in the negative right as Adam's father said, "Ashley. Right?"

Adam nodded at his dad awkwardly then glanced over at Clay's dad, curious if the name meant anything to him. At first he didn't seem to make the connection, but then his expression changed and Adam realized he must have seen her hanging around the marina.

"You're dating the Kensington girl," he said, his voice devoid of any expression.

"Ah, so you do know her," Adam's dad said.

Clay's father wiped his mouth. "No, not personally. Her family is pretty well known around these parts." He turned to Adam. "I hadn't realized you two were an item."

Adam opened his mouth to say something but couldn't figure out what.

"And this is just getting weird," Clay interrupted. "Not that I don't want to spend my entire Friday night discussing this dude's love life, but we should let them have this table."

Adam shot his friend an appreciative glance, and the rest of the night went smoothly.

The next morning, he took his dad out on the boat for a quick tour of the island, returning just in time to pick up food before Ashley arrived. Adam was excited to see her, but nervous as hell. He knew his dad would like her, but wasn't positive how she'd act around his dad. Thankfully, his dad went out onto the balcony with a book, leaving Adam to greet her alone.

Ashley arrived right on time. Adam relaxed when he saw her and leaned in to kiss her before checking out her outfit. She wore a lavender and pink floral dress, and she looked beautiful in it, of course, but it was nothing like the sort of thing she normally wore. It took a few years off her age and offered no hint whatsoever of her perky boobs, tiny waist or long, lean legs. Adam tried to stifle a laugh, but she sensed something was wrong.

"What?" She immediately blushed and looked down. "You hate the dress?"

"No, it's pretty," he said. "You look great. It's just…a little more conservative than you usually dress."

She narrowed her eyes. "Did you want me to wear a tube top and breakaway shorts? I'm meeting your dad!"

Adam shrugged. "Sure. And if we want to go crochet something with the ladies in the church group after, you'll fit right in."

Her expression changed and Adam immediately panicked that he'd taken the taunts too far, but then she smiled.

"Jerk," she muttered under her breath, thrusting a plate towards him. "Here. I made brownies."

"You can bake? Why am I just now learning this?" Adam wondered aloud, following her into the apartment.

Ashley paused near the kitchen, clearly having spotted Adam's dad. "He looks like you," she said.

Adam glanced over right as his dad turned, gave a little wave, and set his book down. He supposed he could see a resemblance, although he was hoping to have more hair when he hit fifty.

His dad pulled the sliding door shut behind him as he entered, smiling warmly at Ashley.

"You must be Ashley. I'm Sam Bricker."

"Nice to meet you," she said politely. "I was just telling Adam I see the family resemblance."

His dad looked at Adam as though he'd never considered it. Finally, he nodded. "I'll take that as a compliment. He's got his mother's eyes, though." He started into the kitchen and pulled out plates. "Come on, let's eat."

They made small talk through the meal, with Adam astounded at how well Ashley held her own with his father. She seemed comfortable around him and didn't even skip a beat when he started asking her about her family. They had just started on the brownies she made when he asked what her family thought about Adam.

If he hadn't known her so well, Adam probably wouldn't have noticed the flicker of panic cross her face. She pulled it together quickly and smiled in Adam's direction.

"My brothers were total jerks to him. They take that big brother role a bit too seriously. And I'm pretty sure the tattoos freaked out my mom," she said calmly. "But, you know Adam. Everyone who gets to know him loves him."

Adam's dad glanced at him, one eyebrow raised. Adam rolled his eyes, eager to change the subject. "Yeah, I'm just such a like-able guy, Dad," he said jokingly. As he thought about it, though, he was impressed with Ashley's answer. She hadn't exactly lied, but she'd done a nice job of omitting the part where she was forbidden to date him.

When they were done with lunch, Adam walked Ashley down to the marina and kissed her.

"Talk later?" she asked.

"Of course," he replied and took the stairs back up to the condo.

Adam stalled, hoping his dad would voice an opinion without him having to ask, but by the time he'd loaded the dishwasher and refilled his water glass, he was too impatient to wait any longer. "So, what did you think?"

His dad raised an eyebrow, almost as though he hadn't expected the question. "She's a very nice girl," he said finally.

"But?"

He shook his head. "No but. I see why you like her. She seems to like you a lot, too."

Adam waited, now certain there was more on his dad's mind.

"You know your mother grew up here," he said finally. "I wonder if Ashley's family is much like hers."

Adam hadn't really gotten to know his grandparents well. They weren't extremely close with his parents, and they died when he was in elementary school. So he didn't really know how to respond to his dad.

"How old did you say she is?" his dad asked after another lengthy pause.

"She'll be eighteen in a week."

His father nodded repetitively, then stood to leave the kitchen.

"That's all you have to say?"

He turned back and shrugged. "Just be careful, son."

Adam rolled his eyes, sick of people assuming he was going to hurt Ashley. It was even more offensive coming from his own father, a man who clearly should know better. "I'm not going to hurt her," he insisted.

A half smile crossed his father's lips. "I wasn't worried about her," he said.

* * *

ASHLEY COULDN'T BELIEVE how perfect everything was with Adam. She had never been sad or lonely, per se, but being with Adam made her feel happy and complete in a way she'd never known possible. She realized for the first time how alone she'd truly been before Adam. Sure, he wasn't with her all the time, but Ashley knew even when they were apart that he was thinking about her as much as she thought of him, and she found herself enjoying even the menial or unpleasant parts of her day, like calculus exams, simply because she would envision telling Adam all about it later. Ashley knew that with Adam in her life, she never had to deal with anything alone. He would listen to any problem she threw at him and he'd help her with anything he could.

Ashley wondered if this was what it meant to be in love. Well, she was positive she loved Adam, but the intensity of her feelings for him made her question what she'd thought she'd felt for Brent. Because while she certainly had said she loved him, Ashley knew she'd never felt this way about Brent and she felt fairly confident he hadn't felt that way for her either. She'd never before been one to believe in soul mates, but maybe that was the answer. Maybe she was that rare person lucky enough to find her soul mate early in life.

The problem, Ashley realized, with that line of thinking was the fear that accompanied it. Her life at the moment was perfect. It couldn't possibly get better, and, therefore, it could only get worse. She found herself worrying about Adam, not all the time in some crazy in need of pharmaceutical assistance sort of way, but just fleeting concerns, especially at night or when he was out on the boat alone. She'd briefly panic at how awful life would be if her were in an accident, or suddenly had to move away, or realized he could do so much better than her.

Luckily, she was too busy and too happy to dwell on the what-ifs for more than a brief moment. And now that her brothers were all back in school, things could only get easier for them. They next evening, they ate ice cream at the marina with friends, but Ashley was soon ready for alone time with Adam.

"Ready to head out now?" she asked Adam. "You could come to my place." Ashley grabbed her purse and said goodbye to Lisa.

"Where are your parents?" Adam asked.

"In Savannah. Some work function. They won't be back for hours."

Adam looked skeptical.

"Trust me, we'll have the house to ourselves for a while."

"Sounds good to me," he said.

When they reached the house, Ashley excused herself to change into shorts and a tee shirt. By the time she emerged from the bathroom, Adam had made himself comfortable.

"Wow, this bed is every bit as fluffy as it looks," he said with a grin, bouncing backwards onto it and resting his head on the pillow. He wiggled side to side for a moment, sinking into the soft mattress that she'd coated with even more cushy blankets. "Although I might never be able to get out again."

"I'm okay with that," Ashley said, locking the door before stretching out beside him.

He traced the back of his fingers along the side of her face while staring admiringly at her. "You're even more beautiful today than yesterday."

Ashley groaned. "I think you have a split personality. If your friends heard you talking like this…"

He reached his arm around Ashley and pulled her closer, lifting her leg over his. "If these sexy legs wrapped around them, they'd turn into mushy romantics, too."

He kissed Ashley before she could think of a witty comeback. As the kiss deepened, the yearning in the pit of her stomach intensified. She couldn't remember ever before having flutters in her chest from kissing a boy. Of course, she hadn't spent hours on end just kissing with Brent. But with Adam, Ashley could literally kiss him until her lips went numb.

He lifted her other leg, shifting her so she was fully on top of him and then he groaned happily. Ashley was self-conscious of having her full weight on him for only a nanosecond before she realized there was no way her tiny frame was squishing his tall, muscular body. She wasn't able to move her hands much in that position, but she did take the chance to knock his hat off his head and run her fingers through his hair. It was a medium brown shade and the softest hair she'd ever felt—not too long, but just enough to actually run her fingers through.

Adam's hands were eagerly exploring her back, but as their kisses grew more frantic, his hands shifted lower. He squeezed her butt firmly and moaned again. Then, his hands both slipped up Ashley's shirt. She inhaled sharply, savoring the sensation as his warm hands touched her bare skin. He inched his hands higher, pausing along the bra strap before scooting over and delicately brushing along the sides of her breasts. Now Ashley moaned, eager for his hands to touch more of her, savoring the warm heaviness pooling in the pit of her core.

Suddenly Adam flipped her over so she was flat on her back. He broke away from her mouth and briefly kissed her neck before scooting her shirt upwards and kissing her bare stomach. Ashley weaved her fingers into his hair, both enjoying the intimacy of his mouth there, so close, and nervously awaiting his next move.

Ashley didn't have to wait long as he quickly thrust a hand back up her shirt, lightly tracing along the outside of her bra before shoving the cups down and gently lifting one breast, then the other, out of the bra. He used the lightest touch imaginable, but it was enough to cause Ashley to bite down on her lip to keep from crying out with pleasure as he brushed across her taut nipples. Adam repeated the motion, gently caressing each breast, while still delicately kissing her stomach.

"Is the door locked?" he murmured in between kisses.

"Mmm hmm," she said, unable to formulate real words let alone process why he might be asking.

"And you're sure we're alone?"

"Yes."

"Good," he replied. He pulled his hands away and grabbed the waistband of her shorts, tugging them down before Ashley even had a chance to lift her hips.

Ashley started to sit up. "Wait! We can't...here?"

Adam pressed his hands against her chest and gently shoved

her backwards. "We're not doing that. Just relax and let me work my magic."

He started to reach for her panties and she panicked, realizing what he had planned.

"Whoa," she said, trying to sit up again.

He gave her a chastising look but stretched out beside her and resumed kissing her. As soon as she'd lost herself in the kissing again, he slid his hand back up her shirt. Her body responded immediately to his touch. His fingers deftly rolled her nipple until she moaned much louder than she meant to. Ashley was embarrassed to have been so noisy, but heard herself make the same noise as he moved to the other breast.

Then his hand slid downward. First he rubbed his hand along the outside of her panties and Ashley quickly found her hips rising to meet him, pressing back against his fingers. Then he pulled his hand away, nudging her thigh to the side some, then brought his hand back down, this time, slipping inside the thin cotton material.

She tensed as soon as he made contact.

"Shh," he whispered in between kisses. He slid his middle finger along her slick epicenter, slowly but rhythmically, until she groaned into his mouth.

"I'll be right back up here," he promised quietly before pulling his mouth away from hers.

Ashley started to protest but before the words came out, he pressed one finger inside her while kissing her neck and working his way lower. Her breath caught in her chest and she felt her body tighten reflexively around him. He groaned appreciatively and Ashley's pulse skyrocketed. She was dizzy with pleasure as he slowly moved his finger in and out then traced along her clit before plunging it back into her. She felt a pressure building in her and warmth spreading through her body. If he didn't stop soon, she was going to explode. Ashley couldn't handle any more of this exquisite torture. He increased his pace slightly, pushing her over the edge.

Ashley grabbed the nearest pillow and pressed it over her face to muffle her cries as shockwaves of pleasure rolled through her. After a minute, she felt Adam smooth her shorts back over her and kiss her stomach one last time before tapping on the pillow.

"Hello in there," he teased, pulling the pillow away.

Ashley tried to hold it firmly in place, embarrassed by her behavior, but he was stronger. He kissed her hard then pulled back.

"What's wrong?"

"Nothing. I just," Ashley fumbled for the right words. "I didn't mean to be so loud."

He groaned. "That was the sexiest thing ever. Don't apologize for that. You have no idea how turned on I am right now."

Ashley knew she was blushing. "I don't usually…"

He waited for her to finish.

"I mean, I've never… Well, it's not usually like that."

Adam frowned and seemed to consider this for a moment. "Wait, are you saying that was the first time you came?"

Now Ashley was certain her face was beet red.

"Ash, are you serious? But I thought you said you and Brent…" He winced instead of finishing the sentence, apparently too disgusted by the thought.

"We did. But it never felt like that. I never…"

"You never came? Holy shit, girl." Adam stared at her with a mix of adoration and pity. "Lay back because I owe you a lot more then."

Ashley laughed and pulled the pillow back over her face. She felt him tugging at her shorts again and she reached for his hand to stop him. He gripped her hand and lifted it above her head, then took the opportunity to tickle her. She shrieked with surprise and then laughed. Ashley freed her hand and rolled over to tickle his neck, and they spent the next few minutes engaged in a frisky tickle match.

When they both stopped laughing, Ashley looked over at him and smiled. It was really unfair that one guy could be so good looking, really. "Can I return the favor now?" She asked, gazing at him with what she thought was her best seductive look.

He smiled but shook his head, pulling her alongside him instead.

"I wanted to make you happy," he said, his voice wavering. "I love you, Ashley."

Ashley froze, not even risking taking a breath for fear she'd realize she heard him wrong. When she stopped panicking, she slowly lifted her head up to look at him. As soon as their eyes met, she knew he meant what he'd said.

"I love you, too," she said.

Adam captured her mouth in a kiss that led to a lot more kisses. This time, he didn't fight her when she unbuttoned his jeans and worked her hand beneath the band of his boxer briefs.

CHAPTER 11

The next few days were phenomenal, and not just because Adam was no longer forced to take multiple showers a day to offset the sexual tension. His dad surprised him with an early birthday present—the rest of the down payment on the boat he'd been saving for since high school. And if the boat itself weren't pure bliss for him—which it was—it also let Adam set the perfect scene for Ashley's birthday.

Adam couldn't compete with Ashley's parents' plans for her birthday—dinner at some fancy place in Savannah, followed by a carriage ride through the city and pricey seats at some fancy musical, but he knew the boat would set the perfect scene for what he did have planned.

Keeping his new toy a secret from Ashley had proved more challenging than he'd anticipated, even though he only had to keep quiet for a week. While it was Adam's dream boat, he knew Ashley wouldn't be impressed. It was a thirty-five foot express yacht, but it was nearly ten years old and lacked the showy upgrades of all the new yachts Ashley's classmates drove around. Adam appreciated that there were things he could do to improve the boat. He wanted to make it his—and doing his own maintenance and improvements were the easiest way to put his own stamp on it.

Besides, it had everything he actually needed: 760 horsepower inboard engine, full head and a galley with microwave, fridge and counter space for any other kitchen gadgets he ever wanted to add, and…of course…the berth. The fixed leather sofa by the table in the galley folded out to create extra sleeping space if it was ever needed, but the true prize of this boat was the raised bed occupying the majority of the stateroom.

Aside from familiarizing himself with the mechanics of the boat and taking a few practice trips with his dad, the only thing Adam had actually done to the boat before Ashley's birthday was swap out the bedding. The boat had come with a hideous brown floral comforter and matching pillow shams, which weren't Adam's style and frankly grossed him out. Besides, used bedding wasn't exactly romantic in anyone's playbook. Adam trekked out to the closest department store—a hefty thirty-five minute drive from the tip of the island—and bought high-end white sheets and pillow cases and a basic grey comforter. It wasn't fancy, but it was new and it matched the predominately cream and mahogany interior of the boat.

Since she was out with her parents on her real birthday, Ashley celebrated with Adam the weekend after. He let Ashley pick the restaurant for dinner and promised a fun surprise after. She chose a hibachi steak restaurant, where the chef prepared their meals on the cooktop at their table. It was cheesy but fun, and suited them perfectly.

Ashley had worn a royal blue dress in a thin, silky material that clung to her while still looking classy, along with strappy silver high-heeled shoes that made her almost as tall as Adam. Having promised her he'd dress up for once, Adam wore black suit pants and a black tie. Miraculously, he'd chosen a light blue shirt, so they matched without planning it. He couldn't bring himself to wear a suit jacket, too, not having dressed up that much since his mom's funeral, but Ashley clearly didn't mind. She couldn't keep her hands off him at dinner and made it very clear she liked his attire just the way it was.

They laughed and flirted their way through dinner, and Adam felt relieved that they didn't have any actual alone time during the meal with the way the table was arranged. Had he been truly alone with Ashley, Adam was certain the anticipation of the rest of the evening would have killed him.

* * *

AFTER DINNER, they drove to the marina. Adam parked and then reached behind his seat, retrieving a hot pink gift bag. He plopped it on her lap proudly.

Ashley gazed over at him, partly excited to see what was inside but mostly feeling guilty that her birthday was costing him so much money. "You didn't have to get me anything," she said. "Dinner was your gift."

Adam rolled his eyes. "Just open it already."

She yanked out the tissue paper, briefly pausing to wonder where he had bought that, and pulled out the first item. She giggled when she saw he had given her a box of candy cigarettes.

"Since you're old enough to smoke now," he explained. "You have no idea how hard it is to track down those. Apparently people don't think it's right to encourage small children to smoke."

Ashley smiled and reached in the back again, this time finding a stack of lottery tickets. "Ooh, very nice. Any winners?"

He shrugged. "You'll have to scratch them to find out."

"Later," she promised. The next item was another cardboard box, considerably larger than the candy cigarettes, though. She lifted it out of the bag and immediately felt her cheeks flush. It was a jumbo box of condoms. Ashley bit her lip and dropped the box back into the gift bag.

Adam was eying her as though trying to gauge her expression. "I can take those back. I just thought it went with the theme of the present. I'm not trying to pressure you…"

"I love it," she interrupted, leaning over to kiss him. "I am glad you didn't have me open this at the restaurant, though."

He laughed. "Yeah. Well and this way I figured my gift was sure to be original."

Ashley nodded. "Indeed it is. Not a single other person bought me condoms."

"There's something else in the bag. It's not exactly a present, though."

She reached in and wiggled her hand around until she felt a jagged metal item. "You gave me a key?"

He gestured for her to follow him out of the car. She set the gift bag on her seat but he reached back in and brought it with him. "In case you're feeling lucky," he said.

Ashley laughed. "I'd have to be feeling really lucky to need all fifty of those," she replied, picturing the gigantic box of condoms.

Adam laughed and pulled her closer. "I was talking about the lottery tickets, dirty girl."

He led her down to the pier where his boat was usually parked, but they walked past his boat and down to the last row.

"Wait, what…" Ashley was so confused. Were they trespassing? Was he borrowing this?

"Remember when I said I had to go see a man about a boat? Well, here's my new boat."

"But you said…"

"I wanted to surprise you."

Ashley was so happy for him at that moment that she probably would've jumped on him and wrapped her legs around his waist, except that likely would have ripped the dress. So instead she leaned in for a classy, reserved kiss.

"Wanna go for a ride?"

"Of course!" She handed him the key. "Can I see the rest?" she asked, peeking down towards the cabin while he started the engine.

"Nope. Let's get out there and then I'll give you the grand tour."

They drove out for a bit and then he killed the engine and came over to kiss her. After a few minutes, he pulled back. "I brought drinks. I was going to do champagne but thought you liked the sweet stuff better."

Ashley smiled, pleased that he remembered. She slipped out of her heels knowing she was less likely to fall down the ladder to the cabin below barefoot.

"I want to get something from down below real quick, so why don't you pour the wine and I'll be right back to give you the tour."

Ashley made her way over to the cooler and saw he'd already uncorked the wine for her, so she just pulled the cork out the rest of the way and filled both of their glasses. They sat on the deck and sipped their wine and talked for a couple more minutes.

"Okay, now can I see the rest?" Ashley asked, growing impatient.

He grinned and helped her up by the hand. "After you," he said, letting her lead the way down to the cabin. It was small and definitely not brand new or flashy, but Ashley was distracted by the bed. It was sprinkled with flower petals and surrounded by glowing battery-operated candles.

"Wow." Flutters filled her stomach and a deep, aching desire started to build deep within her as she knew what this all meant. Suddenly, Ashley was nervous. Too nervous to turn to face Adam. She'd been wanting this for weeks, but now that the time was here, and this whole uber-romantic scene was laid out in front of her, Ashley was panicking.

He wrapped his arms around her waist and began kissing her neck. It was the way he'd kissed her dozens of times before, but this time meant something different. Everything from this point on, Ashley realized, was foreplay.

Adam slowly turned her to face him. "You're trembling," he said.

Ashley considered making up an excuse like she was cold, but knew he'd see through it.

"We don't have to do anything different tonight," he said softly. "I will be really happy if you just let me kiss you for the next hour."

Ashley nodded nervously and they started kissing. As they kissed, she lost herself in his arms. She tasted the sweet red wine on his tongue, smelled his fresh aftershave, and felt his warm breath fall onto her cheeks in repetitive pitter patters like drops of rain. She roped her arms around his neck to pull him closer, then started to fumble with his tie, wanting it looser.

He pulled back, stepped out of his shoes and quickly removed his tie. "Better?" he asked, a cocky smirk plastered on his face.

God he was sexy. Ashley pressed her lips against his, wedging her hands in between them so she could unbutton his shirt and then slip it off. He had a sleeveless undershirt on beneath, which only made him look even hotter, as if that were possible. He pulled back and flashed a lopsided grin.

Ashley reached forward, passing her hands over his chest, appreciating every inch of his perfection. She slipped her hands under his shirt, feeling goose bumps on her skin as she touched his bare flesh. Adam responded by firmly groping her butt then passing his hands upwards.

Impatiently she tugged his shirt up, breaking away from his wet lips just long enough to pull it over his head. Ashley threw herself back into the kiss, overwhelmed with a new sense of urgency. She had been waiting for him for ages, and she couldn't wait any longer. Ashley fumbled with his belt buckle and successfully unfastened his button before he grabbed her hands.

"You're in a hurry now aren't you?" he teased, whispering the words into her mouth and holding her hands in his own at hip level.

She lowered the zipper on his pants while still restrained by his hands.

"That's just unfair," Adam said. He swiveled her around and quickly unzipped her dress while kissing her neck in a way that made her knees weak. A soft moan escaped her lips. Adam slowly slipped the dress straps off her shoulders, running his tongue across her flesh. He worked the dress down gradually, kissing his way down her body until he reached her lower back and had to kneel. Her dress dropped to the floor.

He then guided her back to face him. He reached for her hands and squeezed them tightly while helping her step out of her dress. Their eyes met and her heart thudded uncontrollably. The look in his deep blue eyes was filled with desire and lust, but also admiration and love. Somehow, even though he'd seen her in bikinis as skimpy as her current bra and panties, this moment felt more intimate and Ashley felt infinitely more naked.

Adam didn't say anything, but he kissed her stomach, first while holding her hands, then releasing them and pressing his hands into her lower back. Her own hands gravitated to his head, her fingers running through his soft, smooth hair. He inched her panties down slightly and Ashley froze, certain her legs wouldn't support her if he offered any more pleasure than she was already experiencing, but he simply planted a chaste kiss right where her legs parted then stood up.

She leaned forward to kiss him, but he stopped her, staring at her eyes with a serious, hungry look she wasn't sure she'd seen before. "You are beautiful," he said.

Ashley kissed him in lieu of answering. It was a forceful, demanding kiss, because while she knew they could easily spend the next few hours just kissing, that wasn't what she wanted to do this time. Adam stepped backwards slightly so the backs of his knees hit the bed. Ashley yanked his pants down the rest of the way as he tumbled backwards, pulling her with him. He kicked his feet free of his pants and situated her on top of him, their bare stomachs pressed together as they resumed kissing.

Adam's hands slowly glided up her back and he deftly unfastened her bra. Ashley smiled through the kiss, knowing that her breasts would tumble free the moment she was no longer pressed against him. Adam clearly reached the same realization, as he placed his hands on her hips and guided her chest upwards. She smiled, watching his expression, as he slid her bra off completely and saw her bare chest for the first time. His lips parted and his eyes rolled back in his head a little, but he quickly regained his cool, flexing his stomach to sit up so he could reach her bare flesh with his mouth.

The moment his tongue danced across her nipple, Ashley groaned loudly, feeling the now-familiar pressure in her groin skyrocketing. He moved to her other nipple and licked it as well before falling back onto the pillow. She yearned for his lips to touch her there again, but quickly found his fingers replacing his tongue. Though he'd touched her breasts before with his expert fingers, this sensation was new, and more intense because of the dampness.

After a moment, he pulled her down again, pressing her breasts against his chest, and they both groaned together as their bodies touched in new ways. His hands slid down her hips and he looped a finger under the band of her panties, shoving them down partway. Then suddenly, he flipped her onto her back with her knees bent.

Ashley giggled at the suddenness of it all but he quickly removed her panties and positioned himself between her legs. He then paused and grinned up at her.

"Now that you have me naked, what are you going to do with me?" she asked coyly.

He raised his eyebrows seductively. "I'm going to make you squeal so loud that sailors across the Atlantic could hear you."

Ashley started to reply, but his tongue touched her there—right at the burning, wanting apex of her desire. Ashley brought one hand to her mouth, biting her finger to keep from crying out too soon, and pressed the other hand into his hair. She felt his head move with each stroke of his tongue and loved the eroticism and naughtiness of what he was doing.

But after only a moment, it was too intense. She couldn't hold off any longer. "Adam, stop, I'm gonna come," she panted.

Instead of complying, he reached one hand up to her right breast, twisting and pinching her nipple between his fingers. It was too much. She groaned again and the next stroke of his soft, warm wet tongue against her flesh pushed her over the edge. Ashley cried out loudly, her hips bucking so wildly she worried she'd hurt him. He kept going for a moment after she stilled, then kissed his way up her stomach.

"That was fucking awesome," he said, taking a swig of water from the bottle on the nightstand.

He lay beside her, licked his finger, then gently traced it across her breast while she caught her breath. Finally, Ashley turned to him and grabbed his hand, stilling it.

"I want you," she said, their eyes locking.

He nodded seriously and reached for the giant box of condoms. Ashley pulled down his boxers, her breath catching in her throat as he sprung free. Ashley had touched it before, but hadn't actually gotten a good look at him. And now that she could, it was clear that he was larger than Brent. Much larger.

Adam froze with the condom poised at his tip. "You sure you want to do this?"

"Yes!"

He rolled the condom down quickly and lowered himself back over her. Ashley bent one leg, sliding her foot up closer to her butt and felt him positioned at her entrance. Without him even touching her, Ashley was nearly at the brink again, but this time her body also trembled with excitement.

Adam leaned in and kissed her hard, pausing only to whisper "I love you," in her ear. He slid in quickly then stilled. Her body tensed at the sizable intrusion then soon relaxed. Adam waited a moment, then pulled most of the way out before slowly pushing back in all the way. He continued the slow, tantalizing pace for a minute, bringing her almost to the peak of pleasure. Her heart was racing and she was already breathless, certain her body couldn't tolerate much more of this delicious torture.

Then Adam increased the rhythm of his hips, rocking the bed to the point where she couldn't tell if the movement was from his thrusting or the ocean current. Within minutes Ashley felt her entire body tighten around him before exploding into loose waves. She cried out loudly, the pleasure too intense to stay quiet, then gently bit into his shoulder to muffle the sound. He moaned suddenly, pressing harder into her for a moment while breathing her name, then relaxing and collapsing on top of her.

Neither of them spoke for what felt like an eternity. Feeling his heartbeat against her chest, Ashley knew the exact point when it finally slowed down, and her own pulse mimicked his.

"Wow," she said. "Why did we wait so long to do that?"

"So it would be perfect," he reminded her.

"That was amazing," she said.

"You're amazing," he said.

"I love you," came her reply.

He smiled up at Ashley then scooted off of her.

* * *

ADAM PULLED a blanket across himself and Ashley as she snuggled against him. They were both still naked, but what they'd just shared had been so perfect that Adam felt fully satiated. He'd been with other girls before, but it had never been like that. Not even close. Doing that with Ashley was so amazing that it nearly made Adam wish he'd waited so she could be his first. He was pretty sure he also wished she would be his last.

He sighed and ran his fingers through his hair, wondering how he'd gone from an independent player to a sappy whipped guy content to just snuggle with his girl in such a short time. But then Ashley sighed too, her warm breath tickling his chest as her breasts shifted ever so slightly against his flesh, and he knew exactly how it had happened.

She was perfect, and she was his. Adam knew he hadn't done anything to deserve a woman like Ashley, but maybe it was some sort of karmic compensation for some of the shit he'd been dealt earlier in life. Whatever it was, Adam knew it wouldn't last as long as he'd want it to, and he was determined to enjoy it while he could.

CHAPTER 12

Since that night on the boat with Adam, Ashley couldn't think about anything else. Being away from him the next day and a half while he took the boat out overnight with his dad was torture. She had zero focus, no appetite, and couldn't even sleep. Every time she even stopped moving for a moment, her mind drifted back to the boat, retracing every step of their intimate dance and recalling every detail from the warmth of his mouth all over her body to the way her skin tingled in response to his expert touch.

"Earth to Ashley," Lisa said, waving a hand in front of her face.

Ashley shook her head vigorously, literally rousing herself from her daydream. She gazed around at her surroundings, confirming she was still outside at the marina with Lisa and Katie, enjoying depressingly virgin cocktails on what was clearly the most gorgeous day ever. She glanced down at her phone to see that she still had at least two hours to go until Adam returned.

"You okay?" Katie asked. "You've been out of it all day."

"Yeah. I'm just…" Ashley let her voice trail off absentmindedly as she watched a boat slide into its spot at the dock. She turned back to her friends just in time to see them exchange a knowing stare.

"Okay, spill," Katie said. "This is obviously about a boy."

"You have been smiling all day," Lisa agreed. "I'm pretty sure Mr. Cooper thought you were cheating when you grinned through the whole calculus test."

Ashley forced herself to think back to the calculus test which, she was pretty sure she failed. Okay, not in the literal sense, but she definitely scored significantly lower than her typical above-average coursework.

Lisa glanced around furtively as though confirming no one they knew was nearby. "Spill it, girl. We know you had a big date with Adam on Saturday night to celebrate your birthday. What happened that's making you so giddy two days later?"

Ashley bit her lip. She could feel her cheeks reddening. It felt a bit trashy to kiss and tell, but, well, she was dying to tell someone. She leaned closer. "Okay, we finally did it, and it was amazing," she blurted out, her voice barely louder than a whisper.

Lisa grinned.

Katie looked flabbergasted. "Wait, you've been dating this hot older guy since July and you just now did the deed?"

"It was worth the wait," Ashley said, giggling.

"So he was good?" Katie guessed.

"Oh yeah."

"Better than Brent?"

Ashley gave her a pointed stare. "I'm not going to compare them."

"But?" Katie prompted.

"But I can't stop thinking about it now. We had trouble keeping our hands off each other before and now…" Ashley faked a swoon and collapsed back against her seat.

"This is just depressing," Lisa said with a huff. "You've already had sex with two hot guys and I'm still waiting for my first."

"Only because you were saving yourself for Tyler for the last two years," Katie reminded her.

That was the truth. And after finally going on a few dates with Tyler, Lisa had realized she didn't like him that much after all, and they'd gone back to being just friends.

"I'm going to die a virgin," Lisa mumbled.

Ashley sighed. "And I'm probably going to flunk out of school and then starve to death because once Adam gets back, I really just want to do that over and over with him. I can't see any logical end point. I'm pretty sure he won't tell me no, so pretty much we could just keep doing it until…well, I guess until my period starts in a couple weeks."

"That doesn't have to stop you," Katie said. "Didn't you and Brent ever…"

"While I was on my period? No way. He would've been way too grossed out. Besides, wouldn't it like dissolve the condom or something?"

"Eww. No! Although I can't believe you're using condoms anyway. Especially if you're planning to binge fuck till the end of time, that could get expensive. Just go on the pill."

"I can't risk my parents finding out," Ashley said, still cringing at Katie's terminology.

"Well you don't need condoms when you've got your period anyway. Unless you're worried about STDs or something."

"I'm not," Ashley quickly said. "But the whole pregnancy thing is the issue."

"You can't get pregnant on your period," Katie said. "Did you sleep through health class or something?"

"Are you sure?" Lisa asked skeptically.

"Yes. Every month your body builds up the uterine lining and then halfway through your cycle your ovaries release an egg. That's ovulation, and that's when you're most likely to get pregnant, although it could happen a few days before or a few days after. If the egg isn't fertilized during that short window, your body expels the egg and the uterine lining and then it all begins again." Katie paused to sip her drink after her technical explanation. "There's actually only a few days each month when you can get pregnant, but the trick is knowing which days those are. You should Google it or something. I'm sure he'd like a break from all those condoms."

Ashley covered her face with her hands. "God, it feels so weird to be sitting here discussing this with you guys."

Lisa shook her head. "Geez, by the time I finally find someone I want to sleep with, you guys will both be on your fourth or fifth partner."

Katie laughed, but Ashley glanced back out to the water. She honestly couldn't imagine having sex with anyone but Adam ever again. If they broke up, she'd have to become a nun because she was certain no one could ever live up to the standards he set.

"So when is he due back?" Lisa asked.

"Ninety-seven minutes," Ashley answered quickly, giggling and adding "Or so."

Her friends laughed and they started chatting about their plans for winter break instead.

* * *

ADAM DROVE BACK to the condo with his dad, then quickly showered. As awesome as it had been to finally get out on his boat, he was dying to see Ashley again. He hurried back to the marina and was just about to text her when he heard her familiar laugh.

He slid his phone back into the pocket of his jeans and walked closer to the beautiful sound, his face already stiff from grinning so widely. Her back was to him, so he motioned for Lisa to stay quiet. He stepped closer and wrapped his hands over her eyes.

Ashley flew out of her chair before he could even say "guess who." She spun around and grabbed his cheeks in her hands and kissed him fast and hard.

"Someone missed me," Adam teased, looping his thumbs through the belt loops on her jeans and pulling her close for another kiss. He kept it brief, acutely aware that her friends were both watching them. "I forgot how good you smell," he whispered into her ear so no one else could hear. He then released her and politely greeted her friends.

"Did you eat dinner already?" he asked Ashley.

"I'm not hungry," she replied.

"Not for anything served here anyway," Katie joked, flashing a mischievous grin at Lisa.

Adam raised an eyebrow and Ashley just shook her head.

"I'll see you guys later," she said, pulling Adam by the hand.

"Do you want to get something to eat?" she asked, clearly leading him towards his boat.

"Later," he said, pretty sure he knew what she had in mind. Although he'd been off the boat less than two hours, he was more than happy to get back on it since it was about the only place they could be alone.

"Do we have to go anywhere?" she asked as soon as they were on board.

"Huh?"

Ashley bit her lip. "What if we just went below deck for a few minutes to catch up and then we could grab dinner somewhere and then go for a ride?"

A grin broke out on Adam's face as he realized what she was suggesting. The fact that she couldn't wait to get out to sea before having him again was probably the hottest thing he could imagine.

"I like the way you think," he said. He glanced around, confirming no one was nearby to see them disappear below deck, then headed down the narrow stairs. Ashley followed and pulled the door shut behind her, locking the door. Adam pulled the blinds over the sliver of a window and then turned to face her.

She was wearing fitted jeans, a sequined tee shirt, and sandals, and her hair was pulled back in a ponytail. He guessed this was probably what she'd worn to school and loved that even though there was nothing particularly fancy about it, she still looked sexy.

"You just wanted to kiss me and nothing else, right?" he teased, praying she didn't call his bluff and say yes.

"Sure, there can be kissing," she said, pressing her lips against his.

He groaned, instantly feeling his groin react to her smooth, soft lips. Their kisses increased in intensity quickly, both of them apparently having felt the two day separation more profoundly than he would've anticipated. He slid her shirt up over her head, trailing kisses over her stomach and chest as he went. As his mouth returned to her lips, his fingers fumbled with her jeans, unfastening the button and sliding down the zipper before roaming up her back to unfasten her bra.

Before he could remove her bra entirely, she tugged on his shirt, and in seconds they were both nude from the waist up. Ashley eyed him hungrily, her chest rising and falling rapidly with each anxious breath.

"God you're sexy," he said. They resumed kissing but quickly finished undressing and moved to the bed. A minute later, Ashley pulled away.

"Enough foreplay," she murmured.

Adam grinned, rolled her over and made his way over to a bag in the corner of the room where he'd hidden the massive box of condoms while his dad was on the boat. He grabbed one and returned to her. This time, she put it on him then positioned herself across his lap.

The sight of her looming above him, her breasts swaying as she lowered herself onto him nearly undid him. He grabbed her hips to help steady her as she moved, slowly sliding his hands up her torso to caress her breasts. She tilted her head back, exposing her neck, and Adam sat quickly, nipping at her breasts before pulling her down on top of him. He couldn't not kiss her for a moment longer, and frankly he couldn't have lasted much longer watching her move above him like a mystical goddess anyway.

She moaned into his mouth as she came, and he followed seconds after. As they both caught their breath, Adam realized they'd been on the boat for less than fifteen minutes.

* * *

EVERYTHING WAS different with Adam from then on. Ashley hadn't realized there was anything missing in their relationship before, but now she was certain it was complete. Perfect. Emotionally, she had felt close to Adam from the start, and there was no denying the chemistry from the moment they met. But this new level of intimacy brought with it a closeness she couldn't have even imagined.

Adam was her world. School, sleep, friends, family—everything else was just a way of passing time before she could get back to Adam. On the rare days Ashley knew she wouldn't see him, she honestly missed him, but without the insecurities that racked her consciousness in the early days of their relationship. She knew that wherever he was when they were apart, whatever he was doing, he was still hers. Being with Adam made Ashley enjoy every other part of her life even more than before.

With one notable exception.

On the Thursday before finals began, Ashley pulled her car into her normal spot on the drive then walked down to the mailbox. She wasn't sure why she even did it—she almost never got the mail. Even weirder was the fact that she actually went through the mail instead of simply tossing it on the desk in the mudroom on her way inside. But she did pick up the mail herself and she did sort through it, so she couldn't ignore the thick manila envelope addressed to Ms. Ashlynne Kensington with a return address label from Duke University.

She inhaled sharply, feeling the corners of her mouth turn upwards as she started to rip open the packet, certain what it said. She quickly skimmed the cover letter, confirming her suspicions, and then squealed and jumped around like a child. And then she stopped, a sudden pang of sadness piercing her joy. How had she not thought of this before?

Of course right then her phone buzzed, letting her know Adam had arrived. She replied for him to come on in, then she scurried upstairs to touch up her makeup and comb her hair. When she came downstairs, he was reading the letter she'd left on the counter.

He gazed up at her slowly, smiling widely. "Oh my God, Ashley, you did it! Congratulations!" He pulled her close for a hug, lifting her feet off the ground and twirling her in circles.

His excitement was so pure that Ashley couldn't help but celebrate with him in the moment. The happiness stuck with her as they drove to the restaurant where they were meeting friends, but as she asked Adam not to share the news with any of her friends just yet, Ashley let herself acknowledge that she wasn't as thrilled about her acceptance as she'd expected.

For as long as she could remember, Ashley had wanted to attend Duke. She loved the campus, loved that she was continuing a family legacy, and loved the location—far enough, but not too far away. She was excited about the courses, the extra-curriculars, and the prestige. Plus she was proud. Ashley knew she hadn't earned most things in her life, but she had actually worked hard in school for this. Not everyone, even in her privileged little circle of friends, could achieve what she had.

But all the times she'd pictured college, she was either happily attending alone, or still involved with Brent. Since Ashley and Adam had become an item, she hadn't really thought much about what it would actually mean to attend Duke, and now that it was an impending reality, she couldn't ignore the obvious. Adam would not attend Duke. Not only that, but there was really nothing for him to do in the Raleigh/Durham area. And unless her geography lessons had failed her, Ashley was pretty sure it wasn't even a commutable distance from the island.

"We're gonna head out," Adam said loudly, snapping Ashley out of her funk. "Do you want a box for that?" he asked softly, gesturing to her untouched salad.

She shook her head, waved goodbye to her friends, then snuggled against Adam as they made their way back to his truck.

"You wanna talk now or on the boat?" he asked as soon as he'd started the engine.

Ashley frowned, uncertain of what they needed to discuss.

"You hardly touched your food. And you were totally spaced out of the conversation anyway. I can tell there's something on your mind," he explained.

"Let's walk on the beach," she replied.

"You won't be too cold?"

She shook her head.

Adam shrugged and turned down the first side street past the security entrance to their section of the island. He parked by a third row beach house and reached into the back of the truck to grab a jacket for Ashley before climbing out.

She started ahead, navigating the pitch black sidewalk with ease.

"You didn't want to just head out by my house?"

"Nope. Too many alligators by the lagoon. Plus I wasn't sure about your parents." He caught up to her and clasped her hand in his.

When they reached the beach, they both slipped out of their shoes. Ashley shivered as her feet touched the cool sand and Adam draped the jacket around her shoulders.

They walked for a few minutes before Adam stopped, pulling Ashley to him.

"Time's up. Spill it," he ordered.

Ashley shrugged. "I don't know what you want me to say."

"Yes you do. I want you to tell me what's bothering you. Why were you so distracted at dinner? Why didn't you want your friends to know about Duke? You just got accepted to the school of your dreams. Why do I feel like I'm more excited about that than you are?"

"Why are you so excited?" she asked, her voice louder and shriller than she'd intended. "Do you have any idea where Duke is? Have you just been waiting for an excuse to be six hours away from me?"

Even in the dim moonlight, Ashley saw the shift in Adam's expression. "Oh, babe," he whispered, pulling her into his arms.

He didn't say anything else, and Ashley felt tears starting to slip down her cheeks. She hated crying, hated being that over-emotional girl, but she already felt like they were breaking up and she hadn't even sent in her acceptance yet.

Adam held her tightly for a few minutes before pulling back, wiping her eyes with his thumb, and kissing her forehead.

"Ashley, I'm excited because this is something you want. You've wanted this for a long time and you earned it. You got into an amazing school and I'm proud of you. You know this is going to make your parents happy, and I know you're going to be happy at Duke."

Something about his response made Ashley want to cry harder.

"Stop, Ashley, come on. You're breaking my heart. I'm not happy to be away from you, but that's not how I'm looking at this. We're not going to break up just because you're headed to college and I'm not." He paused, guiding her chin upwards until she made eye contact with him. "I don't ever want to break up with you."

Ashley let him kiss her, comforted by his last statement, but still hung up on the obvious obstacles.

"Duke is really far away. And even if you came up for week-ends to visit, there's no water nearby for your boat."

Adam shook his head as they started to walk again, slower now. "Ashley, if anyone can make a long distance relationship work, it's us. But if it's not working, or even if we decide not to try, that's okay. That's the benefit of my life. I don't have anything firm holding me to Hilton Head. If you want me closer to Duke, I'll get a job closer to Duke. No big deal. I'll do summer work at the marina when you're back home. They don't need much winter help anyway."

Ashley frowned, troubled by the thought of Adam giving up his ability to spend at least part of each day on the ocean. "You love being on the water. I would never ask you to give that up."

"Ashley, I love you. The ocean will always be there. We can spend the weekends on the water. It's not a problem for me."

She inhaled sharply as her foot hit a piece of driftwood. Adam pulled out his cell phone and aimed its flashlight at the sand as they walked.

"There's other schools I can apply for," she said. "There are tons of schools in Florida along the coast. I'd looked at some in Virginia, too."

"No. Absolutely not," Adam said, his voice firm. "You are going to Duke. That part is non-negotiable. The only thing you have to decide is whether you want me to come with you or just visit every weekend. And you don't have to decide that now."

Ashley stopped, leaning in for another hug. "It's really annoying how perfect you are all the time," she said. "And rational. Like, are you sure you're not actually 25?"

Adam laughed under his breath. "Can we head back to the truck now? I think I just smushed a crab between my toes."

"Yes. Take me to the boat," she replied.

"Yes ma'am," Adam replied before suddenly hoisting her into the air and over his shoulder. Ashley shrieked but secretly appreciated dodging the rest of the obstacles on the way back to their shoes.

* * *

ADAM THOROUGHLY DISTRACTED Ashley once he got her alone in the cabin of the boat, but after, when they were cuddled together, quiet, he started to think again. Ashley was right—Duke was far and land-locked. Adam had meant what he'd said—he would move up there and find something to do if she asked him to, but he couldn't imagine that being ideal. There was nothing for him up there—nothing he'd enjoy anyway, and moving someplace just for a girl seemed like a good way to kill the relationship.

Either he'd start to resent her or she'd get bored by him having nothing but her to occupy his time. Adam figured he could do work like his father, traveling up and down the coast, and make it back to see Ashley a few times a month, but he'd have to look into it more. Later. For now, he was going to continue convincing her he was this perfect guy she saw him as, happy for her with no reservations.

Adam glanced down at Ashley. She was still blissfully nude, her head resting on his chest with her hair fanned out across his torso and biceps and her breasts pressed against his stomach. Her eyes were closed, but he could tell she wasn't asleep by the way her fingers absentmindedly traced his heritage tattoo. Adam wished they could spend the night out here, together. He loved the sex with Ashley, obviously, but he craved more of this—more time holding her after, when they were both quiet and still and he could just appreciate the perfection of her human form.

"I have to get you home soon," he whispered.

Ashley groaned.

"I know, babe," he agreed, kissing her forehead. Just then, an idea came to him. "Hey, since your parents are going to be so excited about Duke, do you think maybe they would consider revisiting the whole issue of us dating?"

Ashley didn't move or answer for so long Adam started to think she hadn't heard him. Finally, she sat abruptly. "Maybe.

And with my brothers coming home for Thanksgiving next week, it would be nice to not have to sneak around." She paused thoughtfully, brushing her hair off her chest and offering Adam an unobstructed view of her rounded pink tits.

Adam bit his lip and looked away, certain they did not have time for another round before her curfew.

Ashley reached for her bra and began dressing. "Yeah, it's worth a try. Good idea!" She leaned in to kiss him before slipping her shirt over her bra.

Adam waited until she was pulling on her jeans before he crawled out of the bed. He knew from experience now that it took her a lot longer to get dressed than him.

"So, when am I going to take you out to celebrate?" he asked.

"Celebrate?"

"Duke! Tonight hardly counts. We need to do something big and fun. It's not every day you get into an Ivy League school."

"Duke isn't Ivy League," Ashley said, combing her hair with her fingers. "But let's go dancing. There's a club on the mainland I've been wanting to go to."

"Dancing?" Adam repeated the word, trying to decide if she was serious. He knew Ashley liked to dance, but he was equally familiar with the type of music she liked and it wasn't exactly what they played in the dance clubs.

Ashley gazed at him and giggled. "Your face is priceless right now," she said, leaning over to kiss him. "And we don't have to go, but I figure you can handle one night of good old American music if you really want to celebrate."

Adam winced. "Oh God—you mean like a club where they play country music? Does that even exist? Isn't everyone there going to be in their sixties?"

Ashley rolled her eyes. "It'll be fun. Even for you."

* * *

ASHLEY WAITED until the next evening to talk to her dad about Adam. "I wanted to talk with you about something," she began nervously.

"You could sit," her dad said, motioning to the couch beside him.

She sat, but angled her body so she was facing him. "I feel like I've done a pretty good job overall of meeting your expectations."

He glanced at her then laughed. "Yes. I would say so."

"I mean, I kept my grades up, I don't get in trouble, I got into Duke…" Ashley paused, realizing he'd already agreed with her.

He eyed her expectantly.

"Well, thanks," she continued. "I'm glad you agree. The thing is, I haven't exactly listened to one rule and while I can't say I'm sorry, I do wish I'd told you sooner that it was a ridiculous rule that I had no intention of following."

Her dad sighed. "Is this about your boyfriend?"

Ashley frowned. "What boyfriend?"

"Adam. The boy you've been dating since I asked you not see him."

Ashley blinked repeatedly. She knew they hadn't exactly gone out of their way to sneak around, but she was shocked that her father had known and hadn't grounded her or banished her overseas. "I…I didn't realize you knew."

"Your mother had some suspicions a while back. And your brothers confirmed it over fall break."

Ashley's eyes narrowed. Those traitorous assholes. Over the years she had kept countless secrets for them. Countless. But could they do her one thing in return? Nope.

Ashley realized her father was waiting for her to say something, so she did. "Then you're okay with it?"

"I'm certainly not going to give you my blessing. He is still too old for you and too different from you. You could do better. But as long as you stay out of trouble, you can keep dating him."

Ashley frowned. "Adam is not the person you seem to think he is. I'm lucky to have him in my life."

He turned back to his program. "It's going to be a moot point in a few months, Ashlynne. You'll move to Durham, North Carolina and be enrolled in one of the most prestigious universities and he'll still be here. You'll have even less in common then than you do now, plus the thrill of the novelty of it all will have worn off and the distance will take a toll on you both. I'm not going to fight you over something that's destined to fail regardless."

Ashley considered replying, but instead let it drop. There was no point trying to tell him he was wrong. Besides, she'd gotten the permission she had come for.

* * *

ASHLEY TOLD Adam the good news the very next day after he got off work.

"I'm glad we don't have to sneak around anymore," he said. "Nice work getting the guts to talk to them."

She shrugged. "It was your idea."

Adam kissed her before stepping back. "I need a shower. I was in the water a lot today with tour groups. Can you…"

"Yeah, it's fine. I have a lot of homework anyway."

"You can come up," he offered, unsure if his dad was home or not.

"No, it's nice out. I'll stay here. I'm going to get a soda though. You want anything?"

He shrugged. "Surprise me."

Adam watched her sprawl out her textbooks on a table by the water before heading up to the bar. He hurried through his shower, certain Ashley would be surrounded by a posse of guys by the time he returned, since that seemed to happen whenever she was alone in public for long. But when he returned, she was alone, and her forehead wrinkled as she scribbled something on a notepad.

He sat at a chair across from her and sipped the soda sitting by his seat. "Thanks," he mumbled.

She nodded. "Sorry, I only have a few problems left."

"No hurry." They hadn't decided what they were actually doing today anyway, so Adam figured they'd probably just hang out and then, if he was lucky, head out on the boat. "Anything I can help with?"

"How's your calculus?"

Adam laughed in response. There was a plate of shrimp on the table across from him, so he scooted it closer and started to eat while she continued working. He chuckled watching the tiny changes on her face as she grew more and more frustrated. Her phone chimed several times over the next few minutes, but Ashley didn't even glance over at it.

Finally, Adam couldn't stand it any longer. He reached over and grabbed it. "Aren't you at least curious if it's an emergency?"

Ashley grunted some response but didn't look up, so Adam clicked on to the screen. He'd assumed it was something from Lisa, or possibly her mom or dad, or another friend. It had not occurred to him that all of the texts would be from Brent. Without thinking, he clicked on the message.

The most recent five were all about Duke. Scrolling up, Adam quickly ascertained that Brent, also, had been accepted by early admission to Duke, and he seemed pretty excited that Ashley was going, too. Adam looked over at Ashley, but she was still engrossed in her calculus, so he kept scrolling. None of the texts were particularly objectionable, but the fact that there were so many—and that Ashley wrote back—annoyed the hell out of Adam.

Suddenly, Adam realized Ashley was staring at him.

"Who peed in your Cheerios?" she asked.

He laughed at her expression, then turned back to the phone. "What does 'HBD' mean?"

Ashley frowned with confusion. He handed her the phone.

She gazed at the screen then turned back to Adam. "Happy birthday," she explained, a stern expression on her face.

Adam knew he had some explaining to do. "It was Brent, all those texts you got in the last ten minutes."

Ashley nodded. "So you thought you'd go back weeks and read all of my messages from Brent?"

Adam suddenly felt like a kid who got caught with his hand in the cookie jar. "I hadn't realized you two were still so close."

"We are friends, Adam. I wouldn't call us close."

"I also didn't know he was going to Duke with you."

Ashley raised an eyebrow. "He's not exactly going with me. But yes, he did get accepted too, and it looks like he's going to go."

Adam snatched the phone back and kept scrolling, convinced he wouldn't feel better until he confirmed the innocence of all the texts between them. But instead, it just made him feel more left out, seeing all that they'd shared in the past two months. Ashley didn't try to get her phone back or say anything, so Adam felt a little silly when he finally handed it back to her.

"I don't like sharing you," he said.

Ashley smiled. "Good. Because you're not." She stood up and started cramming everything back into her backpack. "And you are lucky you're cute when you're jealous."

"I'm not jealous," he insisted, taking the backpack from her once she zipped it and wrapping his arm tightly around her.

Ashley giggled and they walked to the boat.

They cruised around for a bit before finally killing the engine to talk.

"Seriously," Adam began, "I never really went out with any girl long enough to consider her a girlfriend, I mean before you. So I don't get this whole "ex" thing. Is it normal to talk with your ex so much? I thought there was supposed to be more bad blood."

Ashley shrugged. "I don't know what's normal. Brent is the only boyfriend I had before you, and we were friends before we went out, so it feels natural to me to stay friends with him. All of our friends are the same, our families go to tons of stupid events together, and we have a lot in common. Plus I think towards the end of our relationship we were basically just friends anyway."

"So do you still have feelings for him?"

Ashley rolled her eyes but pulled Adam close for a kiss. "No. I don't. And I never had the sort of feelings for him that I have for you."

Adam was momentarily distracted by the warmth of her lips against his own. He knew he should just let it drop, but he couldn't. "But you must have told him you loved him. You were together more than a year."

"Yeah, and I did love him. But sort of in the same way I love Lisa, or my brothers even."

"Eww."

Ashley laughed, her breasts bobbing as her chest heaved in and out. "That is my point, Adam. I never felt passionate about him. I never craved him like dessert. I never daydreamed about running my tongue along the length of his entire body. It was totally different."

Adam reached for her hand. "Let's go back to that part about your tongue..."

* * *

ASHLEY GIGGLED but let him guide her down below the main deck. They stretched out side by side, alternating between kissing until they were both winded to staring quietly at each other from mere inches away.

Ashley lost herself in the kissing but snapped out of it the moment Adam's hand drifted below the waistband of her jeans. "Wait," she murmured, opening her eyes briefly before regretting doing so, wanting him even more than before now that she could see him. "We can't today."

Adam groaned and moved his hand up an inch. "Why not?"

Ashley hesitated. "I'm on my period."

"Oh," Adam said. Then he thrust out his bottom lip and pouted. "Please?"

Ashley wavered. "You still want to?"

"Hell yes, I still want to."

Ashley had some other reservations, but before she could share them, he'd slipped her shirt up over her head and was kissing her through her lacy bra. She moaned inadvertently and he immediately glanced up and grinned mischievously. She knew then that he'd won, but by this point, Ashley wanted the same thing, too, so it didn't even matter. Ashley stripped down to her matching black lace panties and bra and Adam watched hungrily, barely taking his eyes off her as he removed his own shirt and jeans.

He pulled her back onto the bed, eagerly resuming the kissing and groping till Ashley was dizzy with desire.

"Shit!" Adam said suddenly, pulling back.

"What?"

"I don't have any protection on me."

"You went through that whole box?"

He rolled his eyes. "No *I* didn't go through that whole box. It's in my bedroom at the condo, I just kept some of them here." He paused. "And you know any that I did use, you were involved in."

He slumped back against the bed, frustrated.

"Stop pouting," she lectured. "I can still make you happy," she said, crawling over him and lowering her head towards his groin.

Adam stopped her by placing a hand on her cheek. "Are you going to let me return the favor?"

"Now? No way," she replied.

Adam scooted her back. "Then no deal. If you don't get any, I don't get any."

"That's a ridiculous rule."

"This obviously just wasn't meant to be today," he said.

Ashley wanted to scream. Of all the damn times to run out of condoms... Then she remembered her discussion with Katie. "Actually, Adam," she began. "I sort of think we might be okay without it."

"Without what?"

"I can't actually get pregnant when I have my period, so if that's the only reason we're using condoms, then..."

He was quiet for a moment. Ashley figured he was trying to recall any details from his high school health class. "Are you sure?"

She hesitated. "Pretty sure."

"I could pull out," he offered.

She nodded.

Adam swallowed audibly. "Well, I really, really want you right now. But if you're not comfortable with this..."

"I want you, too," she said without pause.

Adam rolled over onto her and kissed her with renewed vigor. Ashley suddenly felt overwhelmed with a nervous excitement. She kissed him back for a moment, then excused herself to the bathroom. She returned a few minutes later, completely naked, and tossed a towel onto the bed.

Adam growled and she swore his eyes rolled back a little in his head when he saw her walk towards him. "You are killing me," he murmured, kissing the side of her face.

Everything felt the same, and yet somehow different, more intimate, more sensitive. Ashley could tell when Adam was getting close and she felt him start to pull away, but she was still enjoying herself too much and didn't want to let him go, so she dug her fingers into his toned butt cheeks and held him close. She cried aloud, content that no one could hear them way out here, and he clutched her arms, releasing his own moan before relaxing over her.

"About that plan to pull out," Adam said after a minute.

"I'm sorry," Ashley said. "It just…that plan sucked. It takes all the fun out of it if we stop before we…"

Adam laughed and kissed her forehead. "I know, babe."

CHAPTER 13

The next few weeks blew by, with finals occupying the first part of December and then holiday festivities filling the rest. Adam and his father were out of town for two weeks at the start of the month, which Ashley reluctantly decided was a good thing since it allowed her to study without any distractions. Even when he returned, and Ashley was out of school for winter break, they didn't get to see each other as much as they'd like. Tourist traffic picked up on the island a little over the break, so Adam was working more. And Ashley had to attend several different galas and holiday parties with her family.

Adam's birthday was coming up, and she had no idea what to do for him. Her birthday had been perfect, thanks to him, so Ashley wanted to return the favor, but she was stumped. Money wasn't an issue, but Adam wasn't really interested in many material possessions, aside from his truck and boat.

In the end, she settled on a romantic night. It was harder to arrange than she had envisioned, since she couldn't use Lisa as a cover. Their moms talked frequently, so Ashley would've been caught if she lied and said she was with Lisa overnight. Instead, she casually asked her mom a week in advance if she could spend the night at Katie's house, wisely choosing a night when Katie was actually having a party and Lisa was sleeping over after. That way, if her mom confirmed any of the details, everything would check out, except for the fact that she would not be attending the party or the sleepover after.

Ashley and Adam took his boat to Savannah, then dined at a fancy restaurant before walking back to a cutesy boutique hotel. Ashley was pretty pleased with her plan, in the end. There had been a slight hitch, in that she'd started her period earlier in the week. But while she'd initially stressed about that killing the romance, she then realized that actually it could free them up even more since they could avoid the whole condom issue. Having tested the theory the previous month, they were both more confident about it now, too.

They made love on the bed minutes after entering their hotel room, cuddling and talking for an hour after before deciding to try out the Jacuzzi tub. That, of course, led to round two. By the time they finally returned to the bed, they were both exhausted. Ashley fell asleep on Adam's chest, his arm draped around her, feeling the happiest and most comforted she'd ever been.

* * *

FOR WEEKS AFTER HIS BIRTHDAY, Adam was walking on sunshine. Ever since he'd met Ashley, he'd been happy, but it just kept getting better and better. He knew things would have to change —that at some point, the bottom would drop out, but he was determined to enjoy the ride while it lasted.

At the end of February, Adam and his father finally set out to do what they'd come to the island for. It wasn't that they'd intentionally delayed scattering the ashes, but Mr. Bricker had decided that Adam's mom's birthday was the best day for the task. Adam agreed it felt fitting, but oddly morbid, to really end things on the same day her life had begun. Plus, as uneasy as he'd initially been, alone in the condo with the urn containing her remains, Adam now felt unsettled by the thought of no longer having any real part of her with him.

Ashley offered to accompany them, but Adam needed to do the task alone with his father. He wasn't sure what to expect, though, either from himself or his father. Years before, at the funeral, he'd bawled like a baby for hours before they went to the church, then pulled it together for the actual memorial. But then, at the cemetery, as he'd stood stoically beside his father and grandparents, Sam Bricker had suddenly covered his face with his hands. Adam turned to see his father's shoulders shake rhythmically as an inhumane howl escaped the man's lips. At that moment, Adam too had lost control, crying until he couldn't catch his breath.

Enough time had passed now that Adam and his father could talk about her without tears. The memories brought happiness again, and while the sorrow was still there, it was tolerable.

Adam's dad led him down an unfamiliar beach path about a five minute drive from Ashley's house. When they reached the water's edge, Mr. Bricker turned and pointed to a grey house they'd just passed.

"That was your mother's house," he said.

Adam nodded, realizing he'd seen it before, probably a decade ago. That did explain why his dad had picked this spot, though.

Mr. Bricker blew out a sigh and swallowed awkwardly. "Do you want to say something?"

"You go first," Adam said, uncertain of what was even appropriate.

His dad nodded, then gazed down at the ceramic vase. "You were the best wife I could've asked for, and I'm eternally grateful that you gave me a son who reminds me so much of you. You will always be the love of my life. I know you told me to remarry, but even if I never do, I'm the luckiest man alive for getting to spend the best years of my life married to you."

He paused and glanced at Adam before carefully reaching into the urn. "I would've been content to keep you on the mantel forever, and I'm pretty sure our son feels the same way, but you were pretty clear with your wishes, and even in death, I'd hate to disappoint you."

Adam watched as his father turned towards the side so the wind was at his back before lightly tossing the contents of his fist towards the ocean. Then, his father handed the urn to him.

Adam gazed at his father, filled with uncertainty, but suddenly, he felt himself smiling. His mother used to laugh more than anyone he knew. She had a striking sense of humor, and that got her through the hard times. If she were alive right now, she'd make a joke. Adam was sure of that. And even though she wasn't here, Adam knew she wouldn't want them to be sad now. They were doing what she'd asked, returning her ashes to her favorite place in the world. They should be happy.

He took a deep breath, then spoke. "You were the best mom I ever had. Obviously, you did a good job, because I turned out really well, despite Dad. But I do miss you a lot, and I hope there's a really big beach in heaven."

His father chuckled and patted Adam on the back. They took turns with the rest of the ashes then backed away from the water. Mr. Bricker sat down in the fluffy sand further back. Adam joined him.

The beach was deserted at the moment, thanks to unseasonably cold weather on the island. Compared to Nantucket, though, each day felt like springtime. Adam loved being outside now, finding the brisk air invigorating, but the locals acted like it was subzero.

They were quiet for a few minutes, then Mr. Bricker spoke.

"Your mother would've loved Ashley," he said.

Adam turned to his dad. "You think so?"

He nodded.

Adam agreed, but hearing his dad say it meant a lot to him.

"You know, your mom's parents didn't like me very much either at first. Didn't think I was good enough for their little girl."

"How did you win them over?"

His dad considered that question for a moment. "I loved her anyway. Once they saw I wanted what was best for her just like they did, they came around." He paused. "You can't stand in the way of her going to Duke."

Adam frowned at the implication. "I wouldn't do that."

His dad patted him on the back again. "I know. I just felt like I needed to say it."

They were quiet during the walk back to the car, and then they drove to a greasy burger joint a half hour away that his father swore was his mom's favorite.

When Adam got home that evening, he called Ashley to tell her how it went, and as soon as he'd hung up, Adam realized something. If his mother hadn't insisted they scatter her ashes in that precise part of that precise island, or if she hadn't made him promise to spend a summer on the island, he wouldn't have found Ashley. If he hadn't been so fixated on the ashes when he'd arrived on the island in the first place, he may not have even noticed Ashley so quickly.

It was funny how things worked out, Adam decided.

When he finally fell asleep that night, Adam felt surprisingly peaceful.

CHAPTER 14

Second semester was flying by, and Ashley was enjoying the start of spring and the freedom that came with her impending graduation. Now that everyone had heard back from their first choice schools, no one was as focused on studying, and Ashley and her friends were living it up. As the weather heated up, Adam was getting busier at work, but still saved plenty of time for her.

Ashley didn't normally track her periods too closely, but she couldn't help but notice her next one was due to start the day before the weekend her parents were out of town. When it didn't come that weekend, she was thrilled, thinking of it as a gift from the gods or something. She and Adam took full advantage of it, making love twice on the boat and feeding each other chocolate completely naked.

By Monday, Ashley was acutely aware that she still hadn't gotten her period, but she felt a wicked case of PMS, so she didn't think anything of it. It actually wasn't until a full week had passed that Ashley started to worry. In between each class at school that day, she rushed to the bathroom to check if it had started and each time, she felt more and more dread when it hadn't.

She went with their normal crew to the marina that day, planning to meet up with Adam a little later. Lisa didn't question her grumpiness, having suffered through the same Lit test Ashley had taken, but the second Adam arrived, it was obvious that he sensed something was up.

He kept trying to make eye contact with Ashley and talk to her, but she didn't want to bring it up with him at a table with all their friends around. Actually, she didn't want to tell him at all. She wanted to be the strong, independent type of woman who could pull herself together long enough to buy and take a pregnancy test, confirm that she was just panicking about nothing, and then laugh about it later with her boyfriend.

"What's wrong?" Adam finally mouthed.

Ashley shook her head dismissively and picked at a piece of chipped paint on the table. Without warning, Adam stood, grabbed her by the hand, and tugged her out of the restaurant.

Ashley winced as the cold air hit her. "What are you doing? Lisa was in the middle of a story!"

Adam shrugged out of his coat and wrapped it around Ashley, oblivious to her accusatory tone. "Ash, you haven't smiled once all afternoon. What is going on?"

She dropped her eyes to her feet. "Nothing. Just a bad day."

Adam wrapped his arms around her and pulled her in for a long hug. Ashley couldn't deny that she felt much better about the world being fully encompassed by his warm body, but she also knew they couldn't stay like that forever.

"Babe, I'm going to need more details. You can tell me what's wrong now and we can head back inside, or we can talk on the boat."

Ashley swallowed. "My period is a week late," she blurted out.

There was a pause before Adam answered. "Oh shit."

Just then Lisa popped her head out. "Food's here," she said, glancing uncomfortably from Ashley to Adam and back again.

"Thanks. We'll be a minute," Ashley said.

Lisa looked concerned, but thankfully went back in.

Adam stepped backwards until he was leaning against the wall. He rubbed his forehead as though trying to cure a migraine. Suddenly Ashley felt bad for telling him. She shouldn't have stressed him out before she knew anything for sure.

"Have you taken a test?"

Ashley shook her head.

"Well, it could just be…nothing, then," he said, his tone undermining his words. "There's no reason to worry now."

Ashley started to agree, but instead burst into tears. Apparently, her sobbing on the side of the pier was all it took to snap Adam out of his trance. He stepped closer to her again and gave her another hug, accenting this one with a soft kiss on the head.

"Come on, let's just go take a test," he said quietly.

Ashley shook her head. "I don't even know where to buy one. I mean, what if someone I know sees me and…"

He nodded. "I'll go do it then."

Ashley started to say that wouldn't be much better when he cut her off.

"Don't worry, I'll go far away, and I'll get a bunch so you can be sure. Now go inside and eat something and don't worry about it until I'm back, okay?"

He wiped her tears on his sleeve then kissed her forehead and started off.

"Your coat!" she called after him.

He gestured for her to keep it. Ashley waited a few minutes to try to pull herself together, then headed back inside.

She had no appetite, so when she asked for a to-go box for Adam's untouched food, she tossed most of hers in there, too. Then she texted Adam that she was heading to his boat and for him to meet her there.

Ashley said goodbye to everyone, but felt bad when Lisa followed her out.

"Hey, I'm sorry I was whining about that exam today," Lisa said. "I didn't know you and Adam were having problems."

Ashley realized how everything must have looked from Lisa's perspective. So she shrugged and gave her friend a quick hug. "It's fine. I'm meeting up with him at his boat now to talk."

When she got to Adam's boat, she pulled out her text books to study while waiting for him. But she couldn't concentrate.

When he finally arrived, he handed her a plastic drug store bag filled with five different boxes of pregnancy tests. Adam laughed uncomfortably, explaining he didn't know what kind was best.

"Those suckers are pricey," he added.

"I'm sorry. I can pay you back."

"Ashley, no. I didn't mean…" He shook his head. "I don't know what the protocol for any of this is."

"Me neither." Ashley sighed then started down the stairs with the whole bag. She shut herself in the tiny bathroom below deck and tore open the first box, reading the directions three times before tearing the plastic wrapper off the stick and peeing on it. She only peed a little, as per the directions, and then she set the stick on a tissue, setting her cell phone timer for three minutes.

She considered heading back onto the deck, where she knew Adam was going crazy waiting, too, but she couldn't bring herself to face him until she knew. By the time her cell phone timer chimed, Ashley felt like vomiting. She reached for the stick, her arm shaking, fully prepared to re-read the instructions to ensure she correctly interpreted the results.

But when she glanced down, there was no room for misinterpretation. The bright blue plus sign was pretty hard to ignore.

Ashley dropped the stick like a hot potato and swallowed the bile rising in her throat. She methodically ripped open three more packages, reading the instructions for each and following the steps to a T, only to get similar results from everything.

She couldn't bring herself to take the last test. It was too much, and besides, what was the point? She wedged all the wrappers and instructional pamphlets back into the plastic bag, suddenly very concerned with cleaning up and hiding the evidence.

There was a quiet tapping on the bathroom door. "Ashley? You okay?"

She took a deep breath, opened the door, and fell into Adam's arms.

She wasn't sure if he guessed the results by her reaction or if he simply saw one of the test sticks she'd left strewn on his bathroom floor, but it was clear he knew.

He kept whispering "it's okay," as though it would magically become true if he said it enough.

Ashley bawled her eyes out as Adam held her. She tried to think of something to say or do in between heaving sobs, but she couldn't even think straight. It felt like only a few minutes had passed when Adam nudged her back a bit and calmly said that he should take her home.

"Your curfew," he said, gesturing to her phone.

Ashley swore under her breath and bent to gather the rest of the test stuff.

"Stop, I'll clean this up later. Don't worry about it."

Ashley sighed but stopped what she was doing. She let Adam grab her backpack and steer her to his truck. She knew what she must look like, having apparently just sobbed like a maniac for over three hours, but she didn't care.

Adam was quiet until they reached her street. He pulled over at the end of the street, several houses away from hers and turned to Ashley.

"Look, I know you're freaked out right now, but worrying about it tonight isn't going to do any good, okay? I will make you an appointment at Planned Parenthood for tomorrow after school and we will go and get everything confirmed and then we will figure out what the next step is from there."

Ashley felt herself nodding in agreement, although the plan seemed ridiculous to her.

"I love you, Ashley. It's going to be okay."

Adam stared at her as though seeking confirmation, but Ashley just couldn't. She was already trying to figure out how to explain her blotchy red eyes to her parents.

Adam squeezed her hand and drove on to her driveway, waiting until she was all the way inside before pulling out. She went in through the garage, quickly ascertaining that her father wasn't home yet. That was good at least.

Her mother, unfortunately, was on the couch and popped up the second she heard Ashley enter.

Ashley swallowed hard, bit back the tears and the equally strong urge to run up to her mom and demand she cuddle her until everything went back to normal, and started towards the stairs. She couldn't hide the fact that she'd been crying, so she didn't even bother.

"I'm not hungry, I don't want to talk about it, and no, nobody hurt me," she said to her mother. "I just want to go to bed."

Thankfully, her mother listened.

Ashley went upstairs, determined not to cry anymore. She dropped her backpack on the bed and then swore, realizing she hadn't cracked open a single book. Just then, she got a text from Lisa asking if she was okay. Flipping through her assignment book, Ashley decided the three page assignment of conjugating Spanish verbs was really the only thing she couldn't postpone another day. She reached for her phone to reply.

"Sucky nite but ok now. Adam just dropped me off now. Did u do Spanish homework?"

Lisa answered a couple minutes later with a photo text of her completed homework. Ashley was overwhelmed with relief. She had the best friend ever.

"Thanks," she texted back.

"No prob. Call if u want 2 talk."

Ashley copied the responses onto a crisp sheet of paper and then dumped her backpack onto the floor. She needed a shower and bed.

But the second the hot water hit her face, Ashley felt herself starting to tear up again. Everything had been going so well in her life lately. She had known this was going to happen. Well, not this, exactly. It really had never crossed her mind that she might get pregnant since they'd always been careful.

Except for when they weren't.

Ashley cringed. She couldn't even begin to fathom what a baby meant for her life, and what did it mean for her and Adam? She couldn't stand to lose him. Ashley couldn't imagine living without Adam in her life, but no matter how this all ended up, she was certain it wouldn't be good news for their relationship. Even if this all turned out to be a fluke, he'd never be able to trust her again. And surely he'd resent her for putting him through all this crap.

She shut off the shower, dried off, and weaved her hair into a thick braid. She changed into her pajamas, brushed her teeth and climbed into bed. Ashley had just flipped off the light when her phone buzzed again. It was Adam. Ashley braced herself before reading his message. She knew by this point he was probably wishing she'd kept her mouth shut. Why hadn't she just dealt with this on her own, gotten an abortion or whatever and then never burdened him with it all?

Ashley clicked on his message. It said: "Go to sleep, Ashley. Stop worrying. We will get thru this together. I love you."

Ashley sighed, wiping her eyes before tears dripped onto her phone. Why did he have to be so perfect all the time? He deserved so much better than some irresponsible high schooler. She switched her phone to silent without replying and snuggled under her covers. Ashley didn't think she'd fall asleep, but she did, quickly. She slept soundly until her alarm blared to life.

* * *

ADAM DIDN'T SLEEP a wink that night. He kept checking his phone, half expecting a text from Ashley saying this was all an early April Fool's joke or something. But he knew it wasn't. And he knew she wasn't faking or making anything up. He had never seen someone so upset about anything before in his life, and it made him sick to think about her hurting that much.

He'd returned to the boat after dropping her off, shoving all the evidence of the pregnancy tests into a bag and throwing it away at the marina, but not before re-reading the instructions and confirming she'd interpreted the results correctly. Adam knew this was a big deal, but Ashley had acted like it was the end of the world. If she was that unhappy about the pregnancy, there was an easy fix. He hoped she'd feel better after talking to someone at Planned Parenthood.

He called first thing in the morning to get her an appointment. The quicker it was all taken care of, the sooner she could stop being so miserable. Adam briefly considered the alternative, Ashley keeping the baby, but dismissed it quickly. Her response left no question as to what she wanted to do. Although really, Adam didn't think it would be so bad if she kept the baby. Her family was loaded, so surely they could hire a nanny to watch the baby while she went to classes next year. Maybe she'd even keep Adam around after leaving for college if they had a baby together.

Adam then texted the appointment time to Ashley, checking how she was, telling her he loved her and asking if she wanted a ride to the clinic. She declined, promising to come over to Adam's right after the appointment. He tried not to be offended or worried by the fact that she wanted to go alone, and then got dressed to head to the marina. It was supposed to be his day off, but if they could find some work for him to do, at least it would keep his mind off things.

It was almost 5:30 when Ashley texted that she was headed his way. Since his dad had left already and wasn't expected back for a few days, Adam said for her to come to his condo, not the boat. Adam jumped up as soon as she knocked. He opened the door and she walked past him, headed straight to the couch. Damn he was nervous, and her face wasn't giving anything away. For the millionth time, he regretted letting her go to the appointment alone.

"What did they say?" he asked, pacing behind her.

She took a deep breath. "They did another test and confirmed I'm pregnant, due in October. Since it's so early, we still have lots of options."

Adam tried to swallow the lump in his throat but it kept rising up. He wasn't sure whether it was good news or bad news, what she was telling him. He needed to see her face. He crouched on the ground in front of her.

"They gave me all these pamphlets about the options," she said.

"Like what?"

Ashley was focused on some unknown object across the room. Her skin was pale and her face expressionless. "Abortion, adoption, or keeping it."

"Oh."

She didn't move, so he took the bag from her and began flipping through the different pamphlets. It was a lot of information, none of which seemed relevant until he knew what they were doing, what she wanted to do.

He dropped the bag on the ground and grabbed her hands, squeezing them in hopes of warming them up. "Ashley, look at me," Adam begged. She complied, though her expression was still distant and unreadable. "No matter what, we're in this together. It's going to be alright. I'm not going anywhere."

She stared up at him, a solitary tear escaping her big green eyes. He lifted her off the couch and pulled her into his arms, holding her tight as the rest of the tears started pouring out. She didn't say anything, and Adam certainly didn't dare speak, but it took an eternity for her to calm down.

When she stopped crying, Adam got a good look at her red, puffy eyes and tear-stained cheeks and felt even worse. Seeing her still this upset made him feel like a weight was dropped on his chest, crushing his lungs so he couldn't breathe.

"You should read the pamphlets and then let me know what you think we should do," Ashley said.

"Okay." Adam promised. "But I'll support whatever you decide to do."

She sighed. "Do you think I should get an abortion?"

Adam had never before felt so put on the spot as he did now. "Do you want to get an abortion?"

Her lip twitched. "It's still early, so the procedure wouldn't be too complicated. I wouldn't have to tell my parents—I could just go after school on a Friday afternoon and be fine by Monday. No one else would ever know. I could pay cash, and it wouldn't affect my ability to have a baby later on in life."

She sucked in a breath. "And I could still go to Duke in the fall as planned. It would be like this never happened."

Everything she was saying sounded good. Really good, actually. Adam didn't see any downside at all to this option, but he knew Ashley, and from her detached description, it was clear that she did not want an abortion.

"But is that what you really want, Ash?"

"What choice do we have?"

He frowned, since she was the one who'd apparently just reviewed all this with the nurse, but he knew what she was really asking. "You could have the baby, if you wanted. We wouldn't have to tell anyone until after you graduated, and you could defer Duke a semester. We could find the perfect parents to adopt the baby. Or we could keep the baby and raise it together."

"I can't raise a baby in college."

"Ashley, you can do anything. You're amazing. And you wouldn't be doing it alone. I mean, I can't help much with the whole pregnancy part but once that baby is born, I can do all the work so you can study and go to classes. I'm not going to be in college."

"How will we earn money if you're watching the baby all day and I'm in class?"

"I will work when you're home with the baby. And I'll work extra over summers when you're home full time, and I'll start working more now to save up for it." Adam was tempted to point out that Ashley could afford to hire someone to watch the baby, but he didn't think that would be comforting to her at the moment.

"It makes more sense for me to have an abortion," Ashley said.

"Do you want to have an abortion?" Adam asked for the third time.

Ashley took a deep breath, looked away, and shook her head. "No."

"Okay," he said. "Then we're not doing that. I'll figure out a plan and we will make it work. I promise."

Ashley nodded.

Adam hated that she was trusting him right now. He had no fucking clue what he was doing or saying and she was counting on him. He felt helpless.

"Did they have any advice at the clinic if we decide to go this route?" he asked.

"Yeah," she said slowly, sounding exhausted. "They said to make an appointment with an OB for a full checkup soon. I guess once I'm six weeks along, they can see a heartbeat on ultrasound or something. And they recommended telling my parents as soon as possible."

"Your parents," Adam repeated, the crushing sensation in his chest increasing to the point where he could barely breathe.

Ashley nodded. "The nurse said the parents almost always

take the news better than you expect so it's better to get it over with as soon as possible. She thought my parents might be able to help make the decision."

"Oh," Adam said. He hadn't quite wrapped his head around this whole pregnancy thing yet, let alone telling her parents. They already hated him. It wouldn't surprise him if they literally killed him after hearing the news. And what good would he be to Ashley or the baby then?

Adam sat back on the couch, pretending to look through the pamphlet about pregnancy, but really just trying to catch his breath and slow his pulse enough so that he didn't keel over.

"I like the idea of getting it over with," Ashley said after a moment. "My mom knows something is up. She probably thinks we're fighting or something."

Adam swallowed again. His throat felt like it was swollen shut. "But do you think they'll take the news well?" he croaked.

"No," Ashley said, almost smiling at the preposterous notion. "I'm sure it will be awful, but once they know, then it's done and I can stop worrying about how badly they'll react."

Adam nodded, although he still preferred the option of waiting until the last minute. Surely Ashley could wear baggy clothes or something and disguise it a while. But he didn't say anything, since he figured this was her decision.

"I thought I'd tell my mom first, and then she can talk with my dad."

Adam considered that, and decided that it was a good idea. He didn't know Ashley's mom really well, but she seemed rational enough. And clearly, Ashley got along better with her mom than with her dad.

He took a deep breath. "Okay. Let me know when and I'll be there."

Ashley hesitated and then shook her head slowly. "I think it would go better if I do it by myself."

"We're in this together. You don't have to do it alone."

"I want to," she said, leaning close to him.

He wrapped an arm around her and pulled her against his chest. Even with puffy eyes, Ashley was still gorgeous, and he enjoyed the chance to feel her warm body against his, even in shitty circumstances like these. Adam wasn't sure what the future held for them, but he figured he should take advantage of any time he had with Ashley, since it seemed like their days might be numbered.

$\mathcal{A}$shley found her mom sitting towards the end of the boardwalk, her favorite place in the world. She was holding an open novel, but Ashley could tell she wasn't actually looking at the page but just slightly above it, at the crest of the waves ahead.

"Can I talk to you?"

Her mother nodded and shut the book. She glanced at Ashley, smiled, then turned back to the ocean. Ashley wondered how long it would be before her mother experienced another peaceful smile like that.

"I have to tell you something, and you're not going to be happy about it."

"Uh oh," her mother said calmly, clearly oblivious to the nervousness in Ashley's voice.

"I'm pregnant," she said.

Her mother didn't react. She was so quiet, so calm still that Ashley wondered if the sound of the waves had carried off her words.

"Did you hear what I said?" Ashley bit her lip, trying to keep her tears to a minimum.

"Yes."

Ashley sat on the edge of the bench. "Say something."

"I don't know what to say."

"You could yell at me."

"It's a little late for that," her mother said with a sigh. "It's Adam's?"

"Yes."

"Does he know?"

"Yes."

Her mother glanced around. "And yet you're here alone."

"I told him I wanted to talk to you by myself. He offered to come."

"How generous of him," she said, her voice thick with sarcasm.

"Have you decided what to do?"

Ashley swallowed. "We're keeping it."

Her mother turned the other direction, hiding her face from Ashley, denying her any hint at all whether she thought she was making the right decision or not.

"It's due in October. So I'll just defer a semester at Duke."

She shook her head. "I stood up for him. I told your father we should let you see him, that forbidding it would only drive you right into his arms. I convinced him to give Adam a second chance." She turned to Ashley. "And all along, your father was right."

"This isn't Adam's fault. I know this isn't ideal, but..." Ashley wasn't sure what else to say. She supposed her mom was feeling everything she'd felt when she first found out. "I'm sorry," she added. "I know this isn't what you wanted for me and I get why you're disappointed. I just wanted to try to be responsible about it and tell you sooner rather than later."

"It's a little late to start thinking about responsibility, don't you think?" Her mother sighed. "You need to tell your father this.

I need time to process all of this on my own before speaking with him."

"We don't have to tell him right away," Ashley said, terrified at the idea of telling her father herself. It hadn't occurred to her that her mother wouldn't offer to do that.

"You will tell him today. I'm not keeping a secret like that from your father, and I'm certainly not going to be the one to tell him."

"He's not going to react well."

"You should have thought of that before you had sex then."

Ashley swallowed. Her eyes felt like they were going to burst from her head and her lip stung from the salty tears dripping down onto the raw patch she'd chewed. Her mother had never been this cold with her. It wasn't fair. She knew her mom wouldn't react this way if one of her brothers had knocked someone up in high school, and probably not even with her if it had been Brent's baby.

* * *

ADAM GOT a text from Ashley after she spoke to her mom. She didn't give details, but it was obvious the talk hadn't gone well and her mom had said she had to tell her father the news herself. Ashley said she wanted to tell him alone, but Adam insisted on coming. As much as he hated the thought of facing Wesley Kensington with bad news about his beloved daughter, he could never make Ashley do that alone.

Ashley was nervous on the drive over, more nervous than Adam had ever seen her before. She mentioned that Jackson was home for spring break and that she hoped that would distract her dad some, but then she simply stared out the window absent-mindedly. Adam reached for her hand, squeezing it tightly as he drove, but he was just as scared as she was.

When they arrived, Mr. Kensington was clearly annoyed as he

motioned for them to enter his office. Adam wasn't sure if it was his presence or the disruption itself that had the man so irked.

He glanced around the office nervously while Mr. Kensington finished his call. The office itself was nearly as large as Adam's condo, but it was sparsely furnished. There was a sitting area by one wall, with a couch and two chairs, a coffee table and some end tables, and then there was the L-shaped desk beside the two massive windows. There was a door off by the far wall which Adam guessed led to a private bathroom. He supposed all of this might make a desk job slightly more tolerable.

"I'll look for it Tuesday," Mr. Kensington barked into the phone, hanging up without a traditional farewell. He took a long sip of water from the glass on his desk before turning to his daughter.

"Ashlynne, my schedule is full today so if this is something that can wait…"

"It can't," she said.

Mr. Kensington let out an exasperated sigh and gave a sideways glance at Adam. "Have a seat," he said reluctantly, positioning himself on the chair facing the couch.

Ashley sat on the couch and Adam hesitantly followed suit.

Mr. Kensington stared expectantly at them. Adam had never been so terrified in his life. He couldn't fathom the courage it must take for Ashley to actually say what she came to say today. He reached over and squeezed her hand to show his support.

Bad idea. Mr. Kensington's eyes widened.

Ashley inhaled slowly. "I'm pregnant. And we're keeping the baby."

Mr. Kensington stopped breathing. Adam actually saw the rise and fall of his chest halt abruptly mid-breath and freeze. Mr. Kensington rose to his feet, turned his back on the couple, and returned to his desk. He stood facing the window and slowly emptied the rest of his glass of water. The silence in the room was painful, and it seemed to stretch on for several minutes.

"Adam," he finally said, shattering the silence. "Could you leave us for a moment? I'd like to speak with my daughter alone."

Adam glanced at Ashley and quickly ascertained that she was not interested in that option. He forced the lump in his throat back down and prayed his voice still worked. "Actually sir, Ashley would prefer for me to stay."

"Anything you want to say to me, you can say in front of Adam," Ashley chimed in.

Her dad set the glass on the desk, clanking it loudly against a crystal picture frame. "Very well," he said. He turned to face them again.

"Ashley, I am disappointed in you. I expected you to exercise better judgment than this and I thought we raised you better than to engage in risky behavior. Obviously, an abortion would be a better solution to this situation, but I assume your mind is made up about that or you would've simply had it done rather than tell me."

He turned to her for confirmation. She nodded. Adam squeezed her hand again.

"And this is your decision?" he asked Ashley, "You were not influenced by…" he glanced to Adam, "anyone else?"

"This was my decision," Ashley said. "Adam would have preferred the abortion but is being supportive of my decision."

Mr. Kensington stared at Adam again. Adam stared right back, wishing he could suddenly become invisible. He wasn't sure how Ashley knew that about the abortion, since he certainly hadn't told her that.

"When is the baby due?"

"October."

He returned to his seat and thought for another long minute, his face giving no indication what he was feeling. "We will make an appointment for you with a good doctor as soon as possible. You will focus on your studies the rest of the year and not invite any distractions by telling anyone else about this situation you've gotten yourself into. You will defer your admission to Duke by one year and you will spend that year in England with my sister so that your transcript and resume will show a year spent traveling and enriching yourself rather than a year covering up your own debauchery and misdeeds."

Mr. Kensington sighed. "We will pay for a nanny to stay with you at an off-campus apartment at Duke. Your studies will not be interrupted after the one year delay. And you will stop seeing this boy immediately."

Aside from the part about him, Adam actually thought her dad's plan didn't sound half bad. And he was impressed that the guy had come up with all this on the spot. That must be why he was paid the big bucks. Adam wasn't really sure what he was supposed to do in England for a year, but then again, Mr. Kensington probably picked a location across the Atlantic just to ensure Adam wasn't with her.

"I'm not going to stop seeing Adam," Ashley said. "And you certainly can't keep him from his baby either."

"Ashlynne, I told you from the start this boy was trouble. I'm sure he has some appealing trait somewhere," he said, eying Adam with distaste, "but he has no future and now he is threatening to destroy yours. Your mother and I have worked hard to ensure that you have the opportunities you deserve and I'm not going to watch you throw it away over some schoolgirl crush." His voice grew louder and more animated with each word that left his mouth.

"I'm not going to stop seeing Adam," Ashley repeated. "This isn't a crush and there isn't any scenario for the future where I'm happy unless it involves Adam. If you had ever bothered to get to know him, you would see that he is not the villain you make him out to be."

Her father snorted. "Yes, I'm sure he's a wonderful young man. That's why he impregnated a girl two years his junior when he should be off at college or working full time and dating women his own age."

Ashley started to open her mouth to protest and Adam squeezed her hand again, harder this time, signaling that it was okay. He didn't need her to defend him. If he were her father, he wouldn't like himself either.

"Look, I'm sure it seems like you are in love right now and you think you can conquer the world," Mr. Kensington continued. "But the world looks very different at eighteen—or twenty—than it does at twenty-five. Statistically your relationship has zero chance of surviving long-term whether or not you keep dating this year. The difference is that in one scenario, you miss your chance to study at the university you've been dreaming of for years and you end up an uneducated single mom stuck in a job you hate just to pay the bills. In the other scenario, you control your destiny and you make the responsible decision for yourself and your child."

He paused and looked straight at Adam. "If he truly loved you, he wouldn't insist on dragging you down."

Adam opened his mouth to speak but Ashley stood up. "I'm not going to sit here and listen to you disrespect Adam. I know we made a mistake and that you're not happy. But I am not breaking up with him just because you tell me to. I'm eighteen now. I'm legally an adult. You can't boss me around anymore."

Mr. Kensington's eyebrow twitched as his gaze hardened. "You are right, Ashley. But as long as you are living in my house and on my paycheck, you will follow my rules. And that means you will not see or speak to Adam."

"I won't agree to that."

"That's your choice," her father said. "I'll expect you to move your things out today."

Ashley stared at her father's cold, angry eyes for a moment before storming out of the office, leaving her purse on the couch.

Adam stood slowly, feeling torn between trying to fix things with Mr. Kensington and rushing out to comfort Ashley.

"I think you're making a mistake," Adam said. "Ashley is an amazing person and she really does respect you. And we have a plan. We can make this work. You don't have to lose her over this."

Mr. Kensington raised an eyebrow. "I won't," he said confidently. "But you will. Shut the door on your way out."

Adam grabbed Ashley's purse and hurried out of the office.

By the time he caught up with her, she was already at his truck, tugging on the handle like it was stuck, and not locked. He wanted to comfort her, but she just needed to get the fuck out of there fast.

Ashley was staring out the window. Adam couldn't see her face and she was completely still, so he didn't think she was crying, but he didn't know what to think.

"Where should…" he started to ask.

"My house," she answered.

He drove to her house, slowing as he pulled into the fancy drive, unsure of the plan.

"Wait for me here, okay?"

"Yeah. Of course."

Adam watched her head into the house. Ten minutes later, she flew out the front door. She had her backpack, a rolling suitcase, and two duffel bags. Adam hopped out to grab the bags and threw them in the back of the truck as she hopped back into the passenger seat.

Adam turned, noticing Jackson stick his head out the door. He must have looked panicked, because Ashley followed his gaze, then tapped his thigh.

"Go," she said.

Adam drove. As they neared the marina, he remembered his dad was coming back that evening. He pictured all of Ashley's stuff, having no clue where it would go on the boat, but they'd make it work.

* * *

WHEN THEY ARRIVED at the marina, Adam began unloading her stuff from the truck. Ashley sifted through it, leaving most of it on the deck and taking only the essentials into the cabin. Adam was watching her like he was concerned she'd suddenly go crazy and jump off the helm.

Ashley knew he was worried about her, but she didn't feel like sitting around wallowing.

"I'm hungry," she said. "Can we go out?"

Adam hesitated as though he couldn't tell if he'd heard her correctly, but then he nodded. She picked an Italian place, ordered a seafood linguini and ate half of it with Adam still eying her warily. After dinner, she sat on the deck of the boat and did her homework, and then they took a long walk around the marina. By nine o'clock, she was exhausted, but proud that she'd somehow managed to mostly keep her mind off her dismal reality for a few consecutive hours.

When Ashley went below deck, Adam followed. She started to undress, planning to change into something more comfortable to sleep in, then paused. Adam was watching her still, but something in his expression had changed. Ashley kept her eyes on him as she unfastened her bra, letting it fall to the floor. As she stepped out of her jeans, his stare intensified even more.

Relief flooded Ashley. "You still want me," she said, surprised.

Adam stepped closer, still eying her fully undressed body appreciatively. "Ash, I will always want you."

"Prove it."

He pulled her in for a kiss and then did just that.

* * *

It was a gorgeous March night, but the temperature was still a little cool, so Ashley had slipped into a pair of Adam's sweatpants and his undershirt before falling asleep. His clothes were ridiculously baggy on her, but she felt so much closer to him wearing them, even though his body was draped over her as they slept. Ashley only slept for a little while before being jolted awake.

She glanced at Adam, confirming he was sound asleep. She crawled out of the bed, suddenly too warm and craving fresh air. Ashley climbed onto the deck, expecting to be greeted by silence and solitude. Instead, she quickly noticed her oldest brother pacing beside the boat. Without warning, he shouted and slammed his foot into the side of the boat, rocking it lightly.

"Shhhh!" she cautioned, certain one of the neighboring boat occupants would call the cops if they heard any disturbance this late. Jackson was obviously both pissed off and drunk, but he still offered a hand to help Ashley over the rope as she approached the boardwalk. She accepted it then shook her hand free as soon as she reached solid ground.

"What are you doing? It's the middle of the night!"

His eyes narrowed. "What am I doing? What are you doing on some guy's boat in the middle of the night?"

Ashley rolled her eyes. "Don't start with me, Jackson. You do not get a say in what I do with my life."

"I have never seen Dad like he was tonight."

"Let me guess—drunk and pissed off, just like you?"

His expression softened. "This ain't right and you know it."

She realized then that he might not know the whole story. "Jackson, go home. There is no easy fix to things between Dad and me right now."

He reached for her hand. "You're coming home with me."

"No, I'm not." She shook her head. "Does Dad even know you're here? Because he was pretty clear earlier that he did not want me coming home."

"What?" Jackson frowned. "Why the hell not?"

Ashley swallowed the lump in her throat, dreading telling him. But he'd find out eventually, so she might as well get it over with. "I'm pregnant, Jackson."

His eyes widened then filled with sorrow. She had expected anger, but this was definite disappointment and sadness. He was quiet for so long she started to think he was going to cry.

And then the anger came.

"Get your ass out here, Adam!" Jackson shouted, starting around Ashley.

Ashley stepped back in front of him. "Shh! Jackson keep your voice down. You don't even know that it's his."

He rolled his eyes. "Who else's would it be? Or are you just sleeping with everyone who wanders into town now?"

"It could be Brent's," Ashley lied.

"Brent would never…"

She laughed out loud. "Oh please. He would've dumped me in a snap if I hadn't slept with him. At least Adam is good in bed."

Jackson winced as though she'd hit him. "That's it, we're done here. You are coming home with me." He grabbed Ashley's wrist hard and started to pull. "You and Dad can work this out, but not if you run away like a child. You belong at home with your family. We will take care of you." He started tugging her towards the parking lot.

Being barefoot, Ashley had zero traction. The gravel stung the bottoms of her feet and her wrist burned from the way he was pulling. "Ouch! Jackson let go. You're hurting me!"

He hesitated for the slightest moment and she thought he'd let go, but instead he just picked her up and flung her over his shoulder.

"Jackson! Put me down!"

As he started to walk, Ashley saw movement out of the corner of her eye. Adam was on the deck of the boat and flew over the rail to the dock in an instant.

"Get your hands off her!" he snarled, charging at Jackson.

Jackson plopped Ashley right onto her feet and a second later the men slammed into each other like two trains off their tracks.

Ashley screamed then covered her eyes as punches started to fly.

"Stop it! Both of you!"

Their fists were blurs and they were so tangled up Ashley could hardly tell where one of them ended and the other started. Jackson shoved Adam backwards but then Adam somehow got the upper hand and all of a sudden they were both on the ground. Ashley screamed again, certain one of them was going to get killed if they didn't stop, but equally certain she couldn't break up the fight on her own.

Ashley stepped closer, trying to eye a way to get in between them in hopes that they'd just stop, since clearly neither of them heard her yelling, but they just kept thrashing around, hitting and kicking each other with every ounce of energy they had.

"Help!" she shouted, sobbing. "Stop it!"

Lights flashed and a siren wailed. Ashley exhaled with relief. It wasn't the help she'd wanted, but it was better than those two killing each other.

Two officers ran over, one right after the other. "Break it up!" one shouted, shining a light on the guys.

Adam immediately pulled back. Jackson turned, then dropped Adam's arm. The officers rushed to the guys and started to lift them to their feet.

"Are either of you armed?" an officer asked as he started to pat down Adam.

Ashley almost laughed at the absurdity of it all. Adam was wearing athletic shorts and likely nothing underneath. He had no pockets, no shoes, no shirt—where exactly was he supposedly hiding a weapon?

He glanced at Ashley apologetically but she squeezed her eyes shut, not even able to look at his bloodied face.

The officers began to handcuff them both and launched into

some spiel about rights. Ashley stood there, stunned for a minute, then realized they were being arrested.

She rushed forward. "Wait, officers, stop! This isn't necessary. They're done now. This is a family matter. Look, that's his boat." She gestured from Adam to his boat, then pointed to Jackson. "And he can just go home. There won't be any more trouble. I promise."

The officers glanced at each other and then one of them turned to Ashley, delicately placing a hand on her back and walking her further away. She saw the other officer walking her brother towards the first police cruiser.

"Miss, are you hurt?"

"No, but…"

He held up a hand. "Miss, I understand what you are saying, but we can't just let them go home now. We had multiple calls for a disturbance and we'd be responsible if we were to leave and something else did happen."

"But they won't…" Ashley grew frantic as she saw the other officer start to walk Adam to the other police car.

"Miss, I need you to answer my questions now." The officer was speaking in a gentle tone, but the look in his eyes told her he was serious.

She sighed.

"Did either of them touch you or injure you in any way?"

Ashley glanced down at her wrist then covered the bruise with her other hand, shaking her head.

"Can you tell me what happened?"

"Adam and I were asleep on his boat, and…"

"Which one is Adam?" he interrupted.

She pointed.

"The one with the tattoos?"

Ashley nodded, reluctantly realizing that was probably all they saw when they looked at him.

She was about to continue her story when she saw something else flicker across the officer's face. "How old are you, miss?"

"I'm eighteen," she said.

"You're sure, now?"

"Of course I'm sure."

He nodded, still skeptical. "What's your full name?"

"Ashlynne Marie Kensington."

His expression changed in recognition of the name. "Okay, Miss Kensington, please continue."

"Adam and I were asleep on the boat when my brother came by and started yelling."

"Which brother?" the officer interrupted again.

"Jackson." She paused but he let her continue. "I came out and told him to go home, but he just wanted to argue and yell at me. Then he started yelling at Adam, so Adam came out. Then, well, you saw the rest."

"Was Adam drinking tonight?"

"No!" Ashley nearly added that Jackson most certainly was, but she stopped herself, not yet willing to throw her brother under the bus.

"Alright, thank you, miss." He folded his notepad and started to turn.

"Wait! Where are you taking them? What happens now?"

"We're taking them to the station. They'll spend the rest of the night in lock up and then the decision will be made whether or not to charge them."

She watched as the cars drove off then went back to Adam's boat. She climbed into the cabin and put on her clothes and grabbed her cell phone. As much as she hated to involve her parents, Ashley didn't know what else to do.

She texted her mom: "Jackson showed up @ marina drunk and threatened me then got in fight w/Adam. Police arrested both."

Ashley knew she'd share the text with her dad, and that he

would be the one to fix the situation, but she wasn't about to ask him for help directly.

She was beyond exhausted and even more stressed than earlier—something she wouldn't have even thought possible. She curled up on the cushioned bench, turning to face the still-dark sky. She doubted she'd fall asleep, but there was nothing else she could do until morning anyway.

CHAPTER 16

Somehow, Ashley fell asleep, albeit briefly. When she awoke, the sun was up, so she crawled back down to the cabin to make herself presentable and then grabbed Adam's keys, cell phone, and wallet. She headed for his truck since her car was still at her house. Ashley drove to the police station and a mixture of dread and relief hit her as she immediately spotted her father's Jag in the parking lot.

Ashley hesitated for several minutes, struggling to garner the courage to go inside, uncertain what she would find. When she did finally push through the solid entry doors, Ashley nearly bumped into her father, standing in the corner, on his cell phone. They made eye contact, but his face remained expressionless, and after a moment, he turned away.

The waiting room was otherwise empty. Ashley wasn't sure what to do next, so she started towards the plexiglass window at the front of the room when all of a sudden, she heard a familiar voice. She glanced up and saw Dex, her father's lawyer and a close family friend. He was thanking someone behind the desk and then made his way out into the waiting room.

"Ashlynne," he greeted her jovially, as though he had no idea what had happened or why she was even there. "How have you been?"

Ashley opened her mouth to answer, uncertain what to say, but thankfully didn't have to speak at all, as Dex patted her on the back and nodded.

"They'll both be out in a moment. You can take your boy home."

"Thanks," she mumbled, now thoroughly intrigued as to what all had transpired.

She watched Dex approach her father, who immediately put his call on hold, spoke with him for a moment, and thanked him loudly. Then Dex left and her father resumed his call, leaving the police station without so much as a second glance in her direction. Ashley stared out the window and saw that her father hadn't gone to his car but rather was simply standing by the front of the building.

There was a buzz then and the doors swung open and out filed Jackson and then Adam. Ashley glared at Jackson, as he sheepishly trudged past her and out the door to where their father was waiting. As pathetic as he looked, with a purplish-black eye, busted lip, and swollen cheekbone, she couldn't bring herself to feel sorry for him.

Ashley was so relieved to see Adam that she flung her arms around him, expecting a warm embrace. Instead he winced, holding her at a distance. Ashley gazed up at his face and cringed, barely recognizing him with all the bruises and blood.

"Let's go," he whispered, slipping into the shoes Ashley held.

They walked outside just as her father drove off. Adam took his keys and started the drive back to the marina. Ashley couldn't stop looking at his injuries.

"That looks really painful," Ashley said stupidly.

"I'll be alright."

"I, um saw my dad in the waiting room. And his lawyer, Dexter Abrams. Did you talk to them?"

"Just to the lawyer. He said your brother wouldn't press charges if I didn't press charges and that your dad was going to pay both of our fines for disturbing the peace."

"So…is that it? I mean, do you have to go to court or anything?"

"No. It's done. I guess I owe your father some money, though."

"You don't owe him anything. You were defending his daughter from his son."

He sighed. "I'd like to pay him back anyway."

Ashley knew this wasn't the time to argue with him. As bad as her night had been, his had clearly been worse. "Fine." She eyed him again, closely. "Are you sure we don't need to go to a doctor about any of these cuts? Maybe you need stitches."

"I'll look back at the boat. It's probably too late anyway."

"You better not have any scars marring your perfect face," she teased.

He mustered a half grin and squeezed her thigh with his right hand.

"Do you want me to drop you off at home?"

Ashley shook her head furiously.

"Ashley, you need some rest. I'd take you to my place, but my dad doesn't leave until tomorrow and I don't want him to see me like this."

"I'm staying with you," she insisted.

They hit the drive through for breakfast but were quiet the rest of the drive. Once on the boat, Adam went down below and cleaned up. He looked much better when he reemerged.

"Can we go someplace? I don't want to stay here all day." Ashley gazed sadly at the patch of dusty gravel where you could clearly tell an altercation had taken place.

Adam didn't answer, but quickly untied the boat and started the motor. Ashley went to the cabin to brush her teeth and wash her face then came back up and sat by the bow, watching the waves as they zipped out into the open ocean. He drove for maybe an extra ten minutes after they'd escaped the more congested waters and then killed the engine.

Adam came to sit by her. She stared at his bruised face again, slowly raising her finger to touch his injuries, hesitating to ask permission silently. He nodded, so she very lightly traced a cut above his eyebrow, then down to his cheekbone, and finished at his lip. She leaned forward and planted the softest kiss imaginable over the split on his lip. Then she lifted his shirt. His ribs were bruised and purple beneath his tattoos and he had a few smaller bruises along his other arm, but all in all, Ashley suspected he looked better than her brother.

"We had a good talk, your brother and I," Adam said, startling her.

"What? They put you in the same cell?"

He breathed a laugh while nodding.

"I am so sorry about everything, Adam. I can't even…"

Adam pressed his finger against her lips. "You don't owe me an apology for anything. I was the one who attacked him."

Ashley rolled her eyes. "He came there looking for a fight with you."

He shrugged. "Yeah, I know. But I don't blame him."

"What? I do. He's a monster."

"Ash, think about it from his perspective. You're his baby sister. Your dad isn't around much and he's always viewed himself as your protector. He thinks it's his role to fill in where your dad's absence leaves gaps. You've got this bright future ahead of you and then this new guy comes along and Jackson is terrified it'll screw up your future but he finally decides maybe it's harmless since you're leaving for college soon anyway."

He paused, but Ashley wasn't sure what to say, so he continued.

"Jackson was certain our relationship had an expiration date on it and then he learned you'd left home to stay with me. He's mad about that and then you tell him you're pregnant, and now he figures I've knocked you up on purpose to make you stay and he sees your entire future gone all because of me."

"That's not what happened."

Adam didn't look convinced. "In his mind, it is. I don't blame him for hating me. If the roles were reversed and you were my little sister, well, I'd kick his ass too. I should be protecting you and taking care of you and doing what's best for you." He shook his head. "This isn't what's best for you, Ashley. You deserve a carefree college experience. You deserve to go out in the world and find yourself and figure out what you want to do with your life. You deserve endless possibilities, not this."

Ashley felt tears welling in her eyes. "I want you."

"I know, babe. It's just…" he hesitated and frowned. "You can have me whether or not you go through with the…" he glanced down at her stomach. "If you had an abortion, you could go off to college just like you planned. I could come with you or whatever you want, but then you could decide. If you decided you wanted someone else or some other life that didn't involve me, you could do that. You wouldn't have to feel trapped because of a child."

Now Ashley was sobbing. They'd already had this discussion. He knew how she felt, but clearly he didn't feel the same.

"Ashley," he wrapped his arms around her. She couldn't even look at him. "Ashley, listen to me. I love you. You know I love you. I will be so happy if you want to keep this baby and spend your life with me. I just want you to know it's okay if that isn't what you want, too. Eighteen is really young to figure all of this out."

She tried to catch her breath so she could talk. He supported her chin with his hand and wiped her tears with the other hand.

"I hate making you cry," he said.

"Adam, I know the timing sucks, but I can't shake the feeling that this is how it is meant to be. I get that it would be easier in ten years, or God, even five years, but it happened now. We made this baby," she said. "I can't…I can't kill it. And I don't think I could give it up for adoption either. I'd always wonder…"

Ashley wasn't sure how he'd respond, but he immediately kissed her, hard at first, then pulling back drastically as her lip pressed into his cut. He shifted, pulling her onto his lap and helping her arrange her legs on either side of his so she was straddling him. She wrapped her arms around him and squeezed him as they kissed, feeling his body tense but not figuring out that she was hurting him until he groaned.

"Oh shit," Ashley mumbled, pulling back. "I'm sorry." She delicately patted his bruised ribs. "I wish I could kiss it and make the pain go away."

"Maybe you can," he replied, lifting his shirt over his head.

She gently kissed his shoulder, ribs and bicep before returning to his face.

"I love you," he said.

"I love you too."

They kissed until they were both exhausted, then they went into the cabin and made love gently, so as not to further exacerbate his injuries. After, they fell asleep curled together. Whatever pain they'd endured the past several days, Ashley was happy for now.

When Ashley awoke, Adam was gone, and she was parched. She stretched slowly and dressed in her bikini before heading to deck. Adam had started the motor again, probably because they had drifted too far during their nap, but he shut it off when he saw her.

She grabbed a Coke from the cooler and came up behind him, kissing the back of his shoulder before sitting down. She took one long, refreshing sip, then saw him eying her warily.

"What?"

He opened his mouth, then shut it again.

Ashley gave him a look that he correctly interpreted as an order to talk.

"I was just wondering if it's safe for you to drink that," he said tentatively.

She glanced down at the can in her hand, unsure of what he meant.

"Because of the baby," he explained.

"Oh." She looked at the drink again, almost expecting some warning label like there was on beer. "I don't know."

He frowned. "I'm not sure either. I'm sure one won't hurt, either way."

Ashley grimaced then shook her head. She handed him the Coke. "I'm completely clueless," she said, starting to panic.

Adam grabbed a water bottle from the cooler and handed it to her, wedging the Coke back in between some other items so it wouldn't spill. "We'll figure it out together," he said.

"How do you propose we do that?"

He shrugged. "I don't know. How does anyone figure out what they're doing? I'll buy a book or something. Or look online."

"You're going to buy a pregnancy book?" She smiled, picturing her tattooed bad boy browsing the baby aisle at the book store.

He grinned back. "So how do you feel so far? Are you nauseous at all?"

Ashley considered that. "No, I feel normal, I think."

They were both quiet for a while, enjoying the peacefulness of the gently rolling waves around them.

"I talked to your brother some about my mom. And my life back in Nantucket."

"Really?"

"Yeah. And did you know he has a girlfriend?"

"Jackson?"

Adam laughed at her shocked expression.

"He's never been a one-woman kind of guy," she explained.

"People change. Maybe he just had to meet the right woman."

* * *

ADAM'S DAD left the next day for a two-week jaunt up the coast, so they moved their sleepovers to Adam's condo instead of staying on the boat. Adam had always assumed he'd stay single until well into his thirties, but there was definitely something to be said about having his girl around all the time. Waking up by Ashley was phenomenal and going to bed with her wrapped around him was even better. Pregnancy certainly hadn't affected her sex drive, either. Adam wondered if her dad realized that by kicking his daughter out, he had brought her and Adam even closer.

Adam's only real concern was that whenever he tried to bring up a serious topic, Ashley suddenly had someplace to be. At some point, they'd need an actual plan. Ashley would have to defer at least a semester, and they'd need a place to live. Adam figured his dad would let them live in the condo, especially over the summer when he wasn't home anyway, but since neither of them was real eager to tell his dad, they couldn't be too sure. Adam had looked online at apartments in the Raleigh/Durham area just to get an idea of price, and it wasn't awful, unless Adam factored in the fact that he had no skills that would qualify him for a job that far inland.

He wanted to ask Ashley if she thought her parents would at least still pay her tuition, but he didn't want to upset her. Adam knew the best solution would be for both of them to start working and saving now, before the baby came, but it broke his heart to think of telling Ashley that, in addition to dealing with all the pregnancy woes, she'd also need to forgo any fun this year and spend every moment she wasn't at school or studying working some lame ass job. And while he knew he could get a second job somewhere at the marina, whenever he brought it up, Ashley started whining about not getting to spend enough time together.

Adam wished he were the kind of man who could figure out what to do. He wanted to take charge, find a solution, and make it happen. Ashley needed him to be able to do that. She needed him to be more like her dad.

They'd only been living together for two days when Ashley casually mentioned that her mom had asked her to come home.

"What?" Adam thought he'd misheard her. "When?"

"Yesterday."

Adam frowned. "And you didn't think it was worth mentioning to me?"

Ashley turned to him, her eyes already starting to fill with tears. Okay, Adam had to admit the weepiness was new. He didn't think he'd ever seen Ashley cry before the pregnancy and now, everything brought her to tears.

"You want me to leave?" she asked.

Oh shit. "No, babe," Adam said, joining Ashley on the couch. "I have loved having you around and I want you to stay as long as you want. But I feel bad about screwing up your relationship with your parents, and I think it is important for you to patch things up with them before the baby comes."

Ashley didn't answer.

"What did she say, exactly?"

Ashley handed him her phone, forcing him to scroll through the dozens of messages she'd received to find the string from her mom. He clicked on the message and read it slowly.

It said, "You've made your point, Ashley. Please come home now. Your father was simply upset at your situation and spoke rashly. We will figure something out together."

"That sounds good to me, Ashley. She basically apologized."

She rolled her eyes. "Except she didn't."

"Ashley, your mom misses you. Her other kids are all at college and she doesn't have much longer with you before you leave. She just wants to spend time with you."

"Well, she should have thought of that before."

"Before her teenage daughter got knocked up? How did you expect her to react? You didn't exactly take the news well right away either," he reminded her.

Ashley stood abruptly. "If you want me gone that bad, I'll go stay at Lisa's."

"Ash, come on," he said, tugging on her hand. She yanked it out of his reach. "That's not what I want and you know it. What I want is for you to fix shit with your parents."

She turned, eyes narrowed. "What happened to all of your talk of how we could do this alone?"

"We could, Ashley. If that's what we need to do, I'll make it work," Adam paused, muttering a silent prayer that he could actually keep that promise. "But you can't throw away everything with your family because of me. Do you know how lucky you are to even have two parents and three brothers who care so much about you?"

Ashley rolled her eyes. "Yes, because everyone wants more people in their lives to judge their every move and make their decisions for them."

"Damn it!" Adam clenched his jaw together, calming himself before continuing. "I would kill for the chance to have my mom back in my life, even if all she did was lecture me about what a screw up I am for forgetting the damn condom. Your mom is right there, she's clearly trying to make it work, and you're too fucking stubborn to let her in your life."

Ashley glared back, the hurt evident in her damp eyes. Then she shoved all her stuff into her backpack and slipped into her flip flops.

"Shit," Adam muttered, realizing he'd pushed her too far. He hated seeing her lose her family because of him and, frankly, it did piss him off. Her parents weren't perfect but they were there, and she just took it all for granted.

"Ashley, I'm sorry. Don't..." Adam began, but she slammed the door behind her before her could finish.

Adam gave himself a half hour to cool off, doing an impromptu boxing workout combined with enough push-ups to feel like his arms were falling off. And then he started the text apologies.

Adam knew he was right. The best solution was for Ashley to move back home and for them to move forward with her parents still in her life. Ideally, he'd still be in the picture, too, but Adam couldn't pretend that Ashley or the baby would be better off with just him than with her entire family's support, even if it meant doing it without him.

But Adam also felt like shit. He'd just yelled at Ashley. However right he was about her family, he was wrong to shout at her. What kind of a guy curses at his pregnant girlfriend? He texted her again, threatening to keep stalking her until she replied and let him know if she was okay and if she was coming home. When she finally answered that she was staying the night at Lisa's, Adam was relieved. Then he went out to find Clay and go get drunk.

* * *

As ASHLEY DESCRIBED her fight with Adam to her best friend, she struggled to avoid any comment about the pregnancy. She hated keeping such a big thing from Lisa, but at the same time, she had no interest in sharing the news. The more people who knew, the more real it was.

"It was our first fight," Ashley said, wiping her eye.

Lisa nodded, but said, "What about that night at the marina a week or two ago? That seemed pretty bad."

It took a minute for Ashley to realize Lisa was talking about the day she'd realized she was pregnant. God, that felt like ages ago, but really only a week had passed. That had been a bad day, but they hadn't fought. Adam had been perfect that day. He was always perfect, except today.

"Maybe you guys just need a break," Lisa said. "Maybe you've gotten the whole bad boy thing out of your system and are ready to move on now. I mean, it's not like this was gonna last forever."

Ashley frowned, annoyed that her best friend would assume such a thing. "I love Adam," she finally said. "And he was a total dick today, but he's not usually."

"I know, but Ashley, you're going to leave in a few months anyway. Is it really worth making yourself miserable to salvage a relationship with a fast approaching deadline anyway?" Her friend paused. "And I know your dad can be a total jerk, but he's your dad. You're going to have to forgive him eventually. You can't give up your family over a guy."

Ashley started to reply, then realized she was now having the same argument she'd had with Adam all over again. She shook her head. "I'm going for a walk on the beach," she said.

Ashley walked for what felt like forever down the beach and then headed back up. As she neared Lisa's, she couldn't help but notice the small figure at the end of the boardwalk at the house just past Lisa's. Her house. Even from the distance, Ashley knew it was her mother, and she suspected her mom was watching her. She paused, then took a deep breath and walked closer.

Her mom smiled as she approached, but didn't say anything at first. Ashley sat on the bench across from her mother, but kept her gaze fixed on the ocean.

"You're staying at Lisa's," her mom said, surprised. "I thought you were at Adam's."

Ashley considered lying, but realized there was no point. "I was, but we had a fight today because he thought I should come home and make up with you, and I didn't think you deserved a second chance."

There was silence. Finally, her mom spoke. "I've missed you. So has your dad, although he'd never admit it."

"I didn't leave because I wanted to. He said I couldn't keep seeing Adam unless I moved out."

"I know."

"Adam is the father of my baby. I can't cut him out of my life."

"I think your father and I didn't understand your feelings for Adam. This whole thing seemed to be some rebellion against us and the way we've raised you. Your father thought you'd come to your senses about Adam if he took a tough love approach."

Ashley started to protest, but her mom continued.

"He should have handled it better," she said. "But you have to understand we were surprised and hurt. We didn't want this for you."

"Obviously we didn't plan for this to happen," Ashley said. "But the fact is, it did happen, and since then, Adam has been nothing except supportive and helpful and you guys…you both made me feel worthless."

Ashley noticed her mom's eyes glossing over.

"I'm sorry, sweetie. We didn't mean to hurt you. But you hurt us, too. And you broke our rules. Rules that we had for a reason, obviously."

Ashley wasn't sure what rules her mom meant, actually. She certainly didn't remember either parent ever explicitly telling her not to have sex.

"Your brother said Adam seems like a nice guy."

"Mason?"

She shook her head. "No, Jackson." She paused, smiling at the look of surprise on Ashley's face. "He also said Adam seems to really care about you."

"He does."

"Does Adam's father know about the pregnancy?"

Ashley shook her head.

"Ashley, your father and I would both like it if you moved home. You can keep seeing Adam, and we can all figure out together what would work best for you and the baby."

Ashley thought about it for a moment and then agreed. Her mother looked like a huge weight had been lifted off her shoulders, but Ashley was glad that she didn't hop up to hug her or anything.

"Have you found a doctor?"

Ashley nodded. "I have an appointment with Dr. Baker in two and a half weeks."

"Good. I can come with you if you…"

"No. Thanks. Adam is coming," Ashley interrupted.

Her mother nodded. "Is all of your stuff over at Lisa's?"

"Just some. Most is still at Adam's."

They were quiet again, and Ashley realized Lisa might start to worry if she didn't come back to get her stuff before sunset. She stood slowly and told her mom she'd be back shortly.

"Okay," her mom agreed. "And Ashley? I think…your father and I would both like to get to know Adam better. But we need more time, if that's okay. We understand that you are just as responsible for your current situation as he is, but it's hard for us to forgive him. He's older than you. He should have known better."

Ashley left to get her stuff before she said something she'd regret. She considered calling Adam to tell him the news, but she was still mad. She got his point, but he didn't have to be so cruel about it. He deserved to keep groveling until the next day.

* * *

ADAM WAS on his second beer before they ran out of innocuous topics to discuss. He tried to think of something else to say, but Clay went in for the dirt.

"So what's up with you tonight? You seem…off." Clay said.

Adam sighed, figuring Clay was putting it nicely.

"Ashley."

Clay's eyes widened. "Oh shit dude. You guys didn't break up, did you?"

"No," Adam said, feeling a little sick at the thought of that. "Just a fight."

His friend nodded knowingly and took a swig of his beer. "Who was right?"

"Me."

"So… you apologize yet?"

They both laughed.

"Hell yeah," Adam said.

"And?"

Adam shrugged. "Not sure she's over it yet. She never used to be like this but since…" He stopped himself in time, rephrasing his thought. "She's just been really emotional lately. No matter what I say, she gets all bent out of shape."

"Sounds like PMS," Clay said.

Adam chewed the inside of his cheek. "She had this big blowout with her parents about a week ago. They told her she had to stop seeing me."

"They said that before though, right?"

"Yeah, but this time they told her she had to move out if she wasn't going to follow their rules." Adam told Clay about how they'd basically been living together and then caught him up to the present, minus the baby part.

Clay considered the facts as Adam had outlined them while he finished his beer. "So I agree you're obviously right, but it's kind of cool, that she's willing to take such a big stand for you. I mean, she's always been pretty tight with her family, so if she's willing to give all that up for you…"

"In theory, sure. But she's not thinking it through. She has her heart set on Duke next year. Even if I find a job there, we could barely afford an off-campus apartment, let alone tuition. Add in textbooks, food, car payments, car insurance, diapers, health insurance and all those fancy ass clothes you know she's used to and…" Adam snapped out of his mental tally as he realized Clay was gawking at him, mouth open.

Adam swiveled around, half expecting to see a zombie or some crazy shit behind him based on Clay's expression, but there was nothing out of the ordinary.

"What?" he asked.

Clay took his time picking his jaw up. "Something you're not telling me?"

Adam was confused for a moment, and then he realized what he'd said. "Fuck." He quickly tried to think of a way to play it off before deciding that would be pointless. And actually, now that someone knew, he felt a little relieved. He hadn't meant to tell, so it wasn't like he'd betrayed Ashley's trust, at least not on purpose.

Clay was still staring at him, shaking his head.

"We agreed not to tell anyone," Adam finally said.

Clay nodded and motioned for the bartender to bring them another round. "My treat," he told Adam. "You need it."

Adam chuckled, but it wasn't funny. Getting trashed tonight might help him feel better, but it wouldn't fix a damn thing. He talked with Clay about it for a while, glad to finally have a rational, non-hormonal sounding board, and then they both walked back to the marina. As he said goodnight to Clay, Adam pulled out his phone to send one last text to Ashley.

"My bed feels empty. I'm sorry. I miss you. Sweet dreams, Angel."

He knew she was still too pissed to reply, but it made him feel better.

In light of what Adam had inadvertently shared with Clay, he had no trouble getting Clay to cover for him at the marina so he could surprise Ashley at lunch. Visitors weren't allowed into the school for lunch, but Seniors could head out, so he texted Ashley and asked her to meet him outside. She was smiling as she walked towards him, so Adam heaved a huge sigh of relief.

Neither of them said anything as they collapsed against each other in a long, firm, hug. Ashley was the one to finally pull back and gaze up at Adam.

"I'm sorry," he said at the precise moment she said the exact same words.

"Jinx," she said with a grin.

Adam kissed her. It was the kind of kiss that bordered on inappropriate given that they were in her school parking lot. Okay, it crossed that line. But Adam didn't care. He was just so glad to have her back in his arms. He was rethinking the wisdom in having encouraged her to go back home, where she'd spent lots of nights away from him.

"Come on," he said. "You need to eat." He helped her up into the bed of his truck and handed her a giant sweet tea and a toasted bagel with cream cheese. Not the most romantic lunch, but bagels were the only carbs she'd actually eat and Adam was worried she hadn't been eating enough lately.

"Subtle," she said with a snort.

"What?"

"Trying to fatten me up?"

"Yes. Eat it."

Ashley smiled and started nibbling the bagel. Adam scooted in beside her, leaning back against the cab of the truck like she was, and started eating his own sandwich. In between bites, she told him more about her talk with her mom and what it was like being back home.

"I'm still not happy about how they reacted, or how they've treated you," she added. "And she said they still blame you for this, that you should have known better."

Adam laughed. "I should. I mean, I do. I knew we shouldn't have…"

"I was the one who said I couldn't get pregnant then," Ashley interrupted.

"I should have been more careful," Adam said. "Anyway, it doesn't matter now."

She nodded. "Well, my mom said they'd like to try to start over with you and get to know you better, when they stop being so mad."

He couldn't not laugh at that. "Sure. I'm up for that."

"And it was sort of nice being back in my old bedroom, although I slept like crap without anyone to snuggle with."

"I don't snuggle," Adam said, fighting back a grin.

She finished her bagel and wrinkled up the wrapper. "And I'm sorry about your mom. I hate that you don't have her anymore. It's not fair. I would've liked to meet her too."

"She would've liked you."

"Really?" Ashley looked surprised.

"Yeah. You kind of remind me of her," Adam said, and then he cringed at how that sounded. While Ashley had his mom's same fun-loving beach-oriented attitude and both women had blonde hair, his mom was definitely not hot or his type. "I mean, in a non-Oedipus complex sort of way."

Ashley giggled.

Adam let his mind drift back to his mom for a minute. Usually he stopped himself from going there because even though it had been a few years, it still hurt. He was equally pissed and sad that she was missing so much of his life.

"Honestly I don't even think she would've been that upset about this whole situation," he said. "I mean, I doubt she would've recommended it or anything, but even before she got cancer, she was really big on the whole carpe diem thing. She always said if there was something you wanted, you should go after it right away and not wait."

He paused. "I wanted you."

"You got me."

Adam tossed all of their trash into the deli bag and shook Ashley's drink to see if it was empty, handing it back to her when he confirmed it wasn't. "She always told me to follow my dreams and make things happen and not get caught up on what other people said I should do."

"I think she'd be really proud of you, Adam."

He squeezed her leg. Then he remembered something his father had said, when he was asking about whether Ashley's parents liked him. He'd known his mother grew up on the island and that her family had been wealthy, and he knew his father had grown up on the New England coast, like he had.

Adam shook his head, surprised he hadn't realized that earlier. Not that it changed anything. Apparently these South Carolina girls held too much appeal for the Bricker men to resist.

"I have to go in a minute," Ashley said. "My car is here though, so I'll meet up with you later so we can hang out. And then I need to take my stuff back to my parents."

"Okay."

"I guess from now until graduation, I'll basically just be living at home but without the stupid curfew and dating rules I had before." She paused. "It's not like they have to worry about you getting me knocked up again now."

Adam mustered a smile, but realized that his having already done to Ashley the worst thing imaginable to her parents was not exactly the best reason for them to lighten up on the rules. He wished it could be because he had proven he was trustworthy, not because he couldn't possibly screw up any more than he already had.

They kissed for a few minutes and then Ashley stood to climb out of the truck. Adam hopped down first, offering his hand for support. And then he remembered Clay.

"Oh shit," he mumbled. "I forgot to tell you. I met up with Clay for drinks last night after you left. I was not in good shape after our fight and I was stressing about everything and I sort of blabbed something about diapers."

"Diapers?"

Adam shrugged. "You know, how they're so expensive. Anyway, I didn't even realize I'd said it but Clay picked up on it and now he knows. He won't say anything to anyone, though. I'm really sorry."

"It's okay," Ashley said. She looked like she actually meant it. "If you keep feeding me bagels, people are going to know before school is out anyway."

She leaned in to kiss him again and then waltzed back into the building. He watched her leave, still no less enamored by her sexy butt than he had been the first time he'd seen her.

* * *

WHEN ASHLEY RETURNED to the building after her lunch with Adam, she had just enough time for a quick stop in the bathroom before class. As Ashley ducked into a stall, she realized her cheeks were already sore from smiling so much the last hour. She had known she and Adam would eventually make up, but the fact that they actually had done so was such a relief.

She turned to flush the toilet then gasped, unable to ignore the bright red stain on the toilet paper. Her breath caught in her throat. With shaky hands, she wiped again, only to confirm that she was bleeding.

Ashley called Adam immediately, hurrying back outside without notifying anyone at the school that she was leaving. Luckily, he hadn't gotten far.

Unsure of where else to go, they'd driven back to the Planned Parenthood clinic. The receptionist had initially refused to even let her sign in, insisting they needed to go to the emergency room. Ashley left Adam to deal with it, locking herself in the bathroom there, afraid to even leave the safety of the small sterile-smelling room until he knocked and told her the doctor would see them.

The next hour was a blur of tests and unfamiliar words. Ashley learned she had a chemical pregnancy or early miscarriage, but she tuned out the explanation of what that entailed. All she knew was that she was no longer pregnant.

Adam drove her to his place, but they didn't talk. Ashley wasn't sure how she felt yet, but she knew she wanted to stay with Adam until she'd sorted through all that. She texted her mother, keeping it brief.

"Miscarried. Not pregnant anymore. Do NOT want to talk about it. Staying at Adam's for a few days then will be home," she wrote.

Ashley braced herself before reading her mother's response, but all it said was "okay."

Ashley still wasn't sure what to say to Adam when they got

back to his place, so they just watched TV until well past midnight and then went to bed. The next morning, Adam called in sick to work and Ashley called herself in sick to school, pretending to be her mother, and then they resumed their binge watching.

After a few hours, Adam caught Ashley yawning.

"Do you want to nap?" he asked.

Ashley considered that option, but didn't actually feel sleepy. She shook her head.

"More Netflix?"

She shrugged.

"Do you want to talk?"

She nodded.

"Okay. Roll over. I'll give you a back rub while we talk."

Ashley complied willingly. They were both silent for several minutes as his hands worked their magic. He rubbed softly at first, as though he was afraid he might break her, but then worked into a light pressure massage.

"So…what do you want to talk about?"

"The baby," she said softly.

He waited, probably hoping she'd say more, but she couldn't. She wanted to know what he thought about it all.

Adam sighed, apparently reading her mind. "I thought a lot last night, but I still don't really know what to say to you. Or how I feel." He paused, but Ashley let him continue. "When you initially told me you were pregnant, my very first thought was, 'damn, I bet we make a cute baby.'"

Ashley smiled.

"But then when I thought about it more, I wasn't so happy. I thought about all the stuff you wanted to do in the next few years and how I want you to do all that stuff. I want you to have a care-free, fun summer filled with sushi and surfing and beer or what-ever other crazy shit you want to do. And then I want you to go off to college and take classes that actually interest you and live without your parents breathing down your neck. I want you to have time to make out on sandbars with me in between classes instead of working some crappy, low-paying job. I want you to wake up tired because you were at a crazy fun party and didn't stumble home till three a.m., not because you were up all night with a fussy baby. I want you to figure out what kind of career you want based on what you enjoy, not based on its flexibility or health benefits."

His massage slowed to a stop and he crawled onto the bed beside Ashley, his stomach and chest pressing against her back.

"But mostly I worried you would stay with me because of the baby and not because you wanted to stay with me. And I worried you would resent me for trapping you into this life so different from the one you deserved," he said.

Ashley swallowed hard, realizing she felt all the same worries, both about herself but also about him.

"So I guess that's a long-winded way of saying I should have felt relieved when they said you weren't pregnant anymore," he continued. "But I'm not."

Ashley rolled over to face him.

"I hate seeing you suffering. But I also keep thinking about how you would've been a good mom, even at nineteen. I can still picture the cute little baby we would've had and this crazy life that I know isn't realistic but would've had us together and happy. And if I'm being completely honest, part of me realizes now you'll figure out that everyone else is right and I'm not good enough for you, and that now that this happened, you are free to live your life as you would've before I waltzed in and screwed it all up."

"You thought about all that?" she asked.

Adam nodded. "Like I said, I didn't sleep much last night."

She wrapped an arm over his side. "I think all of that was exactly what I needed to hear."

He smiled and kissed her forehead. "How are you feeling?"

"I guess okay. Still a little crampy."

"I meant, um, emotionally," he clarified.

"Oh. Well, pretty much the same as you. I'm sad, but I'm relieved. And then I feel guilty about feeling relieved."

"Yeah," he agreed.

"Also, I'm worried about the future, for us. With the baby, I knew whatever happened in the next year, we would be together, but now it feels like everything is up in the air again. If I go away to school and you stay here…"

"You're not going to lose me, Ash. I can find work anywhere. If you want me to come with you, I will. If you want me to stay here so you can have a normal college experience, I will. I'm still yours, however far apart we are."

Ashley smiled. "That's really romantic."

Adam smirked.

"I feel like," Ashley started, then she stopped herself, aware she was oversharing. "Like way down the road when I'm like thirty-five or a normal age for babies, if I have a baby with someone else, I'm always going to be wondering what the baby with you would've been like and what she would've looked like."

"She?" he repeated.

"That's what I always pictured. You know, like if she'd have your bright blue eyes but lighter hair like me."

"Your perfect smile," he added. "Or whether she'd be born with tattoo-like birth marks all over her biceps."

Ashley giggled despite the tears rolling down her cheeks.

* * *

ASHLEY STAYED at Adam's house until Sunday, when Adam returned to work. He welcomed the distraction. Adam thought that sharing this awful experience with each other, and really no one else, would've brought him and Ashley closer together. Instead, he ended up feeling guilty and somewhat more distant from her. He knew she had told her parents, and that he'd have to tell Clay, but he felt like he couldn't share any intimate details about it or how he was feeling without betraying Ashley. And he certainly didn't want to burden her anymore with his thoughts about it all, since whatever he was feeling she had to be experiencing tenfold.

Ashley called him before bed Sunday night, as promised. After spending so many days and nights with her, it felt weird to say goodnight by phone, but Adam figured he should get used to it and be grateful that she'd reconciled with her parents. He asked how her parents had taken the news, and Ashley said her father hadn't mentioned a thing about it, but that when her mother was alone with her, she'd actually said she was sorry for everything they'd gone through. She also told Ashley that she'd had two miscarriages before conceiving Jackson, and that was why Ashley and her siblings were all so close in age. Apparently, her mom had expected to have more miscarriages after Jackson but, luckily, never did.

Adam wasn't sure what to make of it all, but he avoided Ashley's house and tried to follow her lead. Within another week, she seemed back to her normal perky self. She surprised him at the marina after school and waited around until he was off so they could take a boat ride.

"You seem happy," he said when they were finally alone.

"I am," she said, smiling and looping her arm through his elbow.

Adam stared intently at her as they walked, but couldn't find any sign that she wasn't telling the truth. "I'm glad," he finally said.

"I'm sorry I've been distant lately," Ashley said, climbing over the rope onto the boat.

"You don't have to apologize, Ash."

She raised an eyebrow as if she didn't believe him.

Adam untethered the boat and started the engine.

"I missed you," he said as they finally reached open water.

Her face lit up. "Yeah? Me too." Then she frowned. "It just felt like, I don't know, I needed to fix things with my parents and sort of forget about all of this. Is that terrible—to want to forget?"

Adam stilled the engine and came to sit by Ashley. "I don't think so. Pretty sure there's not a manual for how we should feel."

Ashley rolled her eyes. "God, it's really annoying how you always say exactly the right thing."

Adam tried to quash the grin. "Sorry."

"No you're not." Ashley swatted him playfully.

Adam caught his gaze slowly drifting down towards the v-neck of her tank top and quickly averted his eyes. He was determined not to ogle her and make her feel more self-conscious, especially right after she praised his perfection. When he finally glanced up again, Ashley was watching him, her bottom lip anchored under her teeth.

"Why do you do that?" she asked softly.

"What?"

"Look away." Ashley sighed. "I know you're probably still traumatized from everything you saw and you don't find me attractive anymore, but..."

"Ashley, stop," Adam interrupted, laughing despite his efforts not to. "Are you being serious right now? I find you immensely attractive now. I have been killing myself trying to avoid staring at you for too long because I'm afraid I'll combust or something."

"Really?"

Adam simply laughed in response.

"Then how come you don't touch me anymore? And you hardly even kiss me."

Before she could say anything else, he flew to her, kissing her until he was dizzy with desire and knew he was close to forgetting what he wanted to say. "Ashley, I want to touch you all the time. I love you more now than ever and I'm more attracted to you every day. I just didn't want to rush you back into anything. I don't even know if it's safe for us to…"

"It is," she said. "I had a follow-up appointment with my doctor this morning."

"Oh," Adam said, slightly miffed that she hadn't mentioned it.

"I'm totally healthy now, and we've got the all clear to resume any and all sexual activity," she said matter-of-factly. "And she put me on birth control pills, which I started taking today, but we have to use condoms for the rest of the month as a precaution."

"I think we can handle that." Adam replied, focusing all his energy on self-control.

"So….?"

Adam gazed down at the ground, certain he'd pounce on Ashley regardless of what she said if he kept staring at her any longer. The way the setting sun reflected off her golden hair reminded him of the first time he saw her, when he'd sworn she was an angel.

"Look, Ashley, just because the doctor says you're physically ready doesn't mean…" Adam cleared his throat awkwardly then gazed back up at her. Her bright green eyes were glistening like the water behind her and her lips curved upwards at one end in a subtle half grin. "Are you really ready? Because I'll wait until…"

Ashley's kiss cut off his words. Adam lifted Ashley onto his lap so she was straddling him and enjoyed the sensations washing over his body. After a moment he stood, carrying her with him, and carefully crept down the stairs into the cabin.

CHAPTER 18

hey lay in bed in the cramped cabin for close to an hour after making love. Ashley never felt more peaceful than she did curled up against Adam's body, her breath and heartbeat matching the rhythm of his own. She traced her finger along the ink decorating his arm and chest as she always did when they lay still like that, and she wondered if she could recreate the entire pattern on a piece of paper from memory by this point.

"I should go soon," she murmured, wishing it weren't true but not enough to risk the wrath of her parents. Since she'd moved back home, they'd left her alone for the most part. She didn't want to rock the boat.

Adam sighed and sat up, reaching for his shorts.

"Hey, actually, I wanted to tell you something first," Ashley said, smiling in anticipation of Adam's reaction to her news. Adam paused but didn't speak, so she continued. "Remember how I told you I applied to the College of William and Mary?"

Adam nodded.

"So, it wasn't the only back-up school I ultimately applied to, and I actually got in everywhere I applied."

Adam's eyebrows raised in confusion as he smiled. "That's great. I always knew you were brilliant. So, where else did you apply?"

"Well, there's Coastal Carolina University, which is the closest, really. Beautiful campus and literally just up the coast from here," she began, gauging Adam's expression although it remained unchanged. "Eckerd, down in St. Pete, oh, and Flagler, in St. Augustine."

"You applied to schools in Florida?" Adam interrupted. "I thought you said the humidity was unbearable."

Ashley shrugged. "It can't be much different than here, right? Anyway, Old Dominion in Virginia and then Endicott College."

Now Adam was frowning. "Isn't Endicott in Massachusetts?"

"Yes."

"Have you ever even seen the campus?"

Ashley shook her head, frustrated with the direction the conversation had taken. She reached for her clothes and started dressing.

Adam laughed then followed her lead, slipping quickly into his clothes. "That's a pretty random group of backup schools. What happened to all the others you'd mentioned?"

"Oh, well, once I got into Duke, I didn't really bother with any of the others. No point, right."

"So you applied to these schools first? I didn't even realize you were looking at any of these."

Ashley hesitated. "Well, no. I applied to these later."

"Why would you apply to back-up schools after getting accepted to your first choice school?"

"I thought maybe I'd be happier at one of these schools. When I picked Duke, I...well I'm not sure I still want the same things I wanted then."

Adam turned abruptly to her, his face solemn. "Wait, Ash, you're not saying you're actually considering going to one of these schools?"

Ashley shrugged. She started up the stairs to the main deck, annoyed that he hadn't reacted the way she'd hoped.

"Ashley, hang on." Adam followed her. "What makes you suddenly so interested in these schools? Do you have any idea how cold it is in Massachusetts in February? Have you ever seen snow?"

She rolled her eyes before turning away. "Don't patronize me."

Adam wrapped his arms around her waist and kissed her cheek before resting his head on her shoulder. "I'm sorry, babe. Help me understand here."

Ashley inhaled slowly then blew out her breath. "They're all on the coast, Adam. If you want to stay here, I can go to Coastal. If you want to move back up north, I can go to one of those schools."

Adam froze. Ashley waited a minute and then swiveled around to gauge his response. He gazed back at her sadly and shook his head.

"Didn't you already send your acceptance back to Duke?"

"Yes, but..."

"No," he said, kissing her before she could protest more. "You are going to Duke, and it will be fine. I told you before, we will work it out. You are not changing your college plans because of me. Understood?"

Ashley broke away and went to start up the engine. "Yes, dad," she retorted.

Adam shook his head, opening his mouth as though he were going to say something else, and then shut it. He took over steering from her, so Ashley went and sat at the bow.

* * *

Ashley's last weeks of school flew by, and before Adam knew it, he was wearing an overpriced rental tux and headed for his second senior prom.

Adam survived the pre-prom beach photo session and actually managed to enjoy himself at the dance. Right after the dance, they ditched their formal clothes and headed to the beach bonfire. Apparently, this was a tradition that seniors from the prep school carried out annually and no one, even the private security for the gated community, protested the loud music, underage drinking, or inevitable mess the following day.

He and Ashley both enjoyed a few beverages, toasted marshmallows for s'mores, and then chased each other around in the sand with gooey marshmallow fingers. There was more dancing, someone having apparently arranged for a pro to DJ the party, and possibly more drinking. By one a.m., the music had switched to softer, more chill tunes that weren't so danceable, and couples had started sneaking off together along the beach. By two o'clock, the party was dying down.

Adam stretched out on a lounge chair carefully placed right where the waves were currently hitting. As the tide was receding, he knew they'd stay dry there till morning. Ashley was still stumbling in a sexy sort of solo dance in front of him, but when she turned and gazed back at him, he patted the chair and she quickly joined him. He tucked the blanket they'd brought over them tightly. The temperature was pretty ideal, actually, and it was too early in the season for the worst of the bugs, but he didn't want to risk them both waking with a billion bites. Ashley was clearly drunk, which made her even more adorable and resulted in her being both very sleepy and oddly chatty, if not altogether coherent.

"I love you," she murmured, slipping her hand just inside the hem of his shirt. "You are the best prom date ever. Tonight was perfect."

"Yeah," Adam agreed, kissing her forehead. He let his eyes drift shut, exhausted from the day. He mumbled random noises in response to the weird comments Ashley made, not fully focusing on anything until she brought up colleges.

"I'm not going to Duke in the fall," she said matter-of-factly.

Adam's eyes popped open. "What? You didn't tell them that, did you?"

"No, but I will. My mind is made up. It's just a school. It's stupid, really. The more I think about it I don't even know why I picked it over the schools on the coast anyway."

"Umm maybe the fact that the academics are a billion times better, and it's more prestigious, and it has a gorgeous campus. Ashley, you love everything about Duke. Do you even know anything about these other schools? Are they even accredited?"

She snorted. "Adam, stop arguing. It's like you said—life is short. You should do what you love. And I love you."

"It's not a choice between me and Duke, Ashley. You can have both."

"You can never have both. It's always one or the other. And I choose you." Ashley yawned loudly at the end of her statement and then her head slumped against Adam's chest.

"Ash," he began, but then he stopped, tilting his head to the side and confirming that she had passed out. "You are going to Duke," he whispered, kissing her forehead.

* * *

ASHLEY AWOKE WITH A POUNDING HEADACHE, a completely numb arm, and a ridiculously dry mouth. She tried to slide off of the chair without waking Adam, but that proved challenging with the wobbly chair and only one fully functioning arm. She stood and stretched, surveying the damage around them. Only about a third of the party-goers remained, scattered along the beach looking every bit as disheveled as Ashley felt. Trash littered the sand, and her headache intensified just thinking about having to help clean it all up later in the day.

She made her way to the table that had served as the bar the night before, finding that it was completely void of any alcohol, but thankfully still had a few sealed bottles of water stashed off to the side. She snagged two and returned to Adam, who was rubbing his eyes wearily.

"Any bug bites?" he asked.

Ashley rubbed her hand along her ankles before shaking her head. "No, I think I'm good. You?"

Adam shook his head, grinning. She handed him a bottle of water then sat beside him.

"My head hurts," she said.

"I bet. I think a few Ibuprofen and a long nap might help."

Ashley nodded. "You okay?"

He shrugged. "More or less."

"We should head out. I'm starving and I want to get out of here before all these drunks wake up and start puking everywhere."

Adam laughed but stood slowly, stretching from side to side.

"How much do you remember from last night?" he asked.

"I think everything. Why?"

He shrugged. "You were saying some crazy shit right before we fell asleep."

Ashley gazed at the celadon sky, trying to remember. "Alright maybe not everything. What did I say?"

"You said you weren't going to Duke."

"Oh." Ashley hadn't remembered saying that, and frankly was annoyed that she had. After how badly he'd reacted the first time she brought it up, she hadn't wanted to start another discussion about it until it was all done.

"So…"

She stared at him, uncertain where he was going with his sentence.

"Is that true?"

"Adam, we shouldn't get into this now," she said, starting up the beach path and pausing for a minute to locate their shoes.

"Wow. So you're actually considering it?"

"Yes, I'm considering it. I don't know why you're being so stubborn about it. It's my decision, not yours."

"Yeah, it is. So do what's right for you, not me."

Ashley slowed her pace and let him catch up. "I'm doing what's right for both of us. In twenty years, it's not going to matter what school printed my degree. But it is going to matter who I'm with."

Adam reached for her hand and tugged her back to him. She tried to avoid his stare but he ducked lower and pulled her close for a long kiss.

When he released her, they walked back up the path in silence. Ashley assumed he was letting it drop, until much later, after they'd eaten breakfast and were parting ways for the day so they could both nap.

"Thanks again for last night," Ashley said, kissing him softly.

"My pleasure," Adam said, his trademark cocky grin on his face. "And you're going to Duke."

Ashley laughed but didn't re-engage in the discussion. She went home and slept until dinner, then helped pick up the beach. The next week was a blur with three days of classes, graduation rehearsal, then graduation, followed promptly by more parties.

Ashley spent her first day as a high school graduate at the beach, surrounded by a handful of her oldest friends. As was typical, the guys were running around playing volleyball and trying to "accidentally" volley the ball onto some cute tourist's towel, while Lisa, Katie and Ashley lounged in chairs, alternating between gossiping, reading, and snoozing.

Ashley was still exhausted from the week, so she leaned back in her chair and closed her eyes. She had nearly fallen asleep when she was overwhelmed by the sensation that someone was watching her. She opened her eyes abruptly and turned to see Mason seated in the sand beside her, his face eerily close.

She jumped, which in turn made him jump.

"Geez Mason, what are you doing?"

"I was trying to see if you were awake."

"Well, I'm wide awake now."

He laughed. "How was the party last night?"

Ashley gave him the quick version, then followed up with more specific answers about all the people he was curious about and the other random details. She knew he loved college, but he was clearly a bit envious of her final high school days, too.

"So, are you counting down the days till Europe?"

She shrugged, wishing he'd change the topic before she started crying.

"Oh, come on. You can sit on the beach when we get back. And there are beaches there."

"I know. I'm not worried about missing the beach," she said, surprised he even thought that.

Mason frowned, then quickly figured it out. "Oh. Adam is the issue. He seriously doesn't want you going to Europe? It's a once-in-a-lifetime opportunity."

Ashley rolled her eyes. It wasn't, of course. They'd taken family vacations to Europe before and surely would again, but that wasn't really the point. "Adam is fine with me going. He has his own stuff going on anyway."

"Does he?"

"Yes. He's going on a boating trip with his dad most of the time we're gone anyway."

"Huh."

Ashley didn't like Mason's tone, but she couldn't pinpoint exactly what was off about it. "What is that supposed to mean?"

Mason laughed. "I don't know. He just doesn't seem to have much of a life aside from you. And before you say anything, I think the exact same thing about you. It's like...you guys are just way too codependent. It's weird. Especially for high school."

"Neither of us are in high school," she reminded him.

He snorted. "You were different with Brent. You still saw your other friends, you worked, played tennis. Now it's like your whole life revolves around Adam. It's like you don't do anything without checking with him first."

Ashley gestured around. "He's not here now."

"Only because he's working, right? And still I'm surprised you're not just loitering around the marina waiting on him to get off."

"Someone seems a little jealous about not having a girlfriend."

Now it was Mason's turn to roll his eyes. "If having a girlfriend means every waking moment is consumed with the same person, I'm fine without. But seriously, you guys are just so intense. You're young. You aren't meant to have such a serious relationship now." He shook his head. "Probably a moot point anyway with you leaving for Duke in a couple months."

Ashley turned back to the water. Mason had effectively killed her good mood.

"Oh come on, don't get all pouty. This trip will be good for you. It'll remind you that you can still have fun when you're not glued to Tattoo Guy."

Ashley opened her mouth to defend Adam, to remind Mason how amazing and supportive Adam had been through everything, but she stopped. Jackson—for some crazy reason—had never told the twins about the pregnancy. She wasn't sure if it was because he was embarrassed of her or something Adam had said when they were stuck in the jail cell together.

"Everything I do, whether or not Adam is with me, is more fun now because he's in my life. And you will understand that someday if you ever find a girl dumb enough to love you," Ashley finally said, lifting her book up to signal the end of the discussion.

Mason snickered but took the hint and stood, spraying sand on Ashley's legs as he scampered back towards the volleyball game.

CHAPTER 19

Adam spent as much time as he could with Ashley over the next few days, but they were hardly ever alone since she had so many graduation open houses and parties to attend. He was working a lot, trying to compensate for the next two weeks that he'd miss when he and his dad went back north by boat. The timing of the trip was perfect, since Ashley would be in Europe while he was gone anyway, but it was going to be weird going so long without talking or texting after being so close for nearly a year.

Ashley was scheduled to leave on a Wednesday. Adam and his father would set sail on Friday morning. Adam worked all day Monday and then Tuesday morning, planning to spend the afternoon and, ideally, the entire night, with Ashley. Since he was leaving early, he hadn't planned on taking a break, so he was surprised when Clay came and said he would take over for Adam at the counter.

"No, I'm good," Adam insisted.

Clay tilted his head towards the dock, where a man in full business attire stood waiting. "Mr. Kensington is here and wants to chat with you."

Adam winced. He had never spoken alone with Ashley's dad, and, since the whole pregnancy thing, actually hadn't spoken with the man at all. Ashley said her parents had forgiven him and were trying to like him, but Adam still felt his pulse quicken at the thought of being alone with him.

"I don't suppose he said what it was about?"

Clay shook his head, looking somewhat sympathetic.

"Crap. Well, if I go missing, have the police dredge those lagoons by her house. Lots of gators that he could probably feed me to."

Clay laughed and Adam ducked around the counter, wishing he had worn something other than shorts and a white sleeveless shirt. Ashley's dad may have been aware of all the tattoos by this point, but actually seeing them might push him over the edge.

He slipped his sunglasses over his eyes as he exited the shop, slowly approaching Mr. Kensington as though he were a rabid animal.

"Mr. Kensington," he said politely. "How are you?"

"Well," the man said, turning and extending his hand politely. "And yourself?"

"Good," Adam said with a gulp.

"If you have a few minutes, I thought we could go have a chat. I can take you to lunch if you have a change of clothes," Ashley's dad said, staring at Adam's attire as though he were naked.

"Uh, this is all I got here. Sort of the, uh, standard uniform for the marina," Adam said. "But we can head over there if you want." He gestured to the café around the corner.

"Okay," Mr. Kensington agreed reluctantly.

They were seated at a booth inside the restaurant where Adam immediately felt even more underdressed. A waitress quickly took their orders and then left.

Mr. Kensington made polite small talk, pretending to be interested in Adam's boat and his work at the marina, until the food arrived. Just as Adam launched into the first bite of his cheeseburger, Mr. Kensington's tone changed.

"I suppose you're wondering why I came to see you today," he said.

Adam nodded, still chewing.

The older man sighed. "Well, first off, I realize the last time we really spoke, I may have said some less than flattering things. I wanted to apologize for that. As you can probably imagine, I was not expecting to hear that news from my daughter and obviously I was not happy. Frankly, when she first brought you over, that was precisely what I envisioned happening—you getting her pregnant and screwing up her chances at Duke."

Adam opened his mouth to speak, but Ashley's father continued.

"Even though it turns out I was right about that from the start, I do see now that I misjudged you. You showed considerable maturity and integrity in the way you handled the entire… situation, and for that I am appreciative."

Mr. Kensington paused now to work on his own sandwich, but Adam no longer knew what to even say.

"I know Ashlynne cares deeply for you, and I can tell you really care about her as well, but I have some concerns."

Adam chugged his soda, determined to get rid of the growing lump in his throat. "What kind of concerns?"

"Well, Duke, for starters. Ashley has been very excited about spending her college years at Duke for as long as I can recall. When her brothers went on college tours, she came along and compared every place we visited to Duke and found nothing really measured up. She frankly never even mentioned the possibility of another university until recently, when we found a brochure for some local college in her room."

Adam felt the lump growing larger.

"Ashley is a bright girl, with a lot of potential. She has big dreams, and they depend on her getting a good education that only a place like Duke can provide."

"I agree," Adam chimed in, eager to have her father know they were actually on the same team for once.

This clearly surprised the man. He leaned back and gazed warily at Adam for a moment. "Did you know she was considering other schools?"

"No," Adam said. "Well, yes, but only recently. I told her she should go to Duke."

Her father nodded. They both ate in silence for a moment before he continued. "My concern is that, at eighteen years old, Ashlynne doesn't have an objective lens for viewing her future and how choosing a relationship over her education would affect her long term. At twenty, you probably have a better handle on your priorities."

Adam still wasn't sure where Ashley's dad was headed with all this, but it couldn't be good.

"Let me rephrase," he continued. "I think Ashley believes she's found her soul mate, and that you two will live happily ever after in your cardboard boxes or whatever it takes, and that she doesn't need anything but you to be happy. But you and I know the reality, that the statistical probability of you both being together in ten years, or even five years, is negligible at best. People change in their teen years, and no matter what she does about college, you'll grow apart and eventually move on. My concern is that, in the meantime, Ashley will make decisions which ruin her life."

"Ashley's a smart girl," Adam said. "I trust her to make the best decisions for her life."

Mr. Kensington chuckled. "She is a smart girl. But she's a smart girl who got herself knocked up in high school. And that's exactly my point. She's so enamored with you that she is reckless. She acts without considering long-term effects of her actions."

Adam wasn't sure what to say. The man seemed to have a point.

"We both have already agreed that the best thing for her is to attend Duke University in the fall. And that's what she truly wants, too."

Adam nodded, still nervous.

"You and I can work together here to make sure that happens."

"Sure."

Mr. Kensington shook his head. "Adam, as long as she's involved with you, she's not going to move five hours away. And even if she did, she still would miss out on most of the college experience. She needs to have time to explore campus, participate in extra-curricular activities, network, and make new friends. At eighteen, Ashley is just learning who she is, and she can't do that if she only sees herself as a part of a couple. She needs to be free to truly engage in everything college has to offer her."

Adam dropped his gaze to the table, now certain exactly where this was going. "You want me to break up with Ashley before she leaves for college."

Mr. Kensington motioned for the check before shaking his head dismissively at Adam. "Are you familiar with the phrase, 'if you truly love something, set it free'?"

Adam nodded.

"That's what I want. I want you to show you love her enough to give her a real chance at a positive college experience. If you two are truly soul mates, fine. She'll have a couple years at Duke and then you can rekindle the romance while she finishes her degree. You'd both be closer than ever then, having had the opportunity to really mature and see what you want for your lives."

"I don't think..." Adam began, but Mr. Kensington cut him off.

"Look, I know how this must sound to you, and I apologize for being brisk here but I have a meeting back on the mainland in an hour, so I'm going to cut to the chase. You have an opportunity here to prove you are the kind of man that is worthy of my daughter. You can make the mature decision and put Ashley and her happiness first."

He paused to scribble his signature on the credit card receipt. Adam was too flabbergasted to speak.

"I understand that you'll be headed out on a boat trip while we are overseas and that you'll return to the island a few days before us. I want you to take that time when you get back to pack up, leave the island, and cut off all communications with Ashley."

"You want me to move away without telling her?"

"No, of course not. You can tell her, just please wait till we are done with our trip. Obviously, I know she's going to be upset for a little while and you don't want to ruin her time in Europe."

"I have a job here," Adam began.

"I understand. And to show you how much I regret inconveniencing you with my request, I've arranged to pay off the remainder of your boat loan and your truck loan, so you should have some time without your normal expenses to look for a new position in a different town."

Adam felt sick. He knew Ashley's dad could be a jerk, but offering him money to abandon Ashley was a new low.

Mr. Kensington sighed, probably reading the disgust on Adam's face. "Just to be clear, there isn't any other viable option here. If Ashley continues seeing you, she will be doing so without my financial support. She will be responsible for her own car, housing, food, clothing and tuition for Duke, or wherever she chooses. I am not going to sit back and let her ruin her life over a teenage romance, so if I have to be the bad guy to make my point, I will."

Mr. Kensington stared pointedly before continuing. "Or, you can choose to be the bigger man and put Ashley's happiness first. Leave town while we're gone, let her mourn the relationship this summer and head off to college in the fall free of any obligations. It's up to you, but if you think my daughter will be happier with you than with a college degree, car, home, and carefree life, you don't know her as well as you think you do."

He stood to leave.

"Oh, and I'd appreciate you keeping this to yourself. If Ashley finds out about the terms of our agreement here, I will not be financing either of your vehicles." He smiled at Adam. "Have a good trip."

Adam sat, slack-jawed, for several minutes, certain he must have misunderstood. When he finally fostered the energy to stand and return to work, Clay eyed him warily.

"Uh oh. What happened?"

Adam shook his head. "I wouldn't even know where to start."

He focused on his work the next two hours, determined not to let what Mr. Kensington had said ruin his last night with Ashley before vacation. He hated the thought of keeping a secret from her, but he knew he couldn't tell her before her trip what her father had said. He wanted her to enjoy Europe, and that wouldn't happen if she knew what a bastard her dad was, especially since she'd be with him nonstop the next few weeks. Adam told himself it didn't matter anyway. He obviously wasn't going to do what her dad wanted, so there was no harm waiting until Ashley returned to tell her.

They'd planned a quiet afternoon at the beach together, kayaking back to the sandbar she'd showed him the summer before, followed by dinner on the boat. Ashley looked gorgeous, of course, and they had a blast together. He could tell she was a little uneasy about her upcoming trip, but they didn't discuss it until that night, when they were snuggled together on the deck of the boat several miles from shore.

"It's going to suck being stuck with my family for the next

three weeks, especially since we can't even talk," Ashley said. "I'm going to miss you."

"I know," Adam agreed. "But with you in Italy and Portugal and Greece, and me cruising along the Atlantic, it's just too hard. If we tell ourselves no calls or texts, it'll be less frustrating than if we both try in vain to get in touch." He traced his finger along her arm. "And you're going to have a blast."

She shook her head, her expression somber. "I'll be missing you too much to enjoy any of it."

Adam gazed out over the dark water. He hoped she was just saying that for his sake, because she deserved a fun vacation. Besides, if her father had been serious earlier about cutting her off, it might be the last nice vacation she'd ever take.

"Ash, I want you to have fun. You can't miss out on stuff because of me."

"I'm sure it won't be miserable, it's just going to be hard because whenever I see something cool or do something really fun, I'm going to think about how much I'd like to be sharing it with you."

She leaned back against his chest and Adam inhaled the tantalizing fruity scent of her hair. He was going to miss that. He was excited about riding the open seas with his dad, but nothing on the boat would smell as good as Ashley.

"Hey, Ashley," he began. "Random, but do you remember when we went to talk to your dad about the baby, and he said he'd cut you off financially if you didn't do what he wanted?"

"Kinda hard to forget."

"Yeah," he agreed. "But you don't think he actually would've done it, do you?"

"Yes."

"Yes?" Adam repeated it, hoping he'd misunderstood.

"Adam, he kicked his pregnant teenage daughter out of the house because I didn't do what he wanted. Of course he was serious."

She snuggled closer to his neck. "My dad means well, but he can be pretty manipulative, and he can be a total jerk if he doesn't get his way. You wouldn't believe some of the things I've heard he's done to business associates who crossed him. I don't doubt for a second that he'd cut me off if it suited him."

Adam swallowed nervously. Ashley was accustomed to really expensive things, and he suspected she had no realistic idea of actual living costs. Her only work experience had been a couple of years teaching tennis to little kids on a very part-time basis. She'd never be happy working a full-time job just to make ends meet, especially with all her friends still living the easy life.

And even if her dad didn't cut her off financially, what did that mean for Duke? If she was dreading a dream trip to Europe because it meant being apart from Adam, how was she going to enjoy the college experience? She'd never try anything new or have any real fun if she was always pining for him.

"Hey," Ashley whispered, cutting into his thoughts. "Earth to Adam. You zoned out there for a minute. Does that mean you're ready to head back below deck for bed? I mean, after round two, of course."

He laughed. "You're up for a second round?"

"Hey, I need to get enough of you to last me nearly a whole month."

Adam grinned. "In a few minutes," he said.

For now, he just wanted to hold her as long as he could. Adam was suddenly overwhelmed with the need to memorize every detail about her—from the way her body curved against his, to the silky texture of her hair. He focused on her laugh, and how she squeezed her eyes shut when something struck her as really funny, and the way she said his name when they were making love, as though she were thanking him and worshiping him all at once.

Everything about Ashley was just so perfect. Too perfect, really. He'd always known it couldn't last.

* * *

ON HER LAST night with Adam, Ashley tried to stay awake, but she must have finally dozed off around dawn. She wasn't worried about being tired, since she planned to sleep the duration of the flight. Adam insisted he'd slept some, but she was pretty certain he hadn't. He kept telling her how beautiful she was, and how happy she'd made him, and even how she could do anything she put her mind to. He was so sappy she knew he must be sleep deprived.

Saying goodbye was brutal, but she did it, and she managed to hold it together until the airport, where she promptly popped a sleeping pill. Throughout her trip, she'd considered calling or texting him a couple times, just to see if it worked, but instead, she emailed. Ashley wasn't sure if he could check email on the boat, so while she was bummed that he didn't write back, it wasn't altogether surprising.

Ashley dialed Adam, the moment her plane landed, not even waiting till they were in the terminal. But instead of hearing Adam's voice, it was a weird recording saying the number had been disconnected. Ashley sighed and sent a text instead, but it bounced back. She tried to get her parents to have the driver drop her off at the marina on the way home from the airport, but her mom insisted she come home then drive herself. Ashley reluctantly agreed, realizing this plan at least enabled her to take a quick shower and changing out of her stale flight clothes before surprising her sweetie.

She had just finished showering and slipped into a tank top and a pair of faded cut off jean shorts that her mom had declared "too short" for the trip when there was a knock on her door. Before she could answer, Austin trudged in, his arms overflowing with envelopes and magazines.

"Yikes. What's all that?"

"Your mail," he said with a groan.

Ashley wrinkled her nose. "I'll look later."

"Looks like you got your dorm and roommate assignments from Duke," he said, waving a thick packet.

Ashley's stomach muscles tightened. She had made her final decision about college over vacation, and it didn't involve Duke. She was waiting till they returned to tell her family so that they didn't try to murder her overseas. She knew she was cutting it close on deadlines, but she figured someone had to drop out of Coastal Carolina last minute and, waitlist or not, a little financial incentive from her family would ensure their spot would be hers.

"Nope. Headed out to see Adam," she said, swiping on lip gloss and grabbing her phone.

"You got something from him, too," Austin said, still leafing through her mail.

Ashley turned and swiped the envelope from him. "Snoop," she mumbled, tearing it open. She had sent him a few postcards but hadn't really expected a letter from him. She smiled as soon as she saw his familiar scrawl:

Dear Ashley,

Over the past year, you have made me happier than I ever knew I could be. You are the sweetest, funniest and most gorgeous woman I've ever met and I still can't believe you ever gave me a chance. I hate telling you this by letter, but I don't have the strength to say it to your face. I am leaving the island for good. By the time you return from Europe, I'll be on a long-term merchant vessel with my father. I'm already miserable without you, but I know in the long run this is better for you. You are vibrant and full of potential and I can't be the one to hold you back. I want you to have a fun summer and a carefree time at Duke.

I never meant to hurt you. I hope someday you realize you are better off without me and you find all the happiness you deserve. I love you more than you'll ever know.

Adam

. . .

ASHLEY SUNK ONTO HER BED, feeling her heart beat erratically, frantically re-reading the letter.

"Ash, what's wrong?" Austin asked.

Ashley felt tears brimming in her eyes and raised the paper to her face, as though she could somehow smell Adam through the ink. Then she shook her head and read it one last time before letting it fall to the ground and staring blankly ahead.

It had to be a joke. There was no other rational explanation. It looked like Adam's handwriting, but obviously it wasn't. Adam would never do that to her. He would never leave without saying goodbye. He would never abandon her.

Austin bent down to retrieve the letter, a concerned look on his face. Ashley knew she must look insane right now but she didn't care.

"Jesus," he muttered, finishing reading the letter.

"I need to go," she said, standing up. The sooner she got to Adam's, the better. Then she would see that he was still there, that this was all some big misunderstanding.

"Ash, you can't..." Austin began, but she was already headed down the stairs. He grabbed her arm as she launched into the garage and snatched the keys away. "I'll drive you," he said.

She was too frazzled to argue.

Thankfully, Austin drove fast, and Ashley jumped out of the car before he'd even parked it, jogging over to the surf shop. She prayed she'd see Adam as she drew closer, but instead she saw Clay.

"Is Adam here?" she asked.

Clay frowned, and the look on his face filled Ashley with dread. She told herself she was seeing things, that it would all still be okay, and she raced over to his condo, pounding on the door until her fist went numb. When there was no answer, she sunk to the floor outside his door and sobbed uncontrollably.

She wasn't sure how long she'd been there when Austin found her.

"Ashley," he began, but she cut him off.

"No. Just no," she said, shaking her head definitively.

He sighed and sat beside her. "I talked to Clay. Adam isn't coming back to work. He quit before his boat trip with his dad."

"He wouldn't do that," she insisted.

"Clay said he packed up the condo and they're renting it out. He's not here, Ashley. He's not coming back."

"Would you stop saying that? He is coming back. You don't know anything! Why are you even here?" Ashley tried to stand up, but was so consumed that her legs wobbled. Austin reached to grab her and held her tightly while she sobbed.

* * *

THE REMAINDER of the week was a blur. Ashley wasn't sure if she got out of bed or even if she ever slept while she was in her bed. It didn't matter. Nothing really did, any more. She read Adam's letter until she'd memorized it, but it didn't make any more sense the hundredth time she read it than it had the first. They'd been so happy, so in love. She knew they were.

What had happened?

*a*dam tried to lose himself in the day-to-day activities on the boat. He didn't want to think about what day it was because he didn't want to think about what Ashley was doing. When he couldn't sleep at night, which was often, he would remember how she was when he first saw her. She was smiling, laughing, and always happy. Adam knew that that was what had attracted him to Ashley in the first place, the way she seemed so carefree and chipper, like nothing could rain on her parade.

Adam told himself that, since Ashley had been happy long before him, she would be happy after him. To some extent, that was comforting, even if he was still miserable.

The two-week boat trip with his dad had been cool, aside from the times where he let himself think about how he was actually leaving Ashley for good, and not just for a few weeks. But being on the merchant vessel wasn't as exciting. The other guys were fine, but Adam couldn't exactly whine about leaving behind the love of his life to a bunch of men who all spent the majority of their days out to sea.

Adam spent hours each day reminding himself that what he'd done had been the right thing. Attending Duke was Ashley's life-long dream. Loving her meant making sure her dream came true. And if he hadn't left the way he had—cutting off all ties, changing his number, and basically disappearing, Adam knew Ashley would've found a way to convince him he was making a mistake.

Even without actually talking to her, Adam heard Ashley's voice in his head all the time. He knew exactly what she would've said when she realized he made a decision about her life without even consulting her. She'd told him countless times how insulting it was that her brothers and father treated her like a child, assuming they knew better than she did. And now, Adam had gone and done the same thing.

And what for? Adam told himself it was for her, but was it really? Sure, Ashley seemed to like her expensive lifestyle. But it wasn't like she'd asked for it. She'd never said she had to have a beachfront mansion, high-end clothes, or a luxury car after graduation. Everyone just assumed she'd always want that.

The more he thought about it, the more he realized Ashley had been perfectly content staying in his crammed condo with him. And whenever she'd had a choice between Adam and anything else in her life, she'd chosen him.

What the fuck had he done?

* * *

ADAM DROVE his boat back down the coast, hoping he'd figure out a plan to get his truck to the island soon enough. It was late afternoon when he reached the marina, and Clay was just closing up shop for the day.

"Well, look what the tide washed up!" Clay teased, leaning in to pat Adam on the back. "Glad to see you, man."

"You too," Adam said, nervously peering around.

Clay followed his glance and then shook his head. "She isn't here. I haven't seen her around here any since you left."

Adam shrugged as though he hadn't been looking for Ashley,

then quickly came to his senses and realized Clay was probably the one person on this island who didn't hate him now. He might as well be honest.

"You haven't seen her at all?" Adam asked, wondering if maybe she just left town too.

"Didn't say that. Just not at the marina. She's on the beach all day every day. Still with her usual crowd as far as I can tell."

Adam blew of out a sigh. "She must hate me."

Clay locked the last cabinet beneath the marina kiosk and then shoved the keys in his pocket. "Her brothers asked about you. The twins. They didn't seem too thrilled about the way you packed up and left with no goodbye."

"They should've been happy," Adam said, gritting his teeth together. Really, he just couldn't win with the Kensingtons. They hated him when he was with Ashley, and hated him when he left her. He couldn't blame them for not respecting the way he'd left, though. It was a shitty move.

"I fucked up," Adam said. "That day at the marina, when Mr. Kensington came to see me…"

"I remember. You left to have lunch with him and then you were all shaken up when you came back."

Adam shook his head, wishing he could go back in time. "He told me to leave town. He…" Adam paused, too ashamed to even tell his friend the rest. "I wasn't planning to do it, but then it really did seem like Ashley was going to bail on Duke if I was still in the picture. I told myself it was the right thing to do, leaving like that."

Clay grimaced.

Both men were silent for a moment.

"You need a lift to her house?" Clay offered.

Adam nodded. "Thanks."

Clay made small talk during the short drive, but Adam was too anxious to say anything. When Clay pulled up in front of the house, Adam wiped his hands on his thighs and inhaled sharply.

This wasn't going to be easy, but he was ready to get it over with.

As he watched Clay driving off, Adam panicked, instantly regretting not having asked Clay if Ashley was dating someone else. But then, he told himself it didn't matter. He owed her an apology, regardless of whether it was too late to salvage the relationship. And he needed to speak with her father.

Adam stood at the door for a moment before ringing the bell, half expecting attack dogs to chase him off the porch. When nothing happened, he rang the bell, only to find himself instantly regretting it.

The light by the front entry flicked on and the door opened. It was Ashley's mom. She seemed surprised to see Adam, but not necessarily in a bad way.

"Adam! What brings you by? Ashlynne's not home," she said, motioning for him to come inside.

"Oh," he said lamely, stepping just far enough inside so she could shut the door. He knew how determined those southerners were to keep the cold air inside and the insects outside. "I actually came to speak to Mr. Kensington, but if he's not here..."

"He's just out back," she interrupted. "Follow me."

Adam nodded politely, reminding himself to breathe as he made his way to the back of the house. He tried not to look around much, the house filled with too many obvious reminders of Ashley and how happy he had been in South Carolina.

"Can I get you a drink?"

"Uh, water would be good, please," Adam said, his throat nearly too dry to speak. He hesitated by the back door as Mrs. Kensington went towards the kitchen.

"You can go on out," she said.

Adam groaned silently but slid the door open. Mr. Kensington was seated with a glass of wine in his hand. Across the table from him sat Jackson, looking even more intimidating than Adam remembered. They both looked up immediately.

"Adam," Mr. Kensington said in a matter-of-fact tone. "I wasn't expecting to see you."

Adam nodded and cleared his throat. "Hello, sir. I just came to give you the boat. I shouldn't have accepted it to start with, so I apologize. I, uh, left the truck up in Nantucket, but I figure if you sell the boat it'll cover what you paid on that too, so hopefully we can call it even." He reached in his pocket and retrieved the keys, dropping them on the table beside Mr. Kensington. "It's parked at the marina, slip 47."

Mr. Kensington glanced down at the keys then back to Adam. "It's a little more complicated than that, I'm afraid."

Adam swallowed. "Well, let me know what I need to do to pay you back. I want out of our deal."

Mrs. Kensington arrived with the water just then. "What deal?" she asked casually, sliding the glass to Adam and motioning for him to sit.

Adam remained standing, unwilling to get any closer to Jackson, who was now eying him like he was seconds away from breaking his jaw. "With the, uh, boat, ma'am."

"Boat?" she repeated, turning to her husband.

Mr. Kensington turned to his wife. "Remember when I said I had that little chat with Adam? I helped him pay off his boat as his parting gift."

"It wouldn't be right for me to keep it because I'm going to talk to Ashley. I was wrong to leave like I did, and um, I want to apologize to her." Adam finally said, bracing himself.

Mr. Kensington remained silent. Mrs. Kensington cleared her throat and turned to Adam, instructing him to sit down. This time, he did. Then she turned to her husband.

"You gave him a boat on the condition that he not speak to your daughter?"

Mr. Kensington sipped his wine in lieu of responding to his wife, so she turned to Adam.

He shrugged. "More or less."

"And you accepted?"

Adam frowned, aware that he had now actually earned the disdain they'd clearly felt for him from the start. "Yes," he said. "At the time, I thought he was right, that Ashley would be better off without me in her life. I didn't want to hold her back and I didn't want her to get cut off financially just because of me."

Mrs. Kensington turned to her husband, an icy stare on her face. "You threatened to cut her off?"

"It was a bluff," he said calmly.

Adam gulped some of the water. Never before had he felt so stupid or weak as he did now. "I did what I thought was best and since then, I realized Ashley is a smart woman and can make her own decisions. I didn't mean to hurt her and I shouldn't have taken anything from you to start with, so I'm sorry."

Ashley's parents sighed in unison. Adam was about to stand to excuse himself when Mrs. Kensington spoke again.

"You know, Adam, when everything happened with…well, in the spring," she began, "I was of course disappointed about it all but I was also impressed with the maturity you showed in handling it all. I thought you truly loved Ashlynne and that we could trust you to take care of her at least."

"I did," Adam said. "I still do love her. I'm sorry that I let everyone down."

"Have you started seeing someone else?" she asked.

Adam hadn't expected that question. "No. I'm…I miss Ashley. Being away has been…hard."

She turned to her husband. "I can't believe you would do this. You saw how miserable she's been."

"She's fine. Kids break up and move on. It's part of growing up."

"She's not fine and you'd know it if you ever spoke to her."

Mr. Kensington frowned. "Anyone who would pick a boat over my daughter isn't worth her love. It's better for her to learn that now."

Mrs. Kensington started to reply but Adam interrupted. He had to get out of there.

"I screwed up and I know I don't deserve her. But I need her to know why I did what I did and that my feelings for her were real.

"Do you expect her to forgive you?" Mr. Kensington asked.

Adam shrugged. "I don't know. But she deserves to know the truth."

Mrs. Kensington glanced at her husband, who sighed reluctantly.

"I don't know if Ashley will even forgive me, but I don't want to sneak around anymore. If she decides she wants to be with me and that means you won't support her, I will find a way to do it. I have my captain's license and completed some courses in boat repair before I moved here so I can get another job or two or whatever it takes. Although I don't think it's fair that she has to pick between me and her family anyway." Adam shifted to stand but was too shaky to even move. He couldn't actually believe he'd just said that to her father.

"Well, Adam, I admire your integrity at least," Mr. Kensington began. "That was very honorable of you to come here first and tell us your intentions and return the boat."

Adam nodded, mumbled a thank you, and stood, praying his legs still worked.

"We'll support her decision, whatever that is. And we will still pay for Duke, obviously." Mrs. Kensington said, flashing a pointed stare at her husband.

Mr. Kensington stood. "When did you take these courses on boats?"

Adam relaxed a bit at the question. "I took nine months of certification classes up north right after high school graduation. And I spent some time on a merchant vessel after leaving here and got my official captain's license."

"Why didn't you mention any of that before? When we met

you, you led me to believe you had no aspiration in life but to rent out jet skis to tourists."

Adam sighed, tempted to just leave now that he'd said his bit. "It didn't seem important. Ashley liked me for me, and not my earning potential. I understand money is necessary—I saw how much my mother's treatments cost and I'm grateful we had the money for that. But if there's one thing I learned from her, it's that life is too short to focus on anything but what makes you happy. And being on the water, and sharing that with other people, that makes me happy. But being with Ashley made me even happier, so if I need to give up all the boating stuff and lock down some 9-5 job to be with her, I'd do it."

Adam started to the door when he felt a hand on his back. He turned to see Mr. Kensington handing him the keys.

"Keep your boat," he said. "No strings attached. It's too big of a hassle for me to sell it anyway."

"I don't…" Adam began.

"I'll walk you out," Jackson interrupted, standing abruptly. He nudged Adam as he brushed by, starting for the steps at the back of the deck.

Adam clenched the keys tightly in his fist, feeling the metal tip digging into his palm as he reluctantly followed Jackson. At the bottom of the steps, a series of concrete stepping stones led towards the beach, giving way to a wooden plank beachwalk after several yards. Adam had followed this path countless times with Ashley, but now as he reached the worn wood, he couldn't shake the doomsday feeling that he was walking the plank.

Abruptly, Jackson stopped and turned. Adam braced himself, fully aware he deserved whatever punches Jackson threw.

"She was a mess when you left," he said. "Still is, really."

"I'm sorry," Adam mumbled, acutely aware of what an understatement that was.

"I didn't like you at first and then somehow you convinced us all that you weren't the jerk we pegged you as. But now it turns out you were just fooling us all from the start."

Adam dropped his gaze to his worn, sandy shoes. Jackson was right and Adam knew it. But he also realized Jackson wasn't the one who deserved his apologies.

"I fucked up, and yeah, she deserves some perfect guy like Brent, but I still love her. And I need to talk to her."

Jackson's expression was completely unreadable as he stared back at Adam. Finally, Adam stepped around Jackson and picked up the pace, but before he got more than a couple feet away, Jackson's fingers clenched around Adam's arm.

"If you hurt her again, I'll kill you," Jackson said. The look in his eyes left no question that he meant it, too.

Adam nodded. "Understood." If he hurt her again, well, he deserved whatever he had coming at him.

Adam planned to take off his shoes as he reached the end of the beach walk, but as he glanced towards the water, he saw her. She sat at an angle, mostly facing the water. Her chair was alone on the stretch of beach, but the tide hadn't yet erased the evidence that others had been with her earlier. Her hair sparkled in the last rays of sunlight, and it fell over her shoulders, obstructing his view of her face.

Adam meant to say something to Jackson, to thank him for leading him there or something, but his feet moved as though he were being pulled towards her.

"Ashley," he said softly when he was only a few yards away.

She glanced up, and he immediately saw it—the sadness in her bold emerald eyes where they used to twinkle. He took a deep breath, stepped closer, then dropped down to his knees beside her.

"Ashley, I'm so sorry," he said.

CHAPTER 21

*A*shley wondered if she was hallucinating. One minute she was staring at the ocean, trying to will herself to pack up her chair and return to the house, and the next minute, Adam was kneeling at her feet apologizing. She stared at him, confused. Was it actually him? Why was he here? She glanced past Adam, hoping to gauge from the surroundings whether he was some apparition or reality.

Adam gazed up at her right as she looked down, locking her eyes on his bold, blue eyes, now damp with emotion. "Are you really here?" she whispered, reaching for his hand. He nodded and breathed a laugh.

Ashley dropped her phone, launching herself forward into his arms. Adam caught her then stood slowly, lifting her with him so she was forced onto her toes.

"God, I've missed you," he said softly, his breath falling on her ear. "I'm so sorry."

Ashley wanted to hold onto his embrace as long as possible, knowing how uncertain the future between them was. If this was the only moment she got, she didn't want to waste it. She squeezed her eyes shut, breathing in his familiar sporty scent and running her hands along his firm arms. She opened her eyes as Adam set her down and realized Jackson was standing in the background.

She gazed over at him, now even more confused.

Adam turned, following her stare, then explained, "I stopped by the house to talk to your dad. Jackson told me you were here."

Ashley nodded. "Thank you," she said to her brother. Her voice came out much quieter than she'd intended, so she wondered if he'd actually heard her or just read her lips, but he nodded and then swiveled around and walked off.

Ashley turned back to Adam, who she realized was clearly checking her out. She wore a plain yellow bikini, but as the sun had set, she'd pulled a gauzy white cover up on over. She hadn't bothered with any jewelry and her hair was just loose on her shoulders, but at least she'd worn a little makeup. She would've made an extra effort if she'd known she would actually see Adam again. Since he left, she hadn't had a reason to dress up.

"I don't understand," she said finally. "Where did you go? And why? Why are you back now? Are you back? For real?" Ashley sucked in a deep breath, realizing she sounded like a whiny child now that she'd started to cry again. "What did I do?" she asked.

Adam grabbed her hands and squeezed them until she looked back at his face. "You didn't do anything, Ashley. Didn't you get my note?"

She shrugged. "Yeah, the one where you said you loved me but you were leaving me?"

"Ashley, I never stopped loving you. I thought about you every hour of every day that we've been apart. I regret leaving so much."

"Then why?"

Adam glanced around. Ashley knew they weren't alone on the beach, but she didn't really care who saw them. She had nothing left to lose. She walked a few yards inland and sat on a dry patch of sand, leaning back on her hands.

"Tell me what I did wrong," she said, turning to him.

Adam winced as though she'd hurt him. "I'm so sorry," he mumbled, lowering himself to the ground beside her.

"Would you stop saying that and just explain? You owe me that, at least."

He nodded and drew in a full breath. "Yeah, I do. Right after graduation, your father came to see me at the marina. He said he knew I wanted what was best for you. He talked about how long you'd been dreaming of going to Duke and how, since I'd come along, you'd considered giving that all up."

Ashley's mind was racing. She tried to recall a day her dad was off work and might have gone to the marina but couldn't. "I'm still going to go to Duke," she said.

"I know," Adam continued. "But it wasn't really about that. Your dad just used that as an example of how my presence in your life was changing your plans and how you might miss out on something wonderful if I was still holding you back. He told me the best thing I could do for you was to let you go."

Adam paused and took a deep, strained breath, but Ashley couldn't speak. She didn't know where to begin or what to say.

"I did really love you," Adam continued. "And I knew I didn't deserve you, and I thought you could find someone better for you if I wasn't in the picture."

"You could've asked me," Ashley interrupted, suddenly finding her voice. "You shouldn't just make decisions about my life without involving me."

"I know," he said. "And that's why I'm so sorry. Because I messed up big time, and I see that now. I thought you'd miss me for a couple weeks and then your summer would be busy and exciting and you'd move on. I assumed by now, you'd find someone new, someone better than me."

"You would've known the truth if you'd talked to me," she said, not even bothering to comment on how insulting it was that he assumed she'd move on so quickly. Did he really think her feelings were that fickle?

His face fell. "I couldn't. I knew I couldn't look at you or even hear your voice without it killing me. And your dad..." Adam blew out a breath and bit his lip. "He paid off my boat and truck and told me to leave town. He said if I contacted you, he would cut you off, and you'd lose everything."

"Except you," Ashley said quietly, letting everything Adam had said sink in. She'd known her dad was a pompous jerk, but this— this was more than she could've ever imagined. This was down-right villainous. "I can't believe he'd say that to you."

"He just wanted what was best for you and he thought if given the choice, you'd pick me over the things that really mattered."

She shook her head, trying to catch her breath. "I will never forgive him."

"Ashley, he knows he messed up. And think about it—if I hadn't agreed and left town, none of this would have happened. If I had just talked with you instead of getting stuck inside my own head, we could've figured something out together. If you're going to be mad at someone, be mad at me."

"I can be mad at both of you," she said, although she was still too surprised by Adam's sudden return to actually feel angry with him. "Wait, you said my dad knows he screwed up?"

Adam nodded then gave her a rundown of the past hour.

Ashley shook her head and stood, stretching slightly. This was all too much to take in. None of it made sense and the pieces weren't fitting together in her mind like she needed them to. She stared over at Adam. He seemed tense, sad, and more uncertain of himself than she'd ever seen him before. But otherwise, well, he was still the same Adam. Maybe a little more muscled, she thought, as he raised the sleeve of his tee shirt a bit while standing.

Then, an unfamiliar mark caught her eye.

"What's that?" she asked, reaching for his arm. She was positive this tattoo was new. It was a black outline of a tulip with what appeared to be a letter A written in scroll inside the petals.

Adam lifted his sleeve for her to view it better. "You said tulips were your favorite, right?"

Ashley glanced up at him then stared back down at his arm. The skin was smooth and no redness remained near the tattoo, so she didn't think it was new. "Wait, but when did you do this?"

"A few weeks ago," Adam answered.

"Is that the letter A?"

Adam nodded. "I wanted to make sure the flower was all you, with no other symbolism mixed in."

"But why?"

He laughed. "Ashley, I'll never love anyone else the way I loved you. Even if you aren't a part of my life, you're always going to be a part of me, and this reminds me of that."

Ashley fought back tears. "Why are you here, Adam?"

His expression grew serious again. "To apologize. I don't want you to ever question what we had together or think I left because I didn't love you because I did. You were my everything, Ashley. I've been miserable since we've been apart. The only thing keeping me going was my stupid assumption that you were happier without me."

"But I wasn't. How could you even think that?"

"I don't know." He shook his head. "I've made a lot of mistakes, Ash. I know I don't deserve you and I probably never will. But I wanted you to know that I would do anything to make you happy. If that means walking away and leaving you alone, I'll do it. But if you'll let me stick around and you give me another chance, I will spend every day earning back your love."

Ashley squeezed her eyes shut, not wanting anything to distract her from his words. Her heart was still pounding in her chest and she was dying to hold him close again, to feel his pulse against her own. But she needed to know for certain. "Do you still love me?"

"Yes. I love you so much it physically hurt me to stay away from you. I love you," he repeated.

Ashley dove into his arms, spraying sand over them both.

"I love you too," she mumbled, her words muffled by his chest. She hugged him so tightly that she worried he'd snap, and then he pulled her back slightly, placed his hands gently on her face, and guided her closer.

He stared at her for a long moment, his bright blue eyes finally sparkling like she remembered, and then he kissed her. Ashley's heart pounded so rapidly once his smooth lips reached her skin that she felt her chest might burst open.

With Adam's mouth against hers, all the memories that she'd tried so hard to block flooded back. She remembered playing in the sand with Adam, kissing him until they were both breathless, and talking to him for hours on end in the middle of the Atlantic on his boat. She recalled the scent of the marsh when they kayaked in high tide and the sweet taste of his kisses even first thing in the morning.

Mostly she remembered the way she felt when he gazed at her with such adoration that she wanted nothing more than to be as ideal of a person as he already thought her to be. It was hard to forget that, since he was staring at her that way now.

Ashley had never been as happy as she was with Adam, and no matter how much she still hated him for leaving her, she'd do anything for a little more time with him, even if there were no guarantees for the future.

The End

EPILOGUE

TRUE TO HIS WORD, Adam figured out a plan. By Thanksgiving, he had secured a job in Wilmington, North Carolina, captaining chartered cruises and teaching sailing lessons. When the weather cooled, he supplemented that with marine technician work. He made enough money to afford an apartment in Wilmington, a mere two and a half hour drive from campus, so he and Ashley could visit every week, if not more often. Over summer, he returned to Hilton Head Island with Ashley. He got a small place with Clay further inland so he could keep renting out the marina-front condo as long as possible.

Adam figured he would return to Wilmington in the fall and work there for another year, and then Ashley planned to spend her junior year at the Duke Marine Lab in Beaufort, so he would look for work and an apartment there next. He wasn't certain about the next step, but he wasn't worried either.

With Ashley by his side, Adam could do anything. Sometimes

she talked about moving up to New England when she graduated. Adam would be fine with that, of course, and relished every chance he got to show her around his old stomping grounds throughout the Cape and Nantucket. But deep in his heart, Adam was pretty sure his island girl would never feel truly at home if she weren't in her South Carolina heaven.

That afternoon, the island was feeling especially heavenly. The humidity was unseasonably low, the sky was clear, and the breeze as they cruised along the shore was almost refreshing as the sound of Ashley laughing beside him while he told her about Clay's attempts at a recent electrical repair in their apartment.

Adam was about to head off on a three-week charter trip. The money was too good to turn down, and when he'd accepted the gig, three weeks hadn't sounded like that long. But now that he was here with Ashley, three weeks away felt like an eternity.

Ashley was tense, he could tell, just like she always was when they were about to be separated. She assured him she wasn't nervous he'd leave her again like before, but he knew it had to be on her mind. Thankfully, he'd finally come up with a solution, a way to show her once and for all, that he was not going anywhere.

While he was gone, Ashley was headed to L.A. She was accompanying her dad on a business trip, but mostly Adam knew she just wanted to check out the Pacific Ocean to see how it compared to the Atlantic.

"I'm the one who should be worried," Adam said, killing the engine and relaxing against the guardrail beside Ashley. "You're probably going to fall in love with some west coast sailor and not even remember my name."

Ashley rolled her eyes. "I already told you I'm not worried."

He squeezed her hand. "Except you are, and it's almost worse that you don't feel like you can tell me."

"I forgave you for leaving, Adam. I just..." she shivered at the breeze.

He reached an arm around her. "I know, babe, and I get it. Sometimes when I wake up and you aren't there, I have this moment of panic. And I hate that. But I promise you it won't be this way forever. I want to wake up every day for the rest of my life with you next to me. Someday, I want to buy a house with you. I want to have babies with you someday. I want to take you on long sailing trips along the coast someday."

Ashley smiled. "I want all that, too."

"But you're still worried you're going to wake up and I'll be gone."

She shrugged. "I'm not too concerned about that on the boat."

Adam laughed and reached into his pocket. "Look, I've been waiting for the right moment to give this to you, but I don't know when that'll happen and I'm hoping it might be the reassurance you need."

He opened his hand, showing her the clear, sparkling diamond he'd been carrying around the past week. Her eyes widened so dramatically that Adam worried she might pass out.

"Ashley, I want you to have this so that whenever you have doubts, you can look at this and know that I am loving you and that I am not leaving you ever. Until the day you decide you are sick of me, I will be there. Every day, for the rest of your life if you let me."

Ashley stared up at him, her bright green eyes glistening. "Where did you…"

"This was my mom's," he explained. "I hope that doesn't creep you out. She gave it to me and…"

"No," Ashley interrupted. "It's gorgeous. And I love that it belonged to your mother."

Adam swallowed and held the ring out towards her.

Ashley giggled awkwardly. "Adam, are you asking me to marry you?"

"No! I mean, I…" he exhaled nervously. "You're only nineteen.

"And a half," she added with a slight grin.

Adam laughed. "But my point is that you're young. I'm not trying to force you into committing to anything. I just know that I want to spend the rest of my life with you, but I'm okay with waiting for you to decide what you want to do. So I'm just asking you to keep this—with no obligation or anything—just so you know what I want."

Ashley frowned. "So you do want to marry me."

"Well, yeah," he said uncertainly. "Probably not for a couple years, since I imagine you'd want to be able to legally toast our marriage, but…"

"And this is your mom's engagement ring?"

Adam nodded.

"It sounds like you're proposing."

He sighed. "I'm not. If I were proposing it would be romantic and magical and all that crap. And I'd be expecting some sort of commitment in return from you and that isn't the case now."

"So you just want me to take this engagement ring with the knowledge that you want to marry me someday," Ashley summarized, biting back a smile.

Adam knew he was blushing now. This was not going according to plan. "Yes," he finally said.

"Am I supposed to wear the ring or just hold on to it?"

He shrugged. "That's up to you. If you wore it, you'd be able to see it and feel it, though, and that might be a better reminder that you have me."

"And which finger do you propose I wear it on?" Ashley asked, giggling at her own choice of words.

Adam stepped closer and roped his arms around her waist, slipping the ring onto his own pinky so he could pull her close. "Well, it's sized for your ring finger, so…"

He bent his head and kissed her, eager to distract her from his garbled proposal with something he knew he was good at.

"Just ask already," she said as they broke apart from the kiss.

Adam eyed her stubbornly, then kissed her on the forehead

before dropping to one knee. His heart was pounding so rapidly he thought it might burst through his chest, but he stayed focused on the words he knew he wanted to say.

"Ashlynne Marie Kensington, you are the most amazing woman I have ever met. You are gorgeous and funny and smart and kind and generous. I want to spend every single day of the rest of my life trying to make you as happy as you make me every time you smile. I love you. I am always going to love you. Will you marry me?"

Ashley bit her lip, tearing up even after taunting him. "Yes," she whispered. "Yes, I will marry you." She pulled him up to stand and gazed up at him, grinning. "I love you so much Adam. And that was perfect."

Adam smiled, slid the ring onto her finger, then kissed her hand.

Ashley wrapped her arms around his neck and nudged him close for a long, hard kiss. It was the kind of kiss that made Adam's knees go weak, especially when he realized he would be able to kiss her like that the rest of his life. Ashley pulled back sooner than he would like, clearly eager to eye her jewelry again.

"You know, as a Captain I'm pretty sure I can conduct legal wedding ceremonies, so we could just knock this off the list right now," Adam said.

Ashley swatted him playfully and smiled mischievously. "Nice try, buddy, but I'm going to need at least three years to find the perfect dress and plan the perfect soirée."

Adam groaned. "So I have to wait three whole years until you're officially mine?"

Ashley shook her head. "I've been yours since the day I first saw you."

ACKNOWLEDGMENTS

I'm so appreciative of my fans, to the friends and family who have supported me through the writing and publishing process, and of my RWA group and critique groups.

I'm grateful for all the bloggers who've taken a chance on a new writer and agreed to review my books, and also for every reader who takes the time to leave a review or recommend my books to others.

Thank you to my editor, Kimberly. I'm glad you aren't yet sick of my writing or my effusive style.

Thanks to my cover artist, JD Book Designs. Your patience with my changes and willingness to electronically paint tattoos onto shirtless hunks for my covers means the world to me.

Thank you to my family. You guys are awesome and you know it.

ABOUT THE AUTHOR

Liza Malloy writes contemporary romance, new adult romance, women's fiction, and fantasy romance. She's a sucker for alpha males, bad boys, dimples, and muscles, and she can't resist a man in uniform. Liza loves creating worlds where her heroine discovers her own strength and finds her Happily Ever After. When Liza isn't reading or writing torrid love stories, she's a practicing attorney. Her other passions include gummy bears, jelly beans, and the occasional marathon. She lives in the Midwest with her four daughters and her own Prince Charming. *Forbidden Ink* is her third published novel.

Visit her website at www.LizaMalloy.com

Sixty Days for Love

She's on the clock to win him back!

Chelsea Craig's life is perfect, until her husband David runs off with his paralegal. During the mandatory sixty-day waiting period before the divorce is finalized, Chelsea decides to transform herself into a woman David can't resist. Revamping her life isn't easy, though, and Chelsea lands in one embarrassing predicament after another. Luckily, Nick, a smoldering local cop, happily rushes to her rescue. Convinced that a fling with Nick couldn't hurt, Chelsea embraces the sizzling chemistry they share. But when the separation period draws to a close, Chelsea begins to question whether she's been working all this time to salvage a relationship with the wrong man.

Available for purchase through Amazon, Barnes & Noble, Apple Books and Kobo.

Sixty Days for Love

* * *

For Love and Italian

An education in amore? Yes, please, Professore

Undergrad Bridget is no stranger to romantic advances from men. But when she meets Owen, an instant friendship forms, even though Owen happens to be Bridget's Italian teacher. Neither of them intends to cross that line, but once they do, they can't deny the passion and chemistry between them. Aware that their tryst is taboo, they keep their relationship clandestine. But like all juicy secrets, this one doesn't stay hidden for long. And once it's out, Owen and Bridget must decide what they're willing to risk in the name of love.

For Love and Italian

* * *

The Awakening

When worlds collide, can love truly conquer all?

The first title in this exciting new adult fantasy-romance trilogy will be available in late 2019.